The Fixer

A Rubber City Caper

Artie Reed

The Fixer

Publishing Social Media Accounts:

Facebook: Rubber City Capers

Email: rubbercitycapersstow@gmail.com

ISBN: 978-0-578-27559-8

Table of Contents

Dedication

IT HAS BEEN a wild ride, and my life is nothing but sincere gratitude. Writing the second book of the Scooter Jeanette Rubber City Capers novels is a blessing. Still, the most significant rewards are the friendships and relationships rekindled through writing the first novel, Track Star, in my Rubber City Capers mystery series. Many friends and family members have moved to different parts of the country, but Track Star rekindled that warm feeling of closeness and love. Friends Jake Ricker, Darris Blackford, Steve Kapusinski, Jeff Miner, Todd Caruthers (Crud), the Sturmi brothers, The Honorable Mayor of Cuyahoga Falls, Don Walters, Walt W., Patty Zupko-Maddox, Kimberly Bahr Hinkle, Debbie Bosley, Andrea Clark, Paula Baeli Volpi, Lorna Miller Henderson and so, so many more. And some of these friends are also part of the storyline. Also, a special thank you to Darris Blackford for his unique insights throughout the process.

A special shout-out to Jake Ricker and his lovely wife, Dawn. When I was getting shoved, kicked, and knocked down in a few parts of my life a little while ago, they were in my corner one hundred percent. They are rock-solid, loving, compassionate, and non-judgmental. They taught me not to take things so seriously and, most importantly, to be kind to myself.

On June 6th of, 2022, I had a critical battle with Sepsis, and it almost killed me. Through that trauma, many invited God into the situation, and he never departed my side. If it had not been for my total gift from God and his wonderful Angel on earth Emily Mueller, and if she hadn't listened to her instincts and come to check on me, the outcome might have been very different. I was unconscious on the living room floor. *Emily,   I   love   you   forever.*

Chapter 1

IT WAS SATURDAY, the second day of September, in Summit County, in my hometown of Ohio, and telephone area code 330. The weather was postcard-perfect; large white puffy clouds lay inside a light blue backdrop that stretched forever. It was warm and sunny, with a delicate breeze seemingly derived from Lake Erie, thirty-nine miles to the North. This made me happy.

That and the fact that I was currently flush with many, many Benjamin Franklins in my checking account, well, our checking account, our team's bank account. We had just solved a heartless murder, a tiny human trafficking ring, and we busted a reasonably large university campus drug operation. On that one, we were compensated by a large cash stipend that we extricated from a drug dealer, a corrupt Cadillac dealer, and a sleazy attorney. The legal lines were somewhat blurry on that part, and usually, when we approach legal lines, most times we are respectful law-abiding officers of the court, but in some cases, we somersault that line as if our asses are on fire. And in most cases, we go into full Robin Hood mode. In our most recent investigative caper, the university cut us an extensive check to not divulge all of the case details to the world. We accepted their substantial offer. Also, we, in the process, supplied the local police force with new crime-fighting supplies anonymously, of course.

I was sitting on the passenger side of a shiny royal blue golf cart with the university mascot logo plastered on both sides. I was also admiring my current Nike red running shoes that adorned my feet and were resting on the front of the previously said golf cart. I looked like I could run fast. Twiggy, the oldest of our furry family members and the matriarch, was sleeping in the back of the golf cart on the white padded bench seat. And since it was an Olympic year and the iconic wardrobe designer Ralph Lauren was once again outfitting our U.S.A. athletes, I chose a white satin tracksuit from my personal Ralph Lauren collection for today's meeting. It had two nifty blue and red stripes running up and down each arm sleeve and each pant leg. My array of Polo by Ralph Lauren was not many, precisely one, but it was a Christmas gift from Kat, short for Katrina, my wife. Underneath the white satin jacket, I was wearing my favorite Akron RubberDucks blue polo shirt with the playful yellow rubber ducky on the front and my famous Tom Ford wire and mirrored sunglasses to help thwart the postcard sun. You couldn't see my favorite handgun, a Ruger .38 Special, resting in a small leather holster on my right hip, covered by my shirt and lightweight satin jacket. Over the years, we have made a list you do not want to be on, the list held by some nasty and awful criminals in the Northeastern Ohio area.

It was still technically summer, and besides looking dapper in my new athletic shoes and sunglasses, I was watching the university football team practice. Drinking a Diet Coke in a plastic bottle also took up much of my time. Still, with the remainder of my time, I watched Gunner Thompson, now, all six-foot-five and two hundred and thirty-five pounds and an all-division quarterback, pick the defense apart with pinpoint accuracy. He was quick and smooth, and there wasn't a throw between the chalk lines he was afraid to attempt. The university football team was in a bye week and sitting atop their division with an undefeated record of two wins and zero losses in this early season.

Sitting next to me in the golf cart driver's seat sat University Chancellor William Wright flexing a three-piece dark brown suit featuring thin, light blue stitching over top of a crispy white oxford dress shirt. His ensemble included brown wingtip shoes and he was topped off with a dark brown driving cap perched precariously on his rather large head. This makes him look like Mr. Potato Head. His thick and bushy dark guardsman mustache was dreadful, and if anyone was secretly keeping score, his sunglasses were generic and weren't nearly as cool as mine. The Chancellor was a massive guy at six-foot-four inches tall and weighing over three hundred pounds. The only thing bigger than William Wright? His enormous ego.

I glanced back at Twiggy, and she was still resting comfortably behind William Wright and me on the rear-facing bench seat. I brought her because she looked like she wanted to join me before we left our home, and she had never been to a Division I football practice. And most importantly, the main reason I grabbed her as a co-pilot was I didn't want to get anywhere near or have our team working around this campus again. So I figured someone would upset me over having

Twiggy with me, giving me an excuse to either shoot them in the lower lip or decline the job.

The university football players practiced in gray shorts, white helmets, and blue and white jerseys over thick shoulder pads. Gunner wore a bright red jersey, signaling he wasn't to be touched. The physical contact was minimal, but now and then, you could hear the crack of shoulder pads colliding, followed by a fierce whistle-blow by one or more of the coaches.

On the sidelines were four large tables with blue linen tablecloths with the university logo draped over each to accommodate assorted supplies assorted white towels, gold and blue bandages in different shapes and sizes, eight large cylindrical, bright orange drink coolers, and hundreds of green and orange cardboard cups that read 'Gatorade.' spaced on each. I could feel the warm Northeastern Ohio sun penetrating the back of my neck and smell the freshly cut grass and the familiar hum of a riding lawn mower in the distance; forty yards away, the automatic sprinklers kicked on the second practice field. Then it gave the view a pleasant experience, a shimmering quality. A bonus, three Goodyear blimps were out floating over Summit County; I liked it all.

There was a surplus of assistant coaches, and I counted twelve. Six or eight too many to be necessary, I thought to myself, but then again, I don't coach college football. Mostly I chase bad guys and girls, and sometimes I shoot them dead.

"Kids amazing, isn't he?" William Wright asked me.

"He surely passes the eye test," I replied.

We watched the half-speed scrimmage for another twenty minutes when I finally asked him, "Sir, why exactly are we needed here?"

The Chancellor took off his sunglasses, glanced back at Twiggy, and after a few minutes, he felt safe enough to talk in front of my dog and said, "That young man out there has emerged as one of the best quarterbacks in college football. He has a cannon for an arm, and he has eyes in the back of his head; he runs well and is the perfect drop-back quarterback for one of ten professional teams next year. And he is local, from Cuyahoga Falls."

I knew Gunner Thompson grew up in Cuyahoga Falls, just a few miles outside of Akron, and was a genuine, homegrown talent. Just eleven minutes from where we sat, he has overwhelmed the local sports pages, social media pages, and television sports channels for the last five years. Gunner was an All-State of Ohio three-sport athlete in high school; football, baseball, and track. However, even knowing all of this, sometimes, in my line of work, it never hurts to appear uneducated on the current topic. Never show all of your cards, never.

The Chancellor continued, "He attended Cuyahoga Falls High School and wasn't heavily recruited in Division I but blossomed into an All-American here with us." Wright said proudly as if he were the reason for Gunner's success.

Again, I was aware of this tedious bit of extra unsolicited information but played along: "That is great. But what is it you are asking of my team and me?"

"The kids got the world by the gonads, the samosas, the…."

"Yes, I get the picture with visuals," I said.

"He could go in the first round of the draft and sign a huge contract…..and he is, well, getting death threats, and we would like you to investigate the validity of these threats."

"Hmmm, please explain."

The Chancellor placed both hands on the middle portion of the golf cart's steering wheel while extending his fingers on both hands and looking and studying them for a minute. William Wright's fingers were long, chubby, and had bony knuckle joints. A black titanium wedding ring adorned the correct finger.

"I received a brief letter stating the threat." The Chancellor said in a low voice without looking up from his hands.

That is the last thing I thought I would hear from the university's Chancellor on this beautiful, summer-like day in northeast Ohio. We watched a few more minutes of practice in silence, then we adjourned to William Wright's office, cruising across the campus in his golf cart.

Chapter 2

THE ENTIRE UNIVERSITY sits on over two hundred acres, and the Chancellor's office is located in a stately red brick historical building on the North end of campus; it sits on a small, restful, and tranquil small tree-dotted piece of land named squirrel hill. A five-foot-tall black metal fence surrounded the property with hundreds of skinny metal posts spaced every twelve inches and ornate gold-painted arrows on the tops of each. The building is a two-story, red brick 18th-century priceless piece of architecture. The nine large and six small front-facing windows made the building look larger. A wrap-around front porch with four gigantic white concrete pillars made the structure look antebellum, but the brickwork made it look meaningful. Four creepy goblins sat etched in stone on the top corners of the building as if they were centuries-old sentries. A large door knocker in black was an ornamental lion in a standing position with a huge head. It was bolted on the wooden front door and befit the entrance of this one-of-a-kind building. I liked it, and I knew this house to be on the National Historic Register, just the perfect place for two men to discuss death threats in collegiate sports.

The massive front door opened into a large round foyer with a stunning crystal chandelier hanging above it. There were several small, delicate glass tables positioned around the circular lobby that held brilliant and distinguished pieces of turn-of-the-century art. A pair of exquisite cobalt blue 18th-century Dutch Delft vases with continuous, hand-painted songbirds circling the entire vases caught my attention. There were also colorful flowers and scrolling vines that made the two octagonal vases bright and alive. I walked closer to the table where they sat and leaned down and studied them at a closer distance.

"Are you a 17th-century art aficionado?" William Wright asked me from the doorway of his office.

I straightened up and said, "I dabble, but these two vases are mid-18th-century artworks."

He gazed at the colorful vases, opened his mouth to say something, and thought better of it. I was showing off and just wanted to see the character of William Wright. He was the self-appointed and supposed expert, but he decided not to engage me on this one. Chancellor William Wright remained silent, scoring one for Twiggy and me.

We walked across the affluent lobby, and the walls were beautified with various-sized Italian Renaissance paintings. Most depicted voluptuous women lying on couches eating fruit. It was apparent that the ample and curvy women in these paintings were happy and confident. Twiggy and I joined the Chancellor in an open office doorway directly across from the front entrance. There was a small black enamel nameplate that read 'Chancellor William Wright' in white lettering.

The office space was everything I thought a Chancellor of a major university would lead and educate from, a feeling of competence and knowledge. The massive office is bathed in natural sunlight that seems to follow us from the practice field and two floor-to-ceiling vertical side-by-side windows, with one larger square window in the middle. In the corner of the large, flashy office stood a six-and-a-half-foot-tall bronze-plated armored guard. This impressive sentry was complete with a four-foot-long stainless steel sword. The armor plating was thick, tarnished from five centuries, but, all in all, the old guy looked pretty good. The office was decorated with ancient artisan settees, fragile end tables, and complex ornate rugs. I knew he fancied himself a 17th-century historian. Still, most of this furniture was created in the 19th century, excluding the full suit of armor that was most likely crafted in the 14th century and imported from another continent. I know this because the local historical society once hired us to retrieve some stolen artifacts, and along the way learned more than we wanted concerning historical furniture and very early 17th-and 18th-century artwork and furniture design.

The Chancellor motioned me to a delicate Queen Ann arm-chair. It was painted beige with bright flowers and butterflies in rich deep colors; it was one of two perched in front of his desk. I pointed for Twiggy to lay at my feet; I thought about pointing to the matching chair next to mine, but I didn't want this academic, overweight scholar to have a coronary event in front of me. Chancellor Wright removed his suit coat, and his underarms were extraordinarily wet from sweat. It looked like he had recently put Shamu from Sea World in a headlock.

He placed the suit coat on a brass hook inside the office door and walked over to a tastefully decorated dark oak wet bar from which he grabbed a large crystal decanter full of purple and deep red liquid. He selected two sturdy wine glasses and signaled to me; when I nodded, he filled them up and handed me a drink. The fortified wine tasted berry with a hint of chocolate and unidentifiable herbs; all in all, it was spicy, acidic, and astonishingly horrible. He then sat behind a mahogany desk slightly smaller than an aircraft carrier. The extended desktop was neat and organized, with three framed pictures of a stern-looking middle-aged brunette with three equally stern-looking children, one male, and two female. The remainder of the items on the desk were a telephone similar to something a switchboard operator at the Pentagon would envy, a silver laptop, and a colorful hardback Italian cookbook by Paula Baeli Volpe that sat on the right corner of the desk nearest to me. Paula is a local cookbook author and food blogger, and a long-time friend.

The Chancellor saw me glimpsing at the Italian cookbook and said, "Excellent book; she is local; I have had the entire family in the university suite for a couple of football games."

I wouldn't say I liked name droppers; I hated them; however, Paula's family are our personal friends, especially Kat and Tilly. Paula has cooked for us at the marina on many unique occasions. I wanted to tell the pompous Chancellor that Paula's Eggplant Parmesan, chocolate chip cannolis, sausage, peppers, and onions were the food of legendary status in our home. I thought that shooting him right now would have been satisfying. But I only sighed and replied, "Yes, her books are great."

"Also, does the dog need to be in this meeting?" William Wright asked while looking down at my furry companion.

"Yes, and again, her name is Twiggy."

The Chancellor placed his beefy hands on his desk and gazed at me for a moment before continuing, "We got us a conundrum, Mr. Jeanette."

I was sure I didn't have a conundrum because as soon as I vacated this meeting, I was going to enjoy myself with a late afternoon pontoon boat ride a cooler of iced beers, some jumbo shrimp cocktail appetizers, and assorted cheeses from Sugar Creek Ohio that we had picked up last weekend. Sugar Creek is twenty miles South of Akron in Stark County and is also referred to as *The Little Switzerland of Ohio'* this small village seeps Swiss and German heritage. I drooled a little, thinking of their country baby swiss, sharp cheddar, chive, and horseradish cheeses. Besides, It wouldn't be long before me and the love of my life and wife, Katrina but goes by Kat, Twiggy, and our other two furry best friends, Sabaka and Iggy, were on the water. Kat was currently getting her hair styled while I was drinking rancid port wine; it didn't seem fair.

While initially, I intended to remain passive and respectfully decline any conundrum-solving requests from Chancellor Wright. Because my team and I had just spent a lot of time on this very campus solving numerous felonies and murders, I found myself responding to his comment, "Okay, what do you know?"

William Wright took a considerable amount of port in one long drink, and as he refilled his glass, he leaned back in his chair, which creaked and croaked loudly in painful defiance of his girth. His large gold cufflinks clinked against the arms of the desk chair, making a clamorous noise in the otherwise quiet room. As he continued to lean back, he gazed at the ceiling, holding the wine glass with both hands as they rested on his tremendous midsection. As he continued to stare, I got a feeling of forced theatrics. As if I was watching the Chancellor starring in his one-person play. It was phony and contrived.

They say patience is a virtue, but it isn't, "Can you elaborate?" I asked, getting closer and closer to grabbing my Wing-Dog and leaving.

"Besides the letter, a young male called into our university radio station, threatening Gunner's life."

"Did the threat against the quarterback go over the air?"

"You mean Gunner Thompson? Chancellor Wright corrected while asking me immediately in a respectful, almost gospel tone. He then looked at me forgivingly; after all, it wasn't my fault I was a simpleton.

"Yes, him."

William Wright Continued, "During the seven to nine o'clock Thursday night sports talk show an unidentified young man made brief threats to Gunner. We think it's the same person."

"Have you notified the Akron Police Department?" I asked.

William took a sip of his port and waved his left arm while saying, "No, no, we do not want that kind of attention."

If all of this were true, I wasn't thrilled with a university Chancellor not having a more organized plan for dealing with this highly volatile situation and referring to it as a conundrum. But that battle was probably best saved for another time. Now I was more concerned about turning this hairball of a case down quickly and getting on the water with my wife, my dogs, and our terrific pontoon boat; heck, I thought, I may even throw a line in the water with a large red and white bobber.

William refilled his port glass again and attempted to hand me the letter; I shook my head as I pulled a white hanky from my pants pocket and carefully grabbed the letter from the top right corner to hold and read. The handwritten note appeared to have been authored on regular, plain standard computer paper that you can purchase at any number of local stores or have delivered to your home or office any day of the week.

I asked to see the envelope that went with the letter. Again, the Chancellor, with no regard for the preservation of evidence, picked it up and attempted to hand it to me. I just stared at him in utter disbelief. He, in return, continued to hold the envelope in front of me. I, in turn, continued to stare at him, and after a few more seconds, I motioned with my eyes toward the desk for him to place it anywhere in front of me. After three times, he finally picked up on my not-subtle-at-all cues and leaned over, and gently placed the envelope in front of me. For his semi-heroic efforts, he leaned back and took a herculean drink of his port. I weep for this institution and these students.

I took a pen from my shirt pocket and used the tip to arrange the envelope right side up and to face me. I had a delivery address but no return address. I took one of the Chancellor's business cards from a metal standing frame to my left and set it next to the envelope. I compared the address on the envelope and the address on his business card, and they were the same.

"The letter and envelope are for you to keep, Mr. Jeanette."

I took a small drink from my glass of port, then said, "Mr. Wright, I am not even close to agreeing to take on this case."

Ignoring me, the Chancellor spoke: "In observance of offering you a contract for your services, I'd like to have Milton Haft, our in-house university council, join us." He picked up the phone's handset, punched a single button on the substantial telephone base, murmured something, replaced the handset, and refilled his wine glass. He reached out with the decanter offering me more, but I declined. I reached down and caressed Twiggy and whispered, "We will be on the water with mommy in no time."

Just like that, a tall, slim man in his early forties who appeared to have at one time played basketball very well walked into the room. He also resembled an all-team country club golfer on the weekends, which I would bet were true. His dark hair was short and stylish. He wore expensive orange slacks with no pleats, a broad, white belt with the Nike swoosh embossed throughout many times in black, a bright yellow polo golf shirt made by Puma, and navy loafers styled to look like golf shoes. He looked terrific if he were thirteen years old and his mom was dropping him off at the local municipal golf course with a brown paper bag lunch.

"You a member at Portage, Firestone, or Silver Lake?" I asked him.

"Firestone," he automatically replied.

I smiled. Always good to stay in practice. I glanced at Milton Haft's hands, and they were large with long, manicured fingers. The cuticles were perfect. The third finger on his left hand was bare.

"Milton Haft, please meet Scooter Jeanette," the overweight educator said.

"Oh, Goody, a lawyer in the mix," I replied.

"Oh, Goody, a private detective in the mix," he responded.

Alright, chalk one up for the in-house barrister. One probably needed to be careful around Milt; he was no stuffy corporate fat cat.

The lawyer stopped in his tracks and glanced at Twiggy, then back to the Chancellor, then back to Twiggy, then back to the Chancellor, then back to me, then back to the Chancellor. It was making me dizzy. The in-house counsel looked like he was watching a tennis match. After another long look at Twiggy, he said, "William, why is this dog here?"

"Twiggy, her name is Twiggy for all future references, and she is here to help me with the big words," I said.

Milton Haft hesitated and then extended his hand; I took hold, and he offered a low-strength, wimpy shake - Milt, the man, was probably holding back.

He then began to pontificate to me post-haste, "This, Mr. Jeanette, is the legal agreement we will be presenting to you. I have taken the liberty of reviewing random samples of private investigative and security service rates hourly and weekly across the Midwest. I have averaged them all out to come up with your fee. A fee the university is comfortable paying," he added smugly and condescending at the same time while handing the legal papers to me with a semi-flourish. Extraordinary, just extraordinary.

The Chancellor made a grunting noise, leaned forward, and took a drink of his port. The port appeared ineffective to his massive frame; he showed no signs of drunkenness. Remarkable, really remarkable. I, on the other hand, have had five small sips and felt like I needed to go to the dentist and then to the emergency room to get my stomach pumped.

Every time I was on this university campus, it amazed me how self-important the faculty and staff thought they were, with an average annual graduation rate of forty-six percent. You would think a little humility would appear, even by accident.

"Milt baby, that's it? No small talk, no personal appraisals, no professional references? All business, no desire to stand and rub zippers to get to know each other, you know what I mean?" Then I winked at him.

"What?... Wait...God no...anyhow, please execute and initial these pages as indicated. Expenses, locations, time spent, and in which manner your time spent. All should be sent to me via email daily by four forty-five every day."

"Milt, now see right there? You don't dress like one, but right now, you sound like an attorney."

I sat my half-filled glass of wine on the end of William Wright's desk and quickly looked at the contract, particularly the fee. After twenty seconds, I took a pen from the attorney's hand and crossed out his fee figure, and added mine. I rounded up very high, as I didn't necessarily want to work for these people. And I especially didn't like some in-house attorney assuming we would jump when he instructed me. Also, there was a feeling of something in this room, a light simmering something below the surface between these people, and in my experience, it would come to a rolling boil. Still, I couldn't place it, but I felt it the moment that this egotistical solicitor of the law strolled into the room. I handed my edited agreement version back to Milton Haft and retrieved my unappealing wine.

I leaned back and begrudgingly took a sip and said, "This is the fee I'm comfortable accepting."

"Unacceptable; this is too expensive." Milton Shot back rather quickly.

"Fine, I don't want the job," I replied.

Crossing my right leg over my left and resting my hands on my right knee, I looked at William Wright; he had a quick decision to make.

"That's it, no negotiating, Mr. Jeanette?" William asked.

"No, and as the top educator of a large university, you, of all people, should know that the word 'no' is a complete sentence."

Milt the Attorney began doing that tennis match thing again, bouncing his head back and forth from William to me, this time omitting Twiggy from his tedious, visual venture. "Wait, why it's easy money? We are never going to hear from that kid again," he said.

"Oh, Milt, my new golfer buddy, there are so many reasons, but for simplicity, I didn't like the way you looked at my dog, and I have a real concern that if I executed this agreement, my wife, at some point would throat punch you repeatedly," Maybe I wasn't so passive after all today, oh well baby steps.

Chancellor Wright leaned forward, his slightly panicky facial expression responding to my refusal. That raised a small red flag for me.

"Surely, Mr. Jeanette, you can compromise and work with us here," the Chancellor pleaded.

"Could, but won't, find someone else," I replied while shifting in my chair. The butt of my handgun was digging into my hip. A large Grandfather clock suddenly tingled chimes and toiled jingles from the corner of the large office.

"Well, back to the drawing board, William," the pompous attorney said with a snarky half-grin.

"Let me see the agreement," the Chancellor said, grabbing the paperwork from Milton Haft's right hand.

The Chancellor perused the contract for a full two minutes. Suddenly, his eyebrows raised simultaneously, and he took a huge swallow from his glass, then looked at me and said, "Mr. Jeanette comes to us in high regard, although extremely expensive; nonetheless, I will sign off on this new amount."

"You certainly will not!" The exasperated attorney claimed.

The Chancellor sighed heavily and said, "Milt, you work for me."

"I beg your pardon William, and I work for the university."

"Yes, for me and under me." The Chancellor replied.

"Well, I never have in my life...."

The ugliness between these two or the unattractive and hideous vibe in this office was not only peeking out, but it was also dangerously close to emerging and doing full cartwheels.

"Oh, for Christ's sake, Milt, it's Saturday; we work six days a week. Pull the stick out of your ass and have a glass of port," William Wright said while executing the contract.

The agitated lawyer did not accept either suggestion but instead exited in an extreme bit of a hurry.

"Sorry, you had to see that. Milt means well, and he loves this university, but he is a tad strident."

I sighed and accepted that we were taking the case, and yes, the odds of Milton Haft getting throat punched by my wife a couple of times were very high. They say the truth sets you free, but now it's acceptance. Besides, my team is nosy.

"No, it's always a good day when you piss off an attorney. I divorced an attorney, an unfaithful one, years ago, and that's an old memory I don't mess with today," I replied.

The Chancellor glanced at me after my divorce admission, and he had nothing to add, so he pulled a small daily planner with a well-worn brown leather cover from his top desk drawer and glanced at the contract. He then wrote a few entries in the planner on today's date. After closing the day planner, he smiled and said, complete with annoying '*Air Quotes*,' "I know, a Chancellor of a major university should get with the times. Computers, computers, and more computers, all that tech stuff." And he raised his right arm and made a dissing move with his right hand.

His statement had nothing for me, so I just remained quiet. Something I am working on today, per my wife. I adjusted the contract so I could bestow my John Hancock.

"Been relying on these for years; I save everything in them, just like my father. I have dozens and dozens," he said as he poured another glass of port and pointed to a small credenza. The medium-sized credenza was open, and I could see it was loaded with dozens of small leather notebooks.

William said, "You know it feels weird talking about this bizarre situation."

I took in a deep, deep breath and, after a few seconds, blew out that same deep, deep breath because I was about to explain to a meaningful university Chancellor that *'weird'* is an adjective, not an emotion, and then get up and leave with my four-legged companion. However, I chose to remain quiet. Again, this is a character trait my wife thinks I should wield more often.

"Does he sleep around, does he tear the labels off pillows, does he not heed the specific instructions on the back of the shampoo bottle? Does he burn ants with a magnifying glass? Does he steal social security checks?"

The Chancellor's face and wide and fleshy neck turned an attractive shade of crimson, and he gasped, "Heavens no, this young man is a saint."

"Gunner, Gunner Thompson," I fired back with a smile.

I didn't know Gunner Thompson personally and had no firsthand knowledge of his sainthood, but he certainly had one disloyal fan.

"What does his football coach say about all of this?" I asked, assuming that during the football season, the coach would occupy the majority of his time.

The Chancellor brushed his right hand at me and said, "That pompous ass doesn't say one word without screaming; he screams everything. That dreadful man is insufferable, and his only devotion is to his winning record. The first major program other than ours to offer him a head coaching position, he will be gone, the loyalty aspect, Coach Dennis Darling lacks."

"Before Gunner decided to enroll in this university, our football team was, for lack of a better word, 'enthusiastic.' They won two games in three years, and Coach Darling was in the final year of his contract." The overweight educator spoke all of this rather hourly.

"Well, Coach Darling must have done a heck of a recruiting job to land Gunner Thompson. Being local and a major sports fan, I know other big schools offered him scholarships."

"They did, and there were many schools from the East Coast to the West Coast, head coaches made many home visits, the Ryan Day's, Nick Saban's, Jimbo Fisher's, Dabo Sweeney's, Lincoln Riley's, and Kirby Smart's, but Gunner wasn't leaving his mother or his hometown."

I didn't know how to process this because most kids can't wait to move away. Especially a gifted athlete that had a pick of many schools in different states. And those coaches are living legends.

"Gunner is an only child, and he grew up without a father. So one day, we get a telephone call from Gunner's high school football coach, Rick Giles, who informs us that Gunner would like to play football and get his education with us. And get this, Gunner and his mother were wondering if any money was available for him; the rest is history."

The Chancellor said, shaking his head with unresolved disbelief. I knew the Cuyahoga Falls High School football head coach Rick Giles well, and he is a top guy.

"What information do you require to begin this private inquiry?" William suddenly asked.

I thought for a few moments and replied, "Gunner's daily schedule, including academic and football commitments, his current home address, the make and model and license plate number of his vehicle, and his last two years of academic transcripts."

William Wright leaned over and grabbed his glass of port. This time he didn't take a drink but just held the glass.

"You are certainly thorough, Mr. Jeanette."

There was nothing to add, so I did not. The Chancellor's gaze on me was different now, and again there was a shift in the room, an unspoken movement, a something; I felt it. His relief that I took this case was seismic. Twiggy probably would have also thought it if not for the apparent fact that she was sleeping, as the loud snoring from her fully validated my suspicions.

"What purpose in your initial investigation does Gunner Thompson's academic profile provide?" Wright asked.

"I don't know until I know," I replied.

"What does that mean?"

"Hell, William, I look at everything I can, I turn over every piece of information I can, and ultimately, I see it."

"See what?" Chancellor Wright implored.

I leaned forward and replied: "It, the pattern, the sense of it all and then the truth, always I finally see the pattern, then the truth."

"Every time?"

"Yes, Sir, every time," I said.

Chancellor Wright reached over to his massive call center and pushed a button with his left index finger, and said, "Miss Bethany, can you please come into my office."

"Saturdays around here are casual but mostly for catching up on detail work, so our project coordinator just happens to be in today," he said.

A female entered the room; she was in her mid-thirties, petite, demure, and delicate. She wore dark leggings, a white skirt, and black short platform boots. Her long sleeve blouse was dark green and silk. A large silver necklace hung loosely around her neck, and small, silver hoop earrings were her only other jewelry, no wedding ring. Her blond hair was cut short, and she wore understated makeup. Her small, round face was unlined and shiny, and she wore red eyeglasses. She stood modestly in the doorway and said, "Yes, Mr. Wright?"

"This is Mr. Scooter Jeanette, and he has been hired for a brief, unique project and requires some information," William nodded in my direction and continued, "Mr. Jeanette, please tell Miss Bethany what you will require to begin our project."

I thought this characterization of investigating death threats of an extremely popular student-athlete as a *special project* was a bit insensitive, and the hairs on the back of my neck tingled - my spidey senses were pinging slightly.

I stood and said, "Hello, My name is Scooter Jeanette; if I could just begin by getting Gunner Thompson's daily class schedule, his current home address, his football practice schedule, his most recent academic transcripts, and any personal vehicle information, that will get me started."

We exchanged business cards, and Miss Bethany said, "I can email all information by five o'clock today."

"That would be fine, thank you."

"Miss Bethany, this can never leave this room, understood?" William Wright said.

"Yes, sir," she responded, shaking her head as she understood, but in that instant, I saw something flash across her face. I have been doing this for a long time, and I saw it. Something passed between them. I filed that away. This case had the makings of one significant babysitting job and headache.

The Chancellor opened his desk drawer and slid two all-access football passes to the team's games. The last bit of business was our retainer fee, and after making known the only amount I would accept to start this job, the job I didn't want in the first place, William Wright raised one eyebrow and gazed at me silently.

We stayed like this for a few sheepish moments, and then he nodded his head up and down a few times before pulling two large brown leather binders that held larger-sized business checks from his desk drawer. He debated between the two binders, then said, "This one will work." He placed the chosen one on top of the other and opened its cover. After inquiring about the correct name to address the check, William Wright carefully wrote it out and signed his name with a flourish. He then slid the check over to me. I picked it up and looked it over, and decided this check would not be embarrassed being deposited into our account to join our many other bucks, and it was a happy, prosperous, and successful-looking check.

Chapter 3

HERE IS WHERE I must tell you that as a young boy, I would lay on the top bunk of my bed and dream of being a member of the original Justice League or G.I. Joe with the yellow amphibious vehicle. I chose the latter because I was terrified of heights, and most importantly, Aquaman had to make the ocean his bathroom. I wasn't doing that. But simple fate had pushed me into a life of private investigations. I ply that trade-in around Northeast Ohio, mostly Akron, Cuyahoga Falls, and Summit County. If the beating hearts of Boston are Fenway Park, baked beans, and the bar from Cheers, then the beating hearts of Akron and the surrounding suburbs are the history of the tire industry, the Akron RubberDucks, free concerts downtown at Lock 3 in the summer, and homemade sauerkraut balls. My hometown is steady, lived in, and dependable, like your favorite after-work sweatpants.

My team is relatively oddball-ish, with my wife Kat, her fraternal twin brother Bam-Bam, her Aunt Tilly, and her Uncle Sully. All four are primarily sweet, helpful, loving, kind, and deadlier than a king cobra bite.

Chapter 4

AFTER LEAVING THE Chancellor's office, I turned the SUV toward downtown Akron and made a beeline to the Peanut Shoppe on Main Street. It was only a few blocks from the university, and we had an unwritten rule that whenever anyone from the family was within a few miles of this peanut gastric oasis, said person or persons must bring pounds and pounds of salted peanut goodies and delicious, decadent chocolates back to our home.

I found an angled parking spot a half block from the Peanut Shoppe on the same side of the street. I left Twiggy with a jerky treat and exited the SUV, and beeped the locks into place. I love downtown Akron; for one, Canal Park, the stomping grounds of the Akron RubberDucks, our hometown professional baseball team, and the AA affiliate of the Cleveland Guardians. The Akron Civic Theatre, The Lock 3 entertainment district, and our favorite, The Peanut Shoppe. I repeat - I love downtown Akron.

The Peanut Shoppe has been in many local and national publications. And has served thousands and thousands of customers and has been an authentic sensational Akron foodie monument and a downtown mainstay for over eighty years.

As I walked through the shop door, a small bell jingled, and the smell of roasting nuts, roasted peanuts, and candied cashews hit me; it was like hearing an old song from high school, a melody shared years ago with someone you cared about, a time you can never get back but a time that never left you, a feeling of a familiar warm embrace.

There were seven other peanut enthusiasts in the store sampling and buying. The glass cases were full of hot pistachios and cashews, walnuts and sunflower seeds, all in all, dozens of assorted salty delights. The store also carried nostalgic candies from the 1950s and 1960s.

I stood and watched Marge, the fabulous owner, deep-fry some delicious cashews and pecans in the front corner of the store closest to the window, looking out onto South Main Street. It doesn't matter my frame of mind. When I walk through that Peanut Shoppe door, my day gets abundantly better.

"Hi, Scooter!"

"Hello, Marge, whatever that is, I want two pounds and another eight pounds of our usual assorted mix."

"Ha, ha, you got it, our favorite private eye man."

Chapter 5

I PARKED THE SUV in our oversized garage that, up until a few years ago, stored pleasure boats for seventy-five years. The Leighton family owned this former marina and boathouse for generations; Sonny Leighton was the father of my high school friend Lenny Staats.

Our marina sits on Turkey Foot Lake, one of many lakes in the Portage Lakes park system. Names like Hower Lake, East and West Reservoirs, Miller Lake, Mud Lake, and Long Lake. We purchased the marina and the surrounding five acres of land. The property had four outbuildings used in a previous life for year-round boat storage, marine parts storage, and extra inventory of marina essentials; fire extinguishers, life preservers, beach towels, and suntan lotions. There was also a tiny, two-story boat house directly on the water that we converted into a small loft condo for Kat, me, and the three canines. It also had a two-stall, open-air boat garage where I had recently killed the Summit County medical examiner and the head coach for the women's track team on our last caper.

The expansive garage splits duty with all our vehicles; Kat's classic black and gold *Bandit* Pontiac Trans Am and her pink Volkswagen Beetle convertible, and our new Mercedes Benz SUV in cobalt blue. We bought the Benz, not from an ego standpoint but from an essential perspective; Kat thought it was cute. Then there's my collector Corvette in gray, a white Denali, Bam-Bam's Ford F-150, Bam-Bam and Kat's matching Ducati racing motorcycles in black, and an older model beige Toyota Camry. We used the Camry for tailing and surveillance purposes. Still more vehicles include Tilly's white Range Rover and Sully's Black Range Rover. In the far corner sat the team's 45-foot Monaco motor home. But the showcase car is Sully's 1965 powder blue Cadillac convertible with white wall tires.

Connected by an adjoining wall was an eight-bed efficiency apartment for Bam-Bam's ex-Army commandos, who go by names like Gator, Mongoose, Snake, Rhino, Smoke, Big Cat, Gigabyte, and Taz. They provide private security for Graceland, our bar oasis, the entire marina, and varied construction skills toward fulfilling our vision for the property. And they deliver assistance on our more challenging cases. They are capital letters *L & L*, Loyal and Lethal.

I unlocked the back door of the marina to the kitchen and dropped the two five-pound bags of peanut and chocolaty goodies on our rectangle-shaped kitchen island. Five pounds are for Bam-Bam's men. Marge was excellent enough to make two equal packages, always protocol.

Besides Twiggy and the human crew gathered in Graceland, we also were joined by our other two four-legged members; Iggy, a ninety-pound German Shepherd with suggestions of Black Labrador, and Sabaka Sunrise, a seventy-pound American Eskimo, and an orange and white extremely mean tabby, named Colonel Tom Parker. Our Graceland is not that famous mansion in Memphis, Tennessee, owned by the dark-haired, iconic King of rock and roll. We did not have the never-ending peanut butter and banana sandwiches and mountains of bacon in large bowls on every table. But our Graceland is our private watering hole, and Sully is our resident home brewer and draft beer architect.

Our Graceland is longer than it is wide; at the wide end is our white pine-wood paneled bar. There are eight high-backed white pine barstools perched against the bar. But these were extraordinary bar stools; each had a white hand-sewn padded seat hand sewn by Tilly that illustrated Elvis and all of her favorite Elvis movies; *Jail House Rock, Love Me Tender, King Creole, G.I. Blues, Blue Hawaii, Girl, Girls, Girls, Fun in Acapulco* and *Viva Las Vegas.* I knew these movies by heart because Tilly had them on a loop on our two 98-inch flat-screen televisions. We spent a lot of time in Graceland, you know, tasting Sully's barley and hops creations. Currently, Sully was holding court standing behind his bar, pouring large draft beers in sturdy Crate and Barrel Portland beer glasses. Sully looked like a commercial for L.L. Bean with his pressed khaki trousers, a blue long-sleeve shirt, and a khaki safari vest. Sully is tall, long, fashionably gray up top, and the most dangerous man I have ever met, ever. He stood inspecting two handguns resting on a white hand towel in front of him. Sully and Tilly are the most dangerous senior citizens in the world.

After telling Tilly that there were ten pounds of goodies from The Peanut Shoppe resting in her kitchen, she slipped past me to begin arranging two peanut, cashew, and chocolate trays, one for us and the other for Bam-Bam's men next door in their dorm room and apartments.

Kat, my wife, and Bam-Bam, her fraternal twin brother, were bellied up to the bar on stools next to each other. When I saw my wife, I got that thing in my solar plexus, and it moved up and danced in my head simultaneously, something that I can't explain when I see her — but it happens every time. Kat was wearing a light blue, sleeveless sundress with yellow butterflies that accented her tanned and toned upper arms. A large, six-stone diamond necklace hung from her neck. Two large, 18k gold hoop earrings that looked amazing dangled from each ear. I was very familiar with these specific pieces of jewelry: Last winter, on a snowy Sunday afternoon, instead of sitting by a toasty fire drinking a hot toddy and watching professional football, I was invited and reluctantly accepted an impromptu invitation to accompany Kat to the Saks Fifth Avenue store in Beachwood near Cleveland.

Bam-Bam was wearing a black t-shirt and gray, and white army camouflage fatigues with a black baseball cap turned backward. His shoulders and biceps were so taut and sculpted that they always looked like they would tear. Kat, even in repose, looked fitness-model-ready. These two were fraternal twins, closer than even the Olsen twins, and I am not sure who would win in a fight. I mean Kat and Bam-Bam, not the Olsen twins. Bam-Bam stood five foot eleven inches, and Kat was five foot nine inches, and both had intensive training in martial arts and hand-to-hand combat. And both had egos the size of the Milky Way galaxy. They are the muscle and demolition experts on our team.

But now, each had a tall pilsner glass containing Sully's Fall batch of homemade draft beer. A darker, amber ale that Sully named Portage Lakes Pontoon-Amber is a full-bodied, semi-heavy beer, but the girls seemed to like it.

After kissing Kat, I complimented her new hair color and hairstyle, something the beauty world called 'almond edges.' I checked out halfway through our conversation about her hair last night. Still, not remembering that she had an early morning appointment and not correctly recognizing the almond edges first thing would have been like not remembering that I pulled the pin on a hand grenade. After said compliment, her eyes lit up like giant sparklers, and her smile was life-changing.

I grabbed an empty barstool while Sully placed a tall Portage Lakes Pontoon-Amber in front of me. Uncle Sam had trained Tilly and Sully early in a world only a few have ever lived to speak. After retiring very young, they made a fortune in private security and consultation, among other highly-paid jobs. As hired security consultants, they took on some assignments that have never been disclosed, but now and then, it can be seen on their faces and voices. As a result of some of this work, a very high admission fee was assessed on these two for the rest of their lives.

I took what I believed was a well-deserved sip of my cold beer after enduring that horrible port wine, and I told the group, "So, we are now gainfully employed by the university to investigate alleged death threats leveled against the football team's starting quarterback, Gunner Thompson."

"At what fee?" Sully asked.

I told him as I passed the extensive retainer check over to Kat, who shared it with Tilly, and she then handed it to Bam-Bam, and eventually, the impressive check arrived in front of

Sully. I explained that Gunner's daily schedule would be emailed later this afternoon. Sully pulled a pen from behind the bar and endorsed the back of the check. He then removed his cell phone from his front pants pocket, opened our bank account app, and took a picture of each side of the check. Now it was safely residing in our bank account, so we had to work the case. Sully inquired about fees as a running joke, and we had more money that we could spend and money that would last three or four luxurious lifetimes. So we had a preference to give a majority of it away. By this evening, a charity will have already been picked out and showered with our expected proceeds from this university job, including the extensive retainer check.

"What's your first move, babe?" Kat said.

"I will compile a short list, but in brief order, I thought a good starting point would be meeting with Gunner Thompson, his mother, his former high school principal, and the university radio station, and then at some point, his football Coach, Dennis Darling, not necessarily in that order," I replied.

"His last name is Darling?" Tilly asked.

"Yes, and Chancellor Wright let the cat out of the bag by strongly suggesting to me that the coach was not a darling but rather a pompous ass, a narcissist, and an egomaniac that screams more than he talks."

"Oh, you two will get along fine," Kat said with dancing eyes and a mischievous grin.

Tilly returned with an enormous peanut platter that also held assorted cheeses, crackers, olives, and some hot Hungarian peppers we bought at a small roadside vegetable stand in Southern Ohio near Cambridge.

I took a bigger sip of my beer and replied with what I thought was confidence and the right amount of gravitas, "I plan on charming the hell out of him."

Kat made what dubiously sounded like a snort while rolling her eyes into the back of her head. If eye-rolling were an Olympic sport, Graceland would have many gold medals.

"Are you implying that Coach Darling and I may not get along?" I said.

"Like sharks and seals," Bam-Bam offered.

"Who's the shark, and who's the seal?" I asked.

"We will see, won't we?" Bam-Bam said.

Bam-Bam and Sully began discussing the merits of the two firearms in front of them. Kat and Tilly discussed a possible shutter and blind renovation in the boathouse. I turned my barstool one hundred and eighty degrees and saw the stunning view through the wall-to-wall and floor-to-ceiling windows and sliding glass doors. The Summit County blue sky seemed limitless, and the lake water was a little choppy, which gave it character and personality. I liked how our pontoon boat rocked gently against our dock, seemingly enjoying it, completely safe with the six rubber boat fenders tied on the dockside. The sun danced off the blue metallic paint. But my very best view was inside Graceland and the marina; there was a reason God created me for this exact time. These great superheroes are my core, my soul, and the reason my blood pumps. These fine humans help people, are grateful, do not take themselves too seriously, and love with a ferocity I have never seen or felt. I thank God every day he picked me so, in turn, they could like me enough to be a part of this beautiful world to help people and do the next right thing. We believe in the current judicial system. However, we also think there are way too many loopholes designed for the rich, delinquents, career criminals, and the powerfully connected. That is where we come in; we close those loopholes. Unfortunately, we have to straddle that line, and that decision sometimes is a bitch.

I turned my head to the left and looked proudly at our pool table with the orange felt surface and the white RubberDucks logo illustrated on the top. I spied Sully's classic Elton John *'Captain Fantastic'* pinball machine. And I also could see on the other side of the room Tilly's treasure of all treasures, her most prized possession, the white sequined jumpsuit from Elvis's July 10, 1975 concert at the Richfield Coliseum in nearby Richfield, Ohio. The audacious suit is encased in insulated protective glass, standing in all of its glory at six feet tall; we have never confirmed if this is the actual jumpsuit Elvis wore and owned or if it is an imitation. Nobody was brave enough to wade into that conversation with Tilly. Sadly, my eyes reached the only piece of art I felt worthy to contribute, a framed and autographed picture of a young and graceful Rocky Colavito standing on first base just before the Cleveland Indians traded him on April 17, 1960. He was before my time, but I am an amateur baseball history nerd. Rocky was a beautiful savior for Cleveland Indians fans. This trade shook the baseball world, but the news decimated fans in Cleveland from the downtown Lake Erie shoreline to the suburbs of Lakewood, Lorain, Parma, Solon, Bay Village, Rocky River, and many more towns throughout Ohio; it was even felt across the nation by some

Cleveland Indians fans who were displaced for one reason or another or had moved away from Northeast Ohio.

"Hey, baby, what are you thinking about?" Kat asked.

I turned my barstool back around and smiled, and then replied, "Baseball, baby, baseball, among other things."

Kat walked up close and stood next to me while I sat, and she said, "Honey, do you like this case?"

I smiled and replied, "Not at all."

Kat smiled and knocked her head against my left shoulder.

Chapter 6

AFTER OUR MUCH-NEEDED boat ride and overindulging in food and spirits, our pontoon boat was now docked, tied down, and covered. And Kat and I were up in our boathouse with our pups. A steady, constant is that Northeast Ohio cools down tremendously in the evenings when summer ends and Fall is around the corner. In that certainty, Kat and I, dressed in comfortable clothes, were lying in front of a crackling fire in the fireplace. I was in mismatched athletic wear; Kat was in a pink, two-piece matching silk pajama set. We looked fetching, or at least she did. We installed the natural rock wood-burning fireplace during the most recent remodel. We could have built an entire boathouse for the cost of the new fireplace, but conveying those thoughts to my wife would be like taking a bath with an electric toaster.

Nonetheless, I was settled in my leather recliner, and Kat was nesting on our matching Ethan Allen couch. I made the past mistake of calling our new Ethan Allen sofa "just the sofa" and was scolded immediately. Won't ever do that again. Twiggy, Iggy, and Sabaka lay on the floor in a fluffy, snuggly jigsaw puzzle directly in front of the fire. It was a moonless night outside, and the deck lights cast a warm, comforting glow in front of the dark lake. We had Pia Toscano on low volume in the background. Pia Toscano is currently touring with Andrea Bocelli. We're huge fans of both.

Kat was on her tablet surfing for deals on anything and everything, but mostly she was shopping on the Neiman Marcus website. I peered over her shoulder a few months back while she was on the site, and the little picture of the shopping cart in the right-hand corner showed she had one hundred and sixteen items ready to buy. This explains why we get an annual Christmas card from Neiman Marcus, and Kat and Tilly each receive personalized birthday cards from the Company's Vice President. Between my wife and Tilly, the marina gets twenty to thirty packages delivered a week, yet every time a new one arrives, they feign shock and surprise that they are for them.

While Kat shopped online, the website I was reviewing informed me that Gunner Thompson grew up about a mile north of Akron in Cuyahoga Falls. Cuyahoga Falls is a small, folksy town located south of Stow, north of Green and Canton.

I was also in possession of all the films from Gunner Thompson's high school football games, beginning with his first year right up through his last game as a senior. I had all of these loaded on my iPad. I knew his former high school football coach Rick Giles, who emailed me a link to Gunner's games plus a complete bio on Gunner Thompson from the team's directory. I pulled up the Cuyahoga Falls versus Barberton high school game from Gunner Thompson's final season, the competition during which the senior players were honored. I like football and want to watch Gunner play tonight, and if I see something, I see something. I can start my detecting work tomorrow. Nonetheless, I had a yellow legal pad and a pen on the table.

The recording began at the start of the first quarter with Cuyahoga Falls wearing their home-field black jerseys and gold pants. Cuyahoga Falls was starting on offense with Gunner Thompson under center. He was tall and lean. I picked up the file folder next to me containing various computer printouts and the information emailed to me by Miss Bethany. After a quick review, I began perusing the physical statistics. He was listed in high school as six foot two inches and one hundred and seventy-five pounds. He didn't look any of it, even wearing his football pads; he was slender. I then returned to Miss Bethany's communication and found the current university football press book that details him as six foot five inches and weighing two hundred and thirty-five pounds. I continued watching while fast-forwarding any action that did not showcase the offense. Gunner threw two touchdown passes in the first half, completed twelve out of fourteen, and had no interceptions. The kid was good.

After thirty-five minutes, I tossed the iPad on the seat of my recliner, and as I stood, I snatched a yellow velour throw blanket from the corner of my chair and draped it over Kat and the couch...er...our Ethan Allen sofa. I bent and kissed her lips lightly before walking to the fire to stoke the logs and motivate the flames. After some stirring, I searched the kitchen to locate a cold Diet Coke and a handful of Tilly's incredible homemade Milky Way brownies. Making my way back to my seat, I was quiet and sly so as not to rile the furry jigsaw puzzle on the floor.

"You're ready to get back to work, aren't you, baby?" Kat said. She was looking at me with her head and neck resting on her hand, arm, and elbow.

"True Dat, " I replied.

I looked at her, and she was shaking her head as she said, "You have just as much street cred as Jimmy Carter."

"Maybe, maybe not, but we both help people," I said smugly.

"True Dat," Kat replied, giggling while holding her iPad against her face, her shoulders shaking uncontrollably. I watched her sneak a peek at me and then hide behind her iPad for a minute. And at that moment, I couldn't quantify how much I loved this woman.

Getting back into a comfortable position in my recliner and focusing back on the football game, I noticed I had forgotten to pause the film, and it had kept playing. The view on my iPad showed Gunner Thompson, without a helmet, walking toward the fifty-yard line with a middle-aged female. The female was holding a dozen red roses, and she appeared to be crying. I believe this is Gunner's mother, and some said I wasn't smart enough to enter the world of private detecting.

Resting the iPad on my lap, I opened my Diet Coke and took most of a Milky Way brownie in one bite. The next frame showed Gunner Thompson walking with his mother back to the sideline; Gunner Thompson and his mom were laughing at something, and she playfully pulled on his right arm. She wore black jeans and a blue denim jacket, and her hair was medium-length strawberry blond. His hair was identical in color but wet with sweat, and his movements were confident. It was apparent he was straining to take shorter strides to allow for his mother's shorter strides. The next frame caught my attention, and I almost missed it; as the camera panned back to the next senior football player walking onto the field with his parents, I suddenly saw mobster Joseph Votto Senior and his number-one wise guy, his at-will executioner, Buster. No last name, just Buster. They were both leaning against the waist-high chain-link fence that surrounds the football field. The crime rate instantly spikes in the zip code where Joey Votto Senior and Buster choose to dwell. My crew had recently put Joseph Votto, Senior's son, Joe Junior, behind bars, although unbelievably, we were on good terms with Joseph Senior on that one. Joseph Votto Senior was a very dangerous human being. It was unsettling seeing this particular high school football game with Joseph Votto in attendance, fifty feet from the prime individual in our new case. It had to be a coincidence. But I didn't believe in them.

Chapter 7

KAT AND I woke early and showered together for a long time, and once I got my sea legs under me, I got dressed for total private eye success in black jeans, a red polo shirt, and white Reebok running shoes. We all tramped over to the marina, including the dogs; it was a beautiful Northeastern Ohio morning, seventy degrees with blue skies dotted with large pillowy white clouds. I lovingly gazed at our pontoon boat nestled up to our dock; out of all modes of transportation, this is one of the simplest and one of my favorites. It wouldn't be long before we had to pull the pontoon and my 1959 Chris Craft Continental from the water and store them for the winter. Maybe I could wrap this case up before the snow begins to fly. The dogs elected to stay outside when they spotted seven ducks at the water's edge; they would come into the marina later when they got hungry and realized they couldn't catch the ducks. As we walked into the marina's massive kitchen, I smelled the greatest gift to the world, breakfast being prepared.

Tilly was cooking mounds of thick-cut bacon, an alarming amount of sizzling link sausages, and a pan the size of a helipad with cheesy scrambled eggs. All of this on Tilly's industrial, restaurant-sized stove. Tilly loves to feed us and Bam-Bam's men. Kat grabbed a spatula and began rolling the sausages in the large pan. When cooking, Tilly wears heavy makeup, and she dresses like she is straight out of a 1950s cooking advertisement. Today she wore a peach shirtwaist dress circa the '50s and multiple gold bracelets on her left wrist. The apron of the day was white with a picture of a young Elvis on his motorcycle wearing his black leathers. Also, I knew there to be at least seven death instruments at her fingertips, not including her favorite pistol resting in her front apron pocket, a Ruger LCP .22 in an orange sherbet steel finish. The small firearm is five inches long and three and a half inches high and weighs less than nine and a half ounces. She named her .22 pistol Dolores Hart after Tilly's favorite Elvis leading lady from the big screen gem, *King Creole.*

"Sully and Bam-Bam are on the range," Tilly declared openly in my general direction.

I grabbed a plastic bottle of Diet Coke from the refrigerator, kissed both women on the cheek, and walked over to the pantry. I reached onto the second shelf on the right-hand wall of the pantry and rotated a large can of V-8 juice until I heard a soft clicking sound. I lifted a large bag of rigatoni pasta and then set it back down on its hidden scale sensor, and then pushed a remote recessed button underneath the shelf. Suddenly, the back wall of the pantry opened to a set of illuminated metal stairs.

The stairs were well-lit, and after reaching the bottom, I turned left and was presented with a metal door and punched #2753 into the electronic keypad. The door opened quietly. The numbers represent my childhood address on Maplewood Street in Cuyahoga Falls. In an instant, the loud hammering of repeated gunshots filled my eardrums. Bam-Bam was standing in the target practice stall nearest me, and Sully was firing in the next booth to the right. Both were wearing eye and ear protection. They stopped shooting when the long tube lights blinked twice as a warning that the door was open.

Bam-Bam was in a black t-shirt, black cargo pants, black combat boots, and a black ball cap. Sully was all Duluth Trading Company today; gray creased cargo pants pressed gray and black-brown checked long-sleeve shirt, tan hiking boots, and a stainless steel compass hanging from his belt loop. Both had handguns hanging by their sides.

"Scooter, try this new compact 9mm., It's simple with a polymer frame striker; I am looking to add to our arsenal," Sully said as he handed the compact weapon to me.

The small weapon had a matte black finish with a soft texture grip and what looked like a three-and-a-half-inch barrel. It was lightweight at about twenty-two ounces with a chamber capacity of fifteen plus one.

I took the .9mm and held it in the palm of my right hand, feeling the weight and balance. I ejected the magazine with one hand, removed the live round, and counted the magazine capacity for fifteen. I held the firearm in my left hand again, feeling the weight, and after a few seconds, I replaced the ammunition and snapped the magazine into the butt of the gun. I put on a set of ear protectors and clear rubber eye goggles. I looked down the barrel, testing the sight lines, and asked Sully to send the number one all-time Northeast Ohio traitor's facial target downrange. We had hundreds of pictures of celebrities and politicians with a red bull's-eye that we used for target practice, and this guy was number one.

Sully laughed and snatched a copy of Art Modell's, the former owner of the Cleveland Professional Football team. His picture still makes my blood boil. Sully then hooked the twelve-inch by twelve-inch photo to two metal clips on the electronic pulley system, and, with a touch of a button on the remote control, he sent it twenty feet to the back of the range.

After the target was set, I took in a solid amount of air, let it out slowly, and raised my right arm, with the pistol firmly sitting in my right hand with my right index finger pointed down the barrel. I then placed my left hand on the bottom of the compact firearm and wrapped it firmly around it and my right hand. I have done these things thousands of times. It was close to being second nature, but I had to make sure every time that it was second nature. If not, that could get me dead real quick. The red light just above and in front of me to my right turned green, and I squeezed the trigger and unloaded all sixteen rounds in three seconds. I set the gun on a side shelf with the barrel pointed down range and removed my ear protectors and safety glasses. Sully retrieved the target electronically, pulled it from the clips, and held it at arm's length while shaking his head.

"Son of a bitch, a new and unfamiliar handgun, and you put fifteen rounds in succession in the center of a three-inch circle."

"It's a gift, and this gun sights a little high and right, or the balance is off on the grip," I handed Sully the handgun and then proceeded to go back upstairs.

Chapter 8

I WAS STANDING just outside of the university resident dining hall. The building itself was newer and could have been stately. However, the boorish designers and architects found a way to waste an obscene amount of money and resources to make it look like a three-story Ohio Turnpike rest stop. There were various glass partitions, a window pattern I could not decipher, and jumbled concrete walls that, as far as I could tell, accomplished absolutely nothing. But on the bright side, it was hideous and expensive. My campus directory had informed me that the dining hall occupied the entire first floor, and the remaining two stories consisted of additional classrooms. Miss Bethany's information affirmed Gunner would be breakfasting at this time.

I walked up to the coffee station and, after nearly exhausting myself, located good old plain black coffee from twenty-seven different choices of flavored, hot, mocha, vanilla, cappuccino, iced, and others I couldn't pronounce. I finally found good old simple black coffee, Christ almighty.

The young female cashier with long dreadlocks, extended silver speckled fingernails, an indescribable silver piercing in her tongue, and astonishingly bright purple eye shadow wasn't buying my story that I was a guest lecturer from Harvard. I paid with cash and went on a quest to find the most popular student-athlete on this campus that just happened to be getting threats on his life.

Gunner Thompson was sitting at a table for six in the center of the room with three other male students. Inferential reasoning and my vast experience as a detective told me the other three diners were football teammates. Being a combined one thousand pounds helped my hypothesis. There were nine empty plastic food trays splayed around the tabletop.

"Hi, Gunner," I said, amazed at what a wordsmith I had become since hanging around the campus.

He looked at me and hesitated for a second before answering, "That's me." It was doing wonders for Gunner as well.

I glanced at Gunner's breakfast companions and thought of how John Madden, the legendary football coach turned legendary game-day announcer turned legendary football video game creator, used to refer to these larger-sized football players as *'The Hog's Upfront.'* These behemoths were paying close attention to my intrusion, except for a big freckled, redhead kid with some small acne spots on his cheeks and neck. He was trying to consume the last molecule of chocolate pudding from a clear plastic cup with a tiny white spoon. I think he was winning, but I couldn't be sure.

"The Chancellor hired me. Is there a place to talk in private?" I asked him and set one of the Chancellor's business cards and one of mine in front of him.

Gunner retrieved both from the table and read them, "I guess we can talk on the way to my class."

We all stood, and I felt somewhat insignificant compared to these enormous young men, but I bet none were carrying a Ruger Max handgun with a ten-round capacity. Point for me.

Gunner and his teammates put their backpacks over their large shoulders, and we exited the dining hall. These four athletes wore various articles of training apparel, all with the university logo and the Nike logo. Gunner was in university blue warm-up pants, a white short-sleeved Nike polo, and white Nike cross-trainers. After walking a few feet outside, the other football players peeled off to attend classes after elaborate handshakes that I had trouble following. As we walked, the cement walkways overflowed with coeds wearing colorful backpacks and wireless earbuds. Many were on their phones. It was sunny and cloudless, an excellent day to talk about death threats in college athletics.

"The university has hired me to confirm or dispel rumors of death threats aimed towards you."

Gunner stopped and looked in each direction to ensure no one had heard my allegations. His face changed from, 'Aw, shucks nice to meet you, sir,' to a hardened 6-foot 5-inch tall, steeled young man. I had to look up to meet his eyes.

"Look, you have no idea what's going on," he said.

"Tell me; we can help you, no matter what it is. Gunner, I promise you that we are very good at what we do. Has anyone personally approached you, conveying you physical harm, or made threats towards you?"

Gunner looked at me, and his face loosened up, showing that maybe I could help him. But then the fear crept quickly back in; his face tightened up, his eyes began to water, and he began to look nervously in each direction.

"Stay out of this, sir, please; you can't help us, nobody can, and they will kill her."

With that, Gunner turned and began jogging away from me, and then it turned into an all-out sprint. 'Oh shit, on this very campus,' one hundred yards from this very spot on our last caper, a female track coach began to murder and mayhem by sprinting from me. At least this sprinter called me 'Sir.' However, I knew fear, and this young man was spooked about something. I got that Spider-Man tingly sensation on the back of my neck. This death threat had credibility.

Chapter 9

LOOKING AROUND TO ensure my dignity was intact, I finished my coffee, found a blue trash receptacle, and dropped my cup into it. I sat on a blue wrought iron bench and found Gunner's schedule on my cell phone for the remainder of the day to review. This young, athletic and healthy man was frightened about something, and we needed to watch his back as best we could while we investigated. The bright side is that the football program and his academic requirements took up most of his time. I called Bam-Bam, and we devised a plan for today using one of his less scary-looking men to follow Gunner between classes until three p.m. Then he would be under the football team's care and supervision until eight thirty this evening. Bam-bam would put another man on him until he got to his residence.

I eased into the campus coed foot traffic and felt silly doing it. I was the only one not carrying a backpack slung over my shoulders, a ball cap turned backward, or giant white headphones buried onto the sides of my head. They were like bright silver shiners in the ocean, scurrying back and forth and often diving into each other's paths. Heads down, looking at their iPhones but never crashing into each other, impressive. After a seven-minute walk past the extensive library, I veered off to my right and stood looking at an ancient, mustard-colored brick, five-story building. I expected my backup to arrive before Gunner's class ended but was willing to risk Gunner recognizing me. I was unwilling to let him die because we were asleep at the wheel. I faked that I was looking at something important on my cell phone, occasionally looking up to appear to be reading the postings on the various corkboards inside the building's massive doors. I did this for forty-six minutes as I waited for Gunner to vacate this building through these doors when I received a text message from Bam-Bam that Smoke was in position.

I started walking in the direction of where I had parked, and there Smoke stood, ready to infiltrate the hallowed world of academia. I almost walked past him. Smoke looked like an actual college student: Baggy blue jeans, red Michael Jordon hoop shoes, and a vintage blue t-shirt with a large white peace sign on the front. There was a white rope necklace with a giant shark tooth hanging around his neck. He wore a black newsboy hat backward on his head. His blue backpack was slung over his left shoulder. I knew he would be prepared for any scenario that might present itself, violent or nonviolent. Smoke stood five for nine inches and weighed one hundred and sixty-five pounds, and his face was unmemorable, nondescript. His features are not worthy of a second glance or consideration afterward. He can hide in plain sight, and with a simple change of a hat, untuck of a shirt, or the addition of sunglasses; he becomes an entirely different person. But he is very, very bad and dangerous if the situation calls for it. I walked past him without acknowledging his presence. I also anticipated Bam-Bam would be somewhere close, adding another layer of surveillance and ensuring another interested party wasn't surveilling Gunner.

Chapter 10

I SET A course for Cuyahoga Falls. The short trip from the university to Cuyahoga Falls High School was usually twenty minutes, and today was usual but with great Northeastern Ohio weather. It was seventy-two degrees and sunny at ten forty-six in the morning; I had Elton John and *'Yellow Brick Road'* on volume number five, the top down on the Corvette, my cool shades adorning my face, and the beginning of a new Rubber City Caper - all was right for right now. I was comforted that we had Gunner covered. It took twenty-four minutes to arrive at a visitor parking space at Cuyahoga Falls High School. The building resides on Fourth Street, across from the ginormous Cuyahoga Falls Natatorium.

A few moments later, I was sitting in Principal Ann Runkle Ritchie's office inside the school. Mrs. Runkle Ritchie did not look like my high school principal back in the day. She strikes immediate confidence, is beautiful, has athletic overtones, and is healthy-looking. Her green and blue blouse had a borderline tie-dye design but was respectable and professional. Her brown hair was curly and spongy; a plain, thin leather strap around her neck posed as a necklace. Her earrings were small and made of pewter. Her fingernails were long and painted a brilliant green. She was one-missed hair appointment, one-missed pedicure, and one good Foo Fighters concert away from wearing grunge clothing and straw clogs to ditch academia and go on tour with Dave Grohl. She would flee this era and revert to when the Foo Fighters formed in Seattle in the early nineties.

My very first impression told me that the school board treads carefully around Ann Runkle Ritchie.

"Is there someone I can call to verify your identity and, more importantly, that your intentions are honorable and proper towards Gunner Thompson?" the Principal asked me as she fiddled with my business card.

"You won't take my word?" I asked, smiling.

She returned the smile showing most of her teeth, and they were white and straight. She had a small scar underneath her lower lip that had turned opaque over time. Her eyes were brown and large and sat close together; her nose was small, and her beautiful face was round.

"No, I am afraid not in this instance; too much at stake; this young man is special and very dear to us in the Cuyahoga Falls community."

I thought for a moment, then I grabbed a pen, and a yellow legal pad from in front of her, turned the legal place towards me, and wrote down two phone numbers. I put the pen back down and turned the yellow legal pad toward her. She looked at it, tore the page from the pad, and said, "I will be right back, Mr. Jeanette."

As I waited, I felt that sensation; maybe it was the antiseptic smell and the calm between each ring of the class bell. Every school that I attended maintained the same feeling of excitement and loss of freedom that I had felt years before in this, even in this very same building. The other emotions ranged from anxiety, fear, nervousness, happiness, first love, hope, and joy all in one single, ordinary day of school, usually before lunch.

I looked around the office as I waited and was immediately conscious of the outrageous amount of times I have sat in offices waiting on people to verify my credentials. The world has become an enormous reservoir of cynics and skeptics. But this office had character. It was the second soul of this Principle of Cuyahoga Falls High School. Her office was a mismatched home for succulent plants, small ferns, and gifts and cards given to her over the years. There were bookcases of varying sizes on each wall. In the bookcases, I spotted the new novel by Adriana Trigiani and books by Lee Child and Jamie Raskin. On a small credenza was a homage to the Foo Fighters, especially Dave Grohl and Taylor Hawkins. There were pictures of past concerts, ticket stubs, coffee mugs, and a blue headband from the '90s. On the wall behind her desk was a large wooden cross, plain, not flashy. On the longest wall, we're hand-painted lyrics in blue paint – *'Chasing birds to get high, my head is in the clouds chasing birds to get by, I am never coming down, my heart is six feet underground.'– Chasing Birds - The Foo Fighters*

On the credenza behind her desk sat two pictures in identical silver frames. It was Ann Runkle Ritchie and her husband at the weddings of her son and daughters. Sully had performed a quick social media peek, and we knew she was married to Gary Ritchie and had a son and daughter who recently wed their sweethearts.

After fifteen minutes, the confident and secure principal returned and took her seat behind the desk while placing two unopened bottles of water in front of us.

"The waters indicate that you have decided to speak with me about Gunner Thompson."

She smiled, a genuine smile, and said, "Wow, you are a detective."

I liked her very much already.

Ann Runkle Ritchie leaned back in her seat and crossed her right leg over her left, reaching down and straightening her short yellow skirt until she got it how she wanted it. Her legs were good. She was wearing white Vans on her feet. She then slid and twisted to get to the far back of her chair and got comfortable before saying, "I called both numbers and spoke to each individual at length concerning you. The first number I called was Summit County Sheriff Inspector William Cunningham. His regards for you are very high, although he indicated that you occasionally cut corners, and your judgment and judgment alone are sometimes the foremost concern when working a case."

"That is true, and he is my biggest fan," I replied.

She held up her right hand and continued, "He also stated that you weren't nearly as amusing or quick-witted as you think." "Am too," I said under my breath.

She gazed at me for a few seconds and then proceeded, "He also explained that your word was gold and that you were the toughest and coldest SOB he had ever met when the situation required it. He also explained that you would kick, scratch, claw, and fight to find the truth. He claims that you and your team are the very best he has ever observed, and the fact that you were currently sitting in my office asking me questions, it was of utmost importance that I should take this as seriously as anything I am doing today. Period." She leaned forward, retrieved her bottle of water from the desktop, opened it, and took a long swig. She drank like Kat occasionally, with no desire, just ameliorating a basic need.

"The second call was quite the shocker, Mr. Jeanette; wow. The fact that this woman personally answered on the third ring, no personal assistant, no staff member, just her on the line, again, for lack of a better word, wow. First, I did not vote for her in past elections, but after speaking with her, I now fully regret my ignorant decision. She said that years ago, with no experience whatsoever, you, as a college student, tracked down her kidnapped daughter, killed the kidnappers with your roommate's crossbow, and then treated her daughter to ice cream at the local Dairy Queen. All while thirty or forty highly trained law enforcement agents, including ones from the F.B.I., sat on their dicks. And that is a direct quote."

Ann Runkle Ritchie took another sip of her water. She paused before continuing, "And that's quite rich considering that presently she now commands and instructs similar units and many more here in Ohio."

"I got lucky," I said.

"She also said that you would say something to that effect."

The educator took another long drink of water and held the bottle close to her chest. "She also asserted that over the years, you have become very, very good at what you do and very passionate about your work. She also said that you do not usually release her cellular telephone number, which I just dialed, so it must be important to you or crucial to someone you are trying to help."

"It is," I replied without fully understanding why this was so important to me, but my gut told me that all background information would help Gunner Thompson.

We sat in silence. Both knew we were opening the door to something important but not knowing what, just that it was.

She spoke first. "Why give me those numbers to call? Why me, Mr. Jeanette?"

I looked past her and out the window onto the four tennis courts just to the right of the parking lot. There were two teenage girls; one with long blond hair and the other with short dyed red hair. Both were wearing blue jeans and colorful t-shirts and were trying to knock the ball over the net and back to one another with little success. Taking turns bouncing the ball and then hitting it underhand and missing an alarming amount of times, they would laugh hysterically when the ball hit the net. They weren't taking the game too seriously - besides the fits of laughter; they were smoking cigarettes.

I focused back on the principal and said, "Why you? Because I believe Gunner's life to be in danger, and the moment I walked into this office, I sensed that you cared for him deeply and you would have cared for him almost as much as his mother does. And I felt you would tell me the truth about Gunner Thompson when he was a student here at Cuyahoga Falls High School."

We sat in silence, and then I told her of the death threats, Gunner's reaction to my asking him about the death threats, and that my gut told me something serious was going on.

"I don't know where to begin," she continued.

"Middle, front or back. It doesn't matter. When I hear something important, I will know I heard it." I replied.

"You will, will you?" she said as she looked at me. Her gaze was tangible, almost physical.

"I will," I replied.

"Mr. Jeanette, before I begin, I must tell you that you are nothing like what I thought a private detective to be."

"Cheap suit, dirty and scuffed brown patent leather shoes, swollen and bulbous bourbon-induced nose, and a worn Polaroid camera hanging around my neck?" I replied.

She tilted her head back and laughed long and loud and said, "I am ashamed to admit it as a person of God and a nonjudgmental pedagogue, but yes. Almost that image, exactly. And I know in my core that you know what pedagogue means."

"In her teachings, she could be a bit pedantic," I said.

"Exactly."

We both smiled, and the atmosphere in the room altered to one of new and trusting friends.

"While Gunner was with us, we found him to be a wonderful person, great student, exceptional athlete, and kind to all. When
Gunner was here in this school, and there was no bullying, none, zip."

"How about Gunner's parents?" I asked.

Ann leaned back and placed her right behind her neck and said, "Gunner has never known his father, but his mother is a wonderful person. She attended every one of Gunner's events here at the school. She actively donated her time to the school for any event, even if Gunner had nothing to do with it. She works at Taylor Memorial Public Library."

"Any best friends, you know, ride-or-die buddies?"

This question made the principal turn complete to me, "Yes, Darris Blackford, Steve Kapusinski, and Todd Caruthers."

Those three names sent a small jolt of electricity into my system. I remembered them from the university football program.

"That was a quick answer," I said.

"Yes, but it's true - they have been inseparable since they were eight, and when Gunner decided to play college football at home, these three followed him. And that was the deal these three get accepted on the team, or Gunner does not play for the university. His loyalty is immeasurable."

We talked for another forty-four minutes, and then I headed back to the marina.

Chapter 11

WHEN I RETURNED to the marina, Tilly was leaning over and spreading a generous amount of brown sugar, honey, and molasses over two ten-pound boneless hams. Kat was sitting on the granite kitchen island crosslegged, eating a turkey sandwich.

"Wow, smells incredible," I said.

Tilly smiled and replied, "Oh, sweetie, that ham store at the mall has nothing on me."

"Come over here," Kat ordered me.

I did as told and was rewarded with an affectionate kiss.

I grabbed a Diet Coke from the refrigerator and walked through Graceland, our patio, and onto our dock. I stood and let the post-summer sun engulf my body; it felt good. I looked around, and the big lake was calm; kids were back in school, so there were only two small fishing boats on opposite ends of the water as far as I could see. I thought about my conversation with Ann Runkle Ritchie. I walked away with renewed relief for the local educational system. She was intelligent, compassionate, emphatic, and realistic. My big takeaway is that Gunner Thompson was a popular, outstanding student and gifted athlete at Cuyahoga Falls High School. He protected other students from bullies, knew the lunch ladies and maintenance men by name, and volunteered on every committee he could, whether his sports commitments would allow him. Kat walked towards me and handed me on a paper plate a giant turkey sandwich on sourdough bread, a mound of potato chips, and a dill pickle. She kissed me and headed back to Tilly and her kitchen.

Chapter 12

I HAD REVIEWED the email that Miss Bethany had sent me again, and I knew Gunner had our protection and would be in classes on campus or involved with the football program until late this evening. I had a great night of sleep, so I was going to get a feel for the death threat accusations from the people closest to Gunner's inner circle. And that put me on head football Coach Dennis Darling's doorstep. Coach Darling currently owns a win-loss record of nineteen wins and twenty-one losses at the university. Still, that record was deceiving because all but two of those wins were with Gunner Thompson at the helm in his first two years, and the first two wins this early season, his junior year as the starting quarterback.

I was thinking these thoughts as I sat in the robust Athletic Field House, more specifically, in Coach Darling's waiting room. I was sitting in a very comfortable blue leather accent chair. Coach Darling had an administrative assistant, and she was sitting behind a black metal desk with a glass desktop. She was not what I expected or the norm I had come to know while working on a previous case at this university and the beginnings of this one. She was considerably older, and I suspected she was alright with being called a secretary. She answered the extraordinarily complicated and extensive telephone system on her desk with courtesy, efficiency, and a little reverence for the office where she worked. I imagined this is what the White House communications director's telephone and demeanor to be. So for shits and giggles while I waited, I pulled out my cell phone and googled the White House's general phone number, I called it, and it was similar to what I was listening to just ten feet away from me. The phrasing was different, but the tone and pace were the same. As to say, 'We are so glad you called us, but please quit bugging us. We are way too crucial for the likes of you,' and Tilly and Kat say I am childish; I say I am fun.

I feared that if I sat here much longer, the phrase '*Coach Dennis Darling's office, how may I direct your call*' would haunt my dreams.

She picked up her phone and spoke briefly and then placed the handset back into its proper resting place and looked at me as if I had just won the lottery. And in a worshiping voice, said, "Coach Darling will see you now."

I resisted the urge to ask if I should take off my shoes before entering and if a genuine and sincere genuflect was necessary, but I fought the urge. Coach Darling was sitting behind his desk and leaning back in a wide leather office chair. He was wearing a blue Nike university football polo shirt with his name hand stitched on the left breast in white script. A matching blue ball cap with the university logo was sitting on his head perfectly. Just as I went to introduce myself, his cell phone that was sitting on his desk vibrated while ringing. He picked it up and immediately began dressing the caller down. There was no hint of amiableness on this particular head coach's face. I waited and looked around the office. It was a standard-issue, egomania-driven male office; trophies, awards, and the prerequisite wall of pictures with local restaurant owners, celebrities, professional athletes, and politicians. I wasn't going to like Dennis Darling, Kat had told me; it was a bad habit of judging people before meeting them, but my gut is not usually wrong.

Coach Darling hung up the phone, placed it on his desk, and said, "Can I help you?"

"I hope so, my name is Scooter Jeanette, and the college has hired me to investigate recent alleged death threats towards Gunner Thompson."

"Who hired you?"

I didn't want to tell him I didn't like him, but he could track it down quickly enough, so I said, "Chancellor Wright."

He leaned forward in his leather chair, scowling at me and smelling like Bay Rum aftershave. Dennis Darling had deep crow's feet around his eyes from squinting, laughing, or being angry. I was betting on the latter. His face was skinny and sharp and deeply tanned from spending hours outdoors.

"Do you have any identification?"

"Sure," I reached into my back pocket and pulled out my private investigator's license and one of my business cards and laid them on his desk.

Coach Darling adjusted my personal information on the desk with his right index finger without actually picking them up so he could read them. I changed my gun on my right side with a quick hip turn and remained silent.

After two minutes, he looked at me and said, "There are no death threats. It was never serious, and it's all a big hoax."

"So, fake news?"

"Absolutely," Dennis Darling replied.

"I spoke with Gunner, and the mere mention of death threats terrified him; why do you suppose that is Coach?" And I emphasized the word 'Coach' a little longer than needed.

The collegiate head coach glared at me, trying to wrap his head around the idea that some stranger had walked into his office and was busting his chops.

"Are you screwing with me?"

"Just a little," I replied, spacing my right thumb and right index finger a half inch apart.

"Watch it, and you stay away from my football team."

"So, there are no death threats?" I asked again.

"Hell no, just some drunken college kid getting his rocks off," Coach Darling replied.

"Ah, so you are aware of the death threats."

The coach knew he just got played and went on the offensive and said, "You're about to get thrown out on your ass, pal."

"That's not going to happen," I replied.

Coach Darling was at a loss; this impromptu meeting went downhill for him quickly. It was much easier to intimidate eighteen to twenty-two-year-old kids by threats of diminished playing time, extra wind sprints, or simply threatening to yank their football scholarships.

I just sat and took it all in; I could almost hear the hamster wheel spinning in his brain. Finally, I said, "So again, a young college male with all the other college experiences at his immediate disposal is getting his rocks off by making death threats?" I asked.

"Yes," the now steaming head coach replied.

"It's enough for Chancellor William Wright to hire us," I replied.

Dennis Darling slammed his hands on his desk and said, "That fat ass has nothing better to do than waste the school's money."

I was at a loss. I sorely wanted to remind this colossal asshat that before Gunner Thompson randomly chose this local university, the great Coach Dennis Darling won a total of two football games. And those two trivial wins cost the students and the State of Ohio, and the federal government appropriations, half of a million dollars in his salary alone. Also, the entire student body gets billed quarterly, so the athletes can walk around campus decked out in Nike gear from head to toe. And mostly, I would have thought Gunner's head football coach would be impartial and committed to proving the validity of these allegations for the imminent safety of one of his players, or at the very least, be open minded. Kat and Tilly have impressed me that sometimes it would be better if my forked tongue stayed still in my mouth on certain occasions. Nope, today wasn't going to be that day; maybe tomorrow.

"I am getting the impression that you are not interested in proving or disproving these allegations," I stated.

"Look, Buddy Boy…"

I laughed and said, "Buddy Boy, I hope you coach better than you talk,"

Coach Darling stood abruptly behind his desk and extended his right arm and pointed his index finger at me, and, through clenched teeth, said, "listen to me, buddy b...er buster, you leave that boy alone. Never speak to him again."

I played shot him with my forefinger and said, "Bang."

He stared at me for a second and said, "What the hell is your problem?"

I leaned forward in my chair while grabbing my information from his desk. I replied, "It means you are officially on my radar. Had Gunner Thompson chosen another college, you freaking twit would be coaching over at Immaculate Heart of Mary elementary in the C.Y.O. League. Now my team will electronically crawl up your ass, working around the giant stick already there. In a few short hours, we will know every aspect of your life, finances, google search trends, who your friends are, and who your associates are, and if we have to, we will harass them because of who you are. We will dig up your academic transcripts from kindergarten through college, the type of toilet paper you use, and if your digital footprint is as annoying as you."

I stood, turned, and exited, leaving him in a state of shock; as I walked toward the door, I silently counted to three, and on three, Dennis Darling began screaming almost in tongues. I smiled to myself. Dennis Darling may have just invented a new language; I thought perhaps this is what Bam-Bam was kidding me about earlier about sharks and seals. But I do believe I established that I was the shark today.

Chapter 13

SUMMIT COUNTY SHERIFF inspector Billy Cunningham and I were sitting at the open bar at Leo's Social Club after my Less than successful meeting with Coach Darling. We were both drinking Rolling Rock in the familiar green bottle. Also, we both had a giant homemade parmesan cheese meatball smothered in spicy marinara sauce in huge bowls, and we each had a large piece of garlic bread in front of us. Leo's Social Club takes up half a city block on Front Street in downtown Cuyahoga Falls. There was a massive outdoor patio with many tables and bright green umbrellas. Leo's is a great spot for happy hour libations, early evening dining, and people-watching. Their Italian food is exceptional. Today soft jazz was piped in, and there was also a pink glass bowl filled with small pretzels. I was one bar stool from Adam LaFaber's personal bar stool. There is a commemorative embossed nameplate confirming it. Adam owns an online advertising agency called 'Digital Sandwich.' Next door. He is a very successful and charming friend, and we have tipped a few back over the years.

Today, I wore a Neiman Marcus misty blue long-sleeved linen sport shirt, light gray twill pants, and Martin Dingman alligator rust-colored leather slip-on loafers. Kat and Tilly both read an article that color clashing is the hottest men's clothing trend of the year. I am currently Kat and Tilly's walking, talking mannequin. But today, I thought I deserved at least an honorable mention on Richard Blackwell's best-dressed list for detectives if he had such a thing.

The happy hour crowd was slinking in at a good clip. The bar seats were filling fast, but no one took the empty seat next to Billy. It didn't matter where we were or how crowded the place was, and there was always an empty stool next to Billy. He radiated authority and toughness, but today he looked exhausted, cranky, and extra dangerous. Some cops could look the same when the day ended as they did when it began, but not Billy; he always looked like this after a long shift with the Summit County Sheriff's Office. Billy Cunningham devotes so much effort, passion, and emotion to every exchange with the public. He believes good always negated evil, believes most people are good, believes he can save people from being hurt, and consequently was always a little frustrated and disappointed at the end of the day.

Billy placed his empty beer bottle on the very edge of the bar, away from his body, the universal sign for hurry the hell up and replace this open beverage. He leaned his Popeyesque forearms on the bar before him and turned to face me.

"Okay, I now have twelve ounces of magical listening fluid in my system and another on the way; what's up?"

"Police work has turned you cynical, " I replied.

"No, Scooter, you turned me cynical years ago."

Our clients get loads of toughness, smartness, determination, and sealed lips from our team. But in addition, they get Billy Cunningham, an invaluable resource for us. Kat, Tilly, Sully, Bam-Bam, and I strive to walk that fine line of the law, but sometimes to save someone's life, we cross that line like Evil Knievel jumping the Snake River canyon on a motorcycle. Billy is sometimes our eyes, ears, and guiding lighthouse, sometimes not.

"Ok, have you heard of any credible death threats targeting anyone on the university football team?"

Our barmaid replaced both our beers and took both empty bottles, smiled at Billy, and ignored me; she probably had a few outstanding parking tickets.

"What the hell is your obsession with the university?" Billy said while making small wet circles on the bar with the condensation from the new beer bottle.

I shrugged my shoulders, smiled, and said, "They pay well."

"Truth bomb," Billy replied, and we clinked our beers.

I began a story with Billy that included most of what I knew to date, but I didn't tell him everything. When I was finished Billy smiled and said, "Scooter you do step in it don't you?"

"I do."

Chapter 14

AFTER ARRIVING BACK at the marina, I was met in the garage by Twiggy, Iggy, and Sabaka. After all three did their version of Elvis shaking, shivering, and jiggling to '*All Shook Up*,' we headed into the kitchen. The smell of Tilly's never-imitated cheesy garlic potatoes smothered in sautéed onions was overwhelming but most welcome. I also knew three ten-pound prime ribs were slowly rotating on an electric rotisserie over an open hickory fire on the patio. Gator was tending to these prime ribs like they were his children.

I went looking and found four homemade cherry pies, and it wasn't difficult as they were on the kitchen counter. Kat and I and I had hand-picked thirty-five pounds of fresh cherries from a farm in Southern Ohio a few weeks ago and sealed and froze most. We liked our food here at the marina. Almost as catching bad guys and girls.

I went into Graceland and was met with Sully standing behind the bar with the Rolling Stones trying in vain to get some satisfaction through the jukebox.

"You, Sully, are the antithesis of the vast representation of the established senior citizen."

"Don't forget it either," Sully replied without looking up. He had the draft beer tap system dismantled, and the parts are lying neatly on the bar on clean white towels and wearing a long black apron with a large front pocket and a lightweight gray mock long-sleeve turtleneck shirt underneath.

"Does Bam-Bam and his men know that Tilly buys your clothes from Neiman Marcus?"

He did not answer me, so I quietly sat at the bar; one does not push Sully too far.

"I thought a little bit of gunk in the tap added flavor over time, like a worked-in barbecue grill does," I said.

"Spoken like a true beer connoisseur novice," Sully answered back while taking a long and thick piece of pipe cleaner to the inside of the gold-plated beer tap. After a few minutes, Sully held the spout up to the light in the room, looked in the opening, nodded his head once, set it down, And said, "I am going to assemble Both of us vodka tonic's, and hopefully we enjoy them."

Sully fulfilled his vision's and we gently clinked glasses and enjoyed our first couple of sips in mutual silence.

Later that evening, we ate an outstanding dinner on the patio sitting around a cozy applewood fire. After dinner, we were sipping coffee, and all four began grinning like ignoramuses.

"Oh, I get it, my meeting with Coach Dennis Darling,"

"Yes." They all chimed together.

"Great White Shark, I was today."

Chapter 15

I STOOD IN front of the university radio station WJFU offices full of piss, vinegar, and questions. I had Sully's version of a super, duper Swiss Army knife in my front right pocket, and I also had one of my favorite lightweight Smith and Wesson .38 caliber handguns on my belt. At the same time, my expanding titanium baton with an easily-accessible velcro strapped to my right lower leg. Overboard, I think not; someone at the radio station may say something unfavorable about The Michael Stanley Band, and I would feel compelled to defend MSB; always be on the ready. If I couldn't quench my investigative thirst today, at the very least, Sabaka, my white furry bodyguard, and I would be getting a couple of M&M Blizzards for our efforts.

I left the SUV running and turned the air conditioning on, placed the *'Official K9 On Duty and he is listening to Abba - All Good.'* signs in each window.

The offices were on the second floor of the newly remodeled Student Union, which sits next to the soccer complex and adjacent to the football stadium. Just a short time ago, my wife tasered a guy in his very personal tool bag in the Starbucks on the main floor of this building for threatening me with a gun. We also halted a campus drug ring, a small sex trafficking operation and put three criminals behind bars. I stood at the desk and observed the radio station's operation, or at least as much of it as I could see. They were running a news segment on current events, which was broadcast throughout the entire radio station, with assorted speakers on the walls, floor, and countertops. I could partially see the back office, where several students were walking around with an occasional phone ringing in the background. The internet has changed hard news permanently, including radio stations, but it felt right that this college radio station was still up and running. I stood at a long counter for a few minutes when a young male came around the corner and asked, "May I help you?"

"Yes, I am working with Chancellor William Wright, investigating the death threat towards a student-athlete that was broadcast on one of your radio programs. Who would I speak with?"

"That would be me. My name is Brian Regan, and I am the station's manager. Do you have some identification?"

I retrieved my driver's and private investigator's licenses and handed them to him. Brian studied both for a bit and handed them back to me.

Brian walked to the end of the counter on my right, his left, lifted a small piece of the counter, and motioned me to follow him while saying, "Let's talk in the conference room; it's open."

This kid reminded me of a cross between Eddy Haskell and Alex P. Keaton.

I walked through the narrow opening between the wall and the counter. There was a row of white office cubicles against the far wall. Only one stall was occupied; a young, blue-haired female with a silver nose ring peeked around the opening to look at us.

Brian and I continued down a short hallway that had certificates of achievements and pictures of musicians hung neatly on the walls. After finding a small conference room, he asked me to have a seat and said he would be right back. I sat with my back to the wall and faced the door. On the far wall was a sign that read, *'None of your Momma's work here - Clean up your Messes.'*

Brian returned with two bottles of water, and after he handed me one, he asked me, do you carry a gun?"

I blew out some air and said, "Yes."

"Have you ever shot anyone?"

I sighed heavily and answered, "Yes. And was the death threat towards Gunner Thompson recorded?" I asked.

"Yeah, I have it right here," Brian replied.

The room was peaceful, with the local news segment ending and then a hip-hop band I could not identify.

Brian looked at me, and I looked at him, and he looked down at his laptop. I placed one of my business cards on the table.

"Oh, shoot, yeah, I can get that." And Brian opened up his laptop, hit two keys on the computer, and a male voice came through the laptop's tiny speakers, *"Gunner knows what he has done, and he will pay with his life."*

The voice was male, late 20s, confident with a silky dialect, Mid-American smooth. "Brian, please play it again."

I listened for any background noises, clocks ticking, car alarms, trains, or outside audible noises. I relaxed and listened to the sounds in the silence of the recording as much as I could, and nothing, no sounds, no extra noises. So maybe the caller wasn't stupid or sloppy; this thought to me, is not good.

"I can email you this link," Brian said.

"That would be a lot of help."

"Sure, what's your email?" Brian asked me, looking up from his laptop. I pointed to my business card again and smiled.

Chapter 16

I WAS DRIVING back from the radio station, and I noticed I had picked up a tail. This one was pretty good. The vehicle tailing me didn't make any unnecessary lane changes and didn't speed up or slow down in spurts. I called Sully on Bluetooth, "Hey, I am returning to the marina, and I have picked up an admirer. Black BMW, semi-smoked-out license plates and windows, occupied twice, both male."

"Which dog do you have with you?" Sully asked.

I looked to my passenger seat, "Sabaka."

I watched the BMW in my mirrors, alternating from side view to rear view with my eyes, not moving my head, while Sully gave me a specific set of instructions. I knew he had asked which dog was with me because our dogs have different thresholds to the sounds and smell of gunfire and violence. Unfortunately, I had a dog that disliked the sound of gunfire and the smell of gunpowder more than the other two.

Ten minutes later, Sabaka and I pulled into the Firestone Metro Parks, about seven minutes from our marina. South Main Street and Jillian Street abutted the park. The Summit County Metro Parks System comprises sixteen parks and fourteen thousand acres. I knew this to be true because Kat had attempted to lure me to every single one of them many times. I wore comfortable tan slacks and a blue polo shirt with my white

Reebok cross-trainers. I switched out handguns from my Smith and Wesson .38 to my Sig Sauer .9mm, and I double-checked my ammo situation; I knew the clip to be packed, but it never hurt to be sure when someone was trying to harm you physically. And my experience told me that these two hooligans weren't the friendly neighborhood welcome wagon of Franklin Township.

I reached into the console and grabbed an earbud, and gently skewered it into my right ear. After attaching a leash to Sabaka's collar, I locked the car, and we headed South down the walking and hiking trail at a leisurely pace. Just a guy and his dog, Sully's plan relied on timing. I felt like I had a huge red bull's eye painted on my back. I wasn't exactly sure what Sabaka was feeling, but he hid any of those feelings by sniffing every twig, bush, and tree. The .9mm made me feel better, but I would have preferred a lot better; sometimes, you take what you can get. The exercise trail wasn't crowded, just the occasional jogger, power walker, or retired senior citizen. After a quarter of a mile, there was a resting station with a green, hard-molded plastic bench and a matching water fountain with a broken spigot. There was also an informational map of the trail mounted on a metal stand in a plastic-enclosed case. The bench had a silver plate that informed me that it was in memory of *'Larry Smith, enjoy the great courtroom and golf courses in the sky.'*

I took a seat and fastened Sabaka's lead to the bench; I didn't want him running when Sully's plan presented itself. I didn't know the entire plan, but it was sure to include violence. I transferred the .9mm from its holster on my right hip and into my lap without Sabaka seeing the gun, and then I waited.

Another seven minutes later, the two guys following us rounded the trail's bend. They were both large with oversized frames and bellies. The one on the right was bald and was wearing black slacks, black leather loafers, and a white long-sleeved oxford dress shirt, untucked. The other one had on a black wool suit, a red dress shirt, and soft black loafers; he had a full head of black hair, and there was a large gold cross hanging around his neck. Both of them legged it uncomfortably and were clumsy. A black wool suit coat and leather loafers were not good hiking gear. It took them another two minutes to arrive at Sabaka and me and the lawyer named Larry Smith's bench upon which I was seated.

"Howdy, an excellent day for a walk, isn't it? I said.

"No, it isn't," Fatty Wool Coat replied between heavy breaths.

"Is too," I replied, stifling a giggle.

"We got a message for you." Fatty Wool Coat replied.

"Who has a message for me?" I asked.

"I just said we, shut up, and we got a…."

I interrupted him, "No, don't do that; let's do this the right way."

The two thugs looked at each other, and Fatty Wool Coat turned back to me and said, "What the hell are you saying?"

"I mean, don't ruin the experience; life is way, way too short; let's enjoy this while we can. Now, you told me you had a message for me. Now I am supposed to say, who is we, then you say, none of your business, then I say, I am making it my business, then you say…."

Fatty Wool Coat pulled a somewhat intimidating .44 caliber magnum handgun from his belt; it had a long, silver barrel and brown wood-sheathed handle. The other thug pulled an identical gun from underneath his dress shirt and held it to his side, probably got the friends, family, and thugs discount at Guns R Us.

This would help explain their initial clumsiness; the .44 magnum is excellent for taking down a 400-pound boar but is large, awkward, and heavy. These were Smith and Wesson Model 29's, each weighing two-and-a-half pounds. It was clear Fatty wool was the one in charge. His voice was rugged and raspy from cigars, cigarettes, and bourbon. Up close, his face was pitted from childhood acne.

"Shut up, wise-ass; we are supposed to send a message to stay away from the university and the football team."

"And if I say something like, have you heard of the new intermittent fasting diet?" I replied pleasingly.

"I would start by killing the mutt and then move on to you," Fatty Wool Coat snarled.

"Okay, okay, I think I understand, and although I envy your fashion sense and sparkling personality, I still must remain steadfast and decline your request at this time. But please feel free to check back in the future," I replied, grinning like the Joker while I continued to hide my .9mm. It wasn't difficult, as these two thugs were so caught up in being tough their sense of observation was limited.

Fatty wool looked at the other thug and said, "Frank, they are always, always, smart with the mouth until we shoot the fucking dog, then they ain't so fucking funny no more."

"You've shot other dogs?" I asked.

He sighed heavily and said, "Yeah," and began to raise the massive gun towards Sabaka.

Roughly twenty yards down the trail from where Sabaka and I had come, two figures walked briskly toward us on the path. These two particular figures were clad head-to-toe in bright colors. One was wearing sunny yellow yoga pants and an equally brilliant blue long-sleeve top, and the other was wearing a rainbow-shaded headband, a pink fanny pack, pink yoga pants, shocking pink cross trainers on her feet, and black fingerless gloves. And she was holding onto and pumping away on two thick walking sticks. These figures were female: One was born with most of the Kennedys, and the other was younger; she was my wife, Kat, and her older companion was our very own Aunt Tilly.

They arrived at us out of breath and spoke loudly to one another, "Are you sure you got no batteries, Ma?" Kat said.

I knew the out-of-breath act was a diversionary tactic to throw the two thugs off. These two women are in extraordinary physical condition.

"What do you think I'm digging around in this thing strapped on my waist for, my health? Hold your britches." Tilly replied.

Kat shrugged her shoulders and placed her large headphones on her head and over her ears.

Tilly straightened up and said to the thugs, "Would one of you young men have four single-A batteries on you? For my Walkman? Duracell's if you got them. Always been a Duracell gal, know what I mean?"

Tilly shook the yellow Walkman a few times and continued, "Darn thing just died on me while I was listening to my *Purple Rain* live cassette from 1985. I love, love that little one named fellow Prince."

"No, we ain't got no fucking batteries; now get lost." Fatty Wool Coat screamed, losing his patience altogether.

Tilly was not deterred and began digging around in her bright pink fanny pack again. "I just know I have a couple of spare batteries in here somewhere."

Sabaka recognized the two of them and started gyrating in place and wagging her tail. He began struggling to pull free from her lead and pull the park bench. Fortunately for us, we weren't dealing with scholastic overachievers.

Kat was chewing gum and gyrating, with some light stretching thrown in to create a distraction as Tilly rooted around in her fanny pack. Kat slowly increased the distance away from Tilly and closer to Fatty Wool Coat, and she continued to dance to a song in her headphones. I knew those headphones to be silent and Kat to be in full focus mode. Her aunt, her husband, and one of her beloved dogs, two hooligans, are now threatening us with weapons. The candle was about to be extinguished, and these two criminals had no idea.

Both men were getting agitated. What they weren't doing was watching this little mature lady shifting her feet slowly into a shooter's stance while distracting them by clumsily searching in her fanny pack. They didn't know that she had already gripped Delores, her favorite pistol for short-range work, and was now buying time.

In the meantime, the two intolerant gangsters were looking in both directions for other trail enthusiasts when Fatty Wool Coat said, "Hey, Jane Fonda's mom and her weird daughter, get the fuck out of here."

Tilly stopped digging around in her fanny pack and slowly raised her head, the earphone in her left ear dangling; I assumed her "assignment" earpiece was firmly in her right ear. Her right hand remained in the fanny pack, and her eyes were much, much different than they had been just a few seconds ago.

"Now, young man, that was rude, and you have been rude to my lovely niece's husband here for the last seven minutes. Threatening to shoot our family pet is the biggest mistake you two posers have ever made. And those large handguns you are trying to hide behind your backs were an even bigger mistake."

"What the hell is going on here?" Fatty Wool Coat exclaimed. And both thugs showed their guns again.

Suddenly, two unusual and simultaneous rare '*Whoosh*' sounds broke the silence of the serene nature trail.

Fatty Wool Coat dropped his gun and reached for the middle of his back, eyes wide and in total shock while reaching, grabbing, and waving at his back until he went to his knees. Fatty Wool Coat groaned loudly while looking at his similarly flailing partner, "What the fuck!"

I quickly stood and kicked the gun out of the other darted thug's right hand and then gave Fatty Wool Coat a first-rate, right-handed uppercut that this particular hiking trail has probably never glimpsed. It sat him on his ass from a kneeling position, and I kicked his gun out of reach. That's a pretty good punch for a shooter, I thought.

The other thug rested on his knees and hands, shaking his head, desperately trying to figure out what exactly had just happened and exactly what he was just shot with, so I told him.

"You have been shot with a high-powered tranquilizer dart mostly used for subduing and transporting large animals at the zoo. Not that you couldn't be mistaken for a hippo, but until I consult with my colleagues, I cannot be sure of the contents. Still, I am assuming from experience the darts were both filled with hallucinogenic drugs that will inundate your brain's neural transmitters for the next twenty hours or so."

"Shot us?" he said with fear, confusion, and astonishment.

"Yes, in about ten minutes, you two will hear strange sounds, see things that aren't there but will terrify you, and you will feel sensations that will make your skin crawl. However, on the plus side, you will love the sick colors." I said.

As all of this went down, Bam-Bam suddenly appeared, pulling a Simone Biles and dismounting from a branch in a large sycamore tree, landing softly twenty yards on the opposite side of the wooded trail. I wished I had a white cardboard sign with the numeral '9.5' on it so I could hold it up for Bam-Bam's dismount. Sully emerged from behind the tree line next to Bam-Bam, holding a long rifle, in fact, a very expensive dart rifle. Sully was in all tan attire with a matching cowboy hat.

"Guys, please meet my two new friends, Fatty Wool Coat and his equal fat-ass friend Frank. And for the record, Fatty Wool Coat was prepared to shoot Sabaka." I jabbed him with my right foot as he sat on the ground.

Sully walked towards him and said, "I heard, but I want to ensure I heard that correctly. Is this true, son?"

"Eat shit, old man." Fatty Wool Coat snarled.

Sully stood behind him, looked at the top of the trees for a second, and swiftly bent over and grabbed both of the mouthy wise guy's shoulders. Sully then placed his right knee in the middle of Fatty wool's back and pushed it forward while simultaneously jerking the fat man's arms back. There was a loud pop, and Fatty Wool Coat began to wail. Sully had dislocated the disrespectful thug's right shoulder. Sully stuffed a black handkerchief in the wailing man's mouth and instructed him to keep it there, or the other shoulder would earn a painful pop and similar dislocation.

Bam-Bam walked over and removed the toxic dart from each man's back, then he retrieved each of their guns and placed them into his backpack. He patted each thug down for other weapons and took two sets of car keys, and said, "No sense risking the public's safety when in a few minutes these two are going to be tripping out; I mean high as hell."

"We will get you to the hospital if you tell us who sent you," I said.

Fatty Wool's wailing was increasing through the mouth gag at a problematic level; it was making the local wildlife flee. We had about another minute before another trail enthusiast ventured onto us.

"Okay, you're now starting to upset me. You were going to shoot our four-legged baby here, so I am going to drag you into the woods over there by your hair, then I am going to hold your mouth and nose shut. Then I will shoot you in your Adam's apple while I watch you gurgle blood. After that, I will repeatedly jump on your enormous belly and watch you resemble a breached whale streaming salt water, but you'll be spraying blood."

I took a noise suppressor from my right pocket and screwed it onto the barrel of my handgun. The other thug Frank was scared; he looked at his partner writhing in pain and said, "Enzo Barra, we work for him."

"Why did he send you? Just the university investigation? I asked.

"Fuck knows, he doesn't tell us shit, he says, and we do. Man, you hurt us bad."

I shook my head in confirmation. I also believe this is why Enzo sent them. No reason for Enzo to tell them anything; they were at the bottom of the food chain.

"How much did Enzo pay you to rough me up today?" I asked.

Both gangsters remained quiet until Sully grabbed Fatty Wool's right arm. The scream through the gag was impressive. Frank, the thug, said, "Christ man, five hundred bucks."

"Each?"

Fatty Wool had his head down while he answered, "No, just the five hundred."

"Ouch, Scooter," Bam-Bam exclaimed.

Bam-Bam, Sully and I looked at each other, and Sully exclaimed, "Enzo Barra. Oh, Vey."

During our chat with Enzo's boys, the ladies had moved to the park bench, and we're giving Sabaka some love. I walked over and unwound Sabaka's leash from the bench and patted his head. Then, Sully, Bam-Bam, Kat, Tilly, and I turned and began heading separately.

"I thought you would help us if we told you who sent us?" Frank the thug mumbled.

I turned and walked backward and said, "We just shot you both in the back with illegal hallucinogenic drugs in broad daylight. What would make you think we could be trusted?"

"For God's sake, you two are stupid," I heard Sully say as I turned forward and skedaddled with my boy Sabaka Sunrise.

Chapter 17

I WENT INTO Graceland and walked behind the bar to construct a Campari and soda; I snatched an orange and cherry pre-sliced garnishment from the refrigerator and added it to my cocktail. I took my drink and went onto the patio, opened the lid of our grill, and peeked at the luscious pork loin, cooking slowly. There were twenty to thirty cloves of garlic sprouting from the luscious meat. I was delighted; it turned a nice charcoal color while rotating above the small flame. I thanked God for everything, just everything. I then chose a comfortable white-cushioned, chestnut-colored rattan seat and decompressed. "Enzo Barra, freaking A," I roared to no one.

Halfway through my cocktail, The Michael Stanley Band began to sing through our outdoor speakers when Kat walked up and said, "Yummy, can I have one of those and sit with you, my handsome and badass husband?"

"Of course, baby." And like Michael Stanley, I, too, thanked God for the man who put the white lines on the highway because I needed them now. This case turned into a hairball, and my lack of progress and clue collecting was embarrassing.

I stood and went into Graceland and constructed Kat's matching cocktail, adding an extra orange wedge. Sully is highly organized and disciplined, so Graceland's large refrigerator is always stocked with fresh fruit and vegetables. Returning to my seat with Kat's drink and my cocktail, I watched Kat pull dead leaves from one of our patio plants. She turned and kissed me long and with a lot of emotion and enthusiasm. She then placed the dead leaves in a small trash receptacle and sat next to me in a patio chair that matched the one I was occupying. She tucked one foot under her behind, took a sip of her drink, and sighed contentment.

After a few minutes of listening to Michael Stanley, I said, "Enzo Barra, fucking Enzo Barra is involved in this thing."

Enzo Barra ran prostitutes, dealt massive amounts of heroin, marijuana, and cocaine, ran numbers, was a confirmed for-hire leg breaker, and was a predatory loan shark. He was independent of the mob and worked on the fringes of their territory's in and around Stark County, twenty miles Southeast of us. He got away with this because he was a psycho and nobody wanted the kind of headache that would come from going to war with him. Rumor has it that he put his cousin in a wood chipper for being twelve days late on a loan payment.

Kat was peering at me over her drink and, after a few seconds, said in a deep mimicking tone, "I am going to repeatedly jump on your enormous belly and watch you resemble a breached whale streaming salt water, but you'll be spraying blood."

"I wasn't sure where I was going with that one, babe; it got away from me," I replied.

She flashed me her number eight smile and said, "Enzo Barra is closer and closer to being dead if he screws with my husband again."

The white lines on the highway just became clear again.

Bam-Bam walked onto the patio and handed me a yellow-green file folder, and said, "Coach Darling may be an obnoxious bastard, but he is a squeaky clean bastard."

Kat stood up and, with her drink in hand, went to help Tilly in the kitchen while I stood and ventured into Graceland. As I walked, Sabaka trailed closely behind me; he sensed danger earlier and was sticking close to me. I made another drink, but this time I chose to run with a bourbon on the rocks. I grabbed a rocks glass, filled it with four ice cubes and three fingers of Old Fitzgerald bourbon, then walked back to the patio with Sabaka and sat back in my chair; he curled up at my feet. I looked out at the lake that sat thirty feet from me, which was calm and vacant. The Northeastern sun lowered and painted a light orange streak on the water. I had my head back and my eyes closed; a thought was racing around my brain, but I couldn't quite get it; when it would prance in close, it would immediately run and hide.

After two minutes, the elusive thought became clear; I leaned up and roared, "Sabaka, son of a bitch! How was Brian Regan able to find and play that particular electronic link in two seconds? I didn't call for an appointment. I just showed up; he wouldn't have any reason to have that clip so accessible." I took a drink from my cocktail and continued, "It's possible that the link just happened to be ready, or the link needed to be readily available for university purposes, but thinking that way does me no good. So this goes in the clue column." I pat Sabaka on the head, and as I celebrated my newfound clue, I headed to our boathouse for a pre-dinner shower.

We all ate outside on the patio; the pork roast, sweet potatoes with butter and brown sugar, and roasted balsamic Brussel sprouts were terrific. The two pitchers of Sangria we downed made Kat get that look in her eyes; we locked eyes, and she raised her glass toward me; I raised mine in mock triumph as to where this evening was headed.

For dessert Bam-Bam grilled fresh banana, pears, and pineapple slices with a zesty raspberry cream sauce accompanied by large bowls of homemade pistachio coffee ice cream. Oh, Mama Mia.

We all took seats around our outdoor big screen projector and streamed Elvis in 'G. I. Blues' for the hundredth time, but it made Tilly happy, and that made us happy. Bam-Bam invited four men for dinner and dessert, and they stayed for the movie. After the film, the guys cleaned up the patio. Kat walked up to me and whispered, "Meet me upstairs in ten minutes."

Bam-Bam was drying a large glass casserole dish with military precision in Tilly's kitchen; he was holding it up to the overhead kitchen lights looking for sneaky food stains, then more wiping and finally drying.

I had Bam-Bam and his team tailing Gunner around campus all morning and afternoon and asked him, "Anything out of the ordinary with Gunner today?"

"All good, the kid…."

"Gunner, Gunner Thompson." I interrupted.

Bam-Bam mean mugged me for a few seconds and said, "Anyhow, Gunner is active, between classes shaking hands with other students, getting to class on time, and instead of lunch, he attended noon mass at St. Bernard's church. Gator and

Mongoose had Gunner until team practice at three-thirty this afternoon. Gunner is bigger than Elvis on this campus."

"Shhh, don't let Tilly hear that," I replied.

After asking Tilly to babysit the dogs overnight, I walked briskly to our boathouse and unlocked the door after four tries because my hands were sweaty and my heart was beating faster than a hummingbird's. I went up the stairs two at a time and found Kat lying on our leather, armless loveseat in the outfit she entered into the world. The only difference was that she was all grown up and not crying and had a red rose between her teeth. Usually, I ask God, 'Why Me?' but on this occasion, I did not question but just loved his greatest masterpiece, which is my wife.

Chapter 18

THE SHORT DRIVE from Portage Lakes to Cuyahoga Falls across the All-American bridge that connects the smaller town to its big city brother Akron takes about twenty-five minutes. The bridge starts at the edge of Akron's North Hill, the former address of JD's Italian Pastry Shop. Once home to many Italian immigrants, North Hill had a primary demographic switch about eighteen years ago, when Bhutanese, Latino, and Nepalese immigrant refugees found it a comfortable place to raise a family.

JD's new location sits on a side street just off State Road, a busy thoroughfare running north and south through Cuyahoga Falls. I pulled into an open parking space in front of the pastry shop and snapped a lead onto Iggy's collar; after a pat on the head, we exited the SUV and walked towards the front door. I neglected to lock my SUV partly because Cuyahoga Falls is a pretty safe city; if a crime occurred on JD's property, the law would be the least of that person's problems. There is no illegal or legal pulse in Northeast Ohio that JD and his social networks aren't in tune. JD freelances his services and old-school contacts to the highest bidder. He could be trusted; his word was gold.

JD was standing at the large glass pastry case that dominated the small space. A young, dark-haired female in her early twenty's, wearing blue jeans, a blue scrunchy t-shirt, and a black apron, was busy placing small, colorful Italian cookies inside the case while JD supervised.

JD turned towards the door and watched us walk towards him. Iggy was in the whole saliva-producing mode, neck, head, and eyes going in four different directions.

"Hi, Iggy," JD said.

I dropped the leash, Iggy ran at JD, and they hugged and kissed for a couple of minutes. I saw seven other customers inside the shop, drinking coffee and eating cannolis.

JD straightened up and shook my outstretched hand, and then walked behind the large glass counter.

"Uh oh, either the ladies of the house have Italian pastry cravings, or you stepped in something that smells."

"Can't a guy just drop by when in the neighborhood?" I responded.

"Well?" JD asked.

"Well, what?" I asked.

"Which one?"

I smiled and said, "Both."

JD poured me a cup of coffee in a heavy white porcelain mug, he refilled his well-worn plastic blue travel mug, and we walked over to a small table by the front windows. The table was black wrought iron with a white tablecloth; next to it sat two small chairs; I took a seat in one while JD leaned against the window; the other small chair would have never stood a chance; JD was a large man, Iggy sat next to me on the floor.

Suddenly two mature women dressed in colorful stretch pants and exercise tops approached our table, and before they reached us, I thought, '*Uh oh, double Karen alert.*' The First Lady contacted us, "Excuse us, but we don't feel this animal should be in a food establishment."

"Iggy," JD replied.

"Excuse me."

"His name is Iggy," JD repeated.

With a toss of her hand, she said, "Whatever, are you going to remove this animal or not?"

"Who, your friend?"

"Excuse me?"

"Leave and never come back," JD replied in a calm and soothing voice.

"Well, I never," The second Karen said.

"Sure you have; now please leave my bakery," JD replied.

Without another word, the two women left hastily.

I took a sip of my coffee; it was hot and rich. The white, thick mug had those small brownish cracks running up and down the top and sides.

"Your customer service is unparalleled, JD," I said.

JD shrugged and turned to look out the window to the North on State Road, "You know I resented leaving North Hill, but now I enjoy it here."

"Seems like it. So, why would Enzo Barra be interested in the university football program?"

JD turned towards me and away from the window and said with a smile, "Christ, Scooter, no segue, and how do you do it? I heard you were trolling around the university again; give them their money back on this one and take a vacation."

"So I just got hired into a hairball?" I asked.

"I am just saying not is all as it seems; either get out or go all in and trust no one. That's all I will tell you about this. I am very fond of you and your family. Yes, this situation will be a dangerous hairball. Also, I know you and your people, and you are just going to pull and pull, annoy and annoy until you get ahold of something and pull it out of its hole. And God knows you have the contacts. But I must remain, and please pardon the euphemism, on the sidelines, on this one. I have alliances with others, and I won't betray that trust just as I wouldn't betray yours."

"I appreciate you, JD."

JD went behind the large pastry case and grabbed two large, unfolded white pastry boxes; he folded them into place and began filling them with cream-filled cannoli, donuts, Italian cookies, and cupcakes. He set them on the pastry case counter and said, "Take them, Robin Hood, take these back to your band of merry men and women."

I put the pastry boxes in the rear of the Benz SUV so as not to torture my buddy. I got in, buckled up my safety belt, patted Iggy on the head, and said, "Iggy, pardon the corny euphemism, but buckle up your chin strap; here we go; JD just cryptically let me know there were big players involved within this thing."

Chapter 19

AS USUAL, WHEN arriving back at the marina, there was a furry mob scene. The two other faithful companions surrounded me, tails wagging, yipping and yapping. After letting Iggy out of the vehicle, I bent down and took the inevitable and rigorous face-licking session from the other two.

"Hey, pooches, leave some for me."

I looked up, and Kat was standing next to us, smiling. I brushed the babies off and stood and kissed my wife. After a few kisses, I said, "Hey, I have two boxes of JD's sweet treats in the trunk."

She pushed me away and said, "Shut the front door; let's get them."

We set the boxes of heavenly delights on the oversized kitchen island while Kat texted everyone about the newfound JD sugary situation. Within three minutes, they all came from three different spots in the house and entered the kitchen.

"Scooter honey, why is there a handwritten note with an address in one of these cannoli boxes?"

Chapter 20

IT WAS A beautiful afternoon in Akron, Ohio, for a college football game. Sunny skies, the temperature in the mid-eighties, and very little wind. Gunner Thompson and our university would host Bowling Green State University in a Mid-American Conference matchup. Both teams have won their first two games of the season. Bowling Green is two hours away, west of the I-80 Ohio Turnpike and fifteen minutes south of Toledo, Ohio.

We arrived about forty minutes before kickoff and stood by the fifty-yard line's railing; Kat and I were wearing our all-access passes around our necks and feeling pretty good about them. Both teams were warming up in their respective end zones with stretches, short sprints, and passing and catching drills. We had entered the stadium through a private entrance due to our firearms. Chancellor Wright had arranged special status and permission for us to carry ours into the stadium.

"Good God, some of these men are gigantic," Kat said.

"They are, and we live with a Rhino and a Gator. See number 19? That's who we are employed to dispel or prove the validity of the death threats."

Gunner was throwing short sideline passes to four different receivers. A young female assistant coach wearing a blue warm-up suit and a white university visor would toss him the football from about two feet, Gunner would bark out a snap count, and the receiver would take off in a sprint. Gunner would backpedal, stop and throw the pass before the receiver even made his cut toward the sideline. The receiver would stop and make a ninety-degree cut toward the sideline, and the football would already be on top of him.

"They each trust that the other is doing the right thing," Kat observed.

"Kind of like us, babe."

"Scooter Jeanette, my darling, you just got all deep up in here right now," Kat said as she interlaced her left hand into my right hand.

The stadium is impressive, even though it is a colossal waste of money. At sixty-one million dollars and only used for five or six home football games a year plus a handful of high school football games, there is no hiding it's a massive waste of money. But it sure is beautiful. The mesmerizing blue artificial turf was intense. It wasn't too long ago there was only green AstroTurf available; times be a-changing. I like football, but not how I loved baseball, I missed playing baseball. I recall, as a youth, proudly standing on manicured grass and rich brown dirt. I remember baseball's written and unwritten rules concerning sportsmanship and traditions. The feeling of being a part of a team on the field with eight other buddies with one purpose, hitting the baseball and running while making all left turns without being thrown out, and the goal of reaching home plate. Baseball is a child's game, and adults love it. That exhilarating feeling of standing at the plate with a two-pound, seven-ounce piece of wood; understanding that an opposing pitcher will throw a baseball ninety miles per hour in your general direction; and knowing that getting a base hit just thirty percent of the time equaled outstanding. There are 12,386,344 possible plays in every baseball game. Baseball is the only sport in which the team on defense controls the ball. True baseball-ers know deep in their souls that there are only two seasons; winter and baseball.

I looked around and began counting the months and days until the Akron RubberDucks retook the field so I could see my good friends, General Manager Jim Pfander and owner Ken Babby. These two are solid, compassionate, energetic, and energetic humans. And Jim is a genuine hometown guy.

The sound of the university marching band's enthusiastic rendition of the Gap band's classic, '*You dropped a bomb on me,*' took my thinking away from baseball and brought me back to the moment.

Kat grabbed my hand, and we searched for the elevator up to the suite level; we found it in the middle of the concourse. The stadium was filling up as the Bowling Green State University fans traveled well, as it's only one hundred and forty-four miles or a little more than two hours between campuses. Holding our 'All Access' passes out in front of us, we were ushered along with nine other adults and four children into a large elevator. The elevator attendant was a young woman with dark hair, black eyeglasses, and a small blue bow in her hair. She was sitting on a black steel bar stool controlling the elevator buttons.

When the elevator began, Kat whispered to me, "Top floor housewares, lady's handbags, lady's undergarments, and one attractive but married male private detective…" she couldn't finish due to her giggling fit. I just eyed the red elevator floor numbers trying to discourage her laughing conniption.

Kat was wearing over-the-calf stretch black jeans and a pink stretch t-shirt with Area Code 330 written on the front in white letters, and I felt that feeling in my solar plexus, a sense of warmth, passion, and excitement. But it was bigger than that, a feeling like I had just met her for the first time and realized that she loved me. In the elevator, as Kat stood facing the doors; the other people seemed to morph into faceless beings, and even the sound of the music rearranged its sound as if wanting to please Kat. Well, that's what I imagined anyway.

The elevator doors opened into a massive air-conditioned space that was very bright and successful looking. The plush carpet color was university blue with gold trim. The walls on our right were decorated with assorted-sized black and white and color depictions of past university football seasons: team pictures and individual players. On the left, there was a smaller room with chairs and tables with white and blue tablecloths. A red velvet rope between two gold pillars and a chalkboard that read 'Reserved for the class of 1981.'

We were met by a slim, athletic blond male attendant wearing light khaki slacks, a white short-sleeved polo shirt with the university's logo stitched in blue on the left breast, and blue Nike cross-trainers with prominent swooshes on each side. He peered at our all-access passes and said, "Hello, my name is Chip welcome to Bruce and Mary Ellen Wright Memorial Stadium. And if you follow me, I will show you to the Chancellor's suite."

We walked down the large carpeted area where large flat-screen televisions displaying the university football network hung on the wall to the right. They were evenly spaced, and two male broadcaster's directly out of casting central, we're on the televisions comparing both teams and the keys to victory for each. A running clock in the right-hand corner of the television screens told us that it was eleven minutes to kick off.

Chapter 21

WE PASSED A small portable bar set up with a young female bartender, probably on the women's swim team, who was busy pouring mixed drinks over ice. She had a conservative amount of liquor bottles, just the staples, on a table behind her. And before them, a line of nine people waiting with varying degrees of patience. This small area was called the '*The Pick Six Bar*' and consisted of about a dozen small tables and chairs arranged without any planned diagrams that I could see. There was also a tiny portable concession food stand that seemed to specialize in loaded nachos, chips, pretzels, and hot dogs. Again, more random blue, gray, and white tables and chairs.

We arrived at our destination, and I attempted to tip our attendant a double fin, but he rejected it due to NCAA rules. Kat snatched my hand, extracting me from the embarrassing blunder I had just made, and we entered the luxury suite. The first thing that hit me was the number of people in the suite. I stopped counting at twenty-two, all eating food and partaking in a beverage from three food and drink stations. I saw hot dogs, corn dogs, grilled chicken sandwiches, hamburgers, cheeseburgers, and large salted pretzels. Also, the diverse drink stations offered assorted beers, soft drinks, Gatorade, and bottled water. The suite's front portion, facing east, was wall-to-wall glass and provided a stunning view of the football field and its bright blue artificial turf. A glass door led to three rows of five gold seats for outside viewing.

I spotted Brian Regan and Chancellor William Wright standing at a small circular stand-up table. My first thought was that this was an odd couple. But most of all, I was struck by a chill thinking that the two people who had received an anonymous letter and an anonymous phone call regarding death threats towards a student-athlete were together. Brian Regan's sense of style remained the same since our first encounter at the radio station; designer blue jeans and a white button-down, long-sleeved dress shirt with the sleeves rolled to the elbows, GQ style. He completed his ensemble with a yellow sweater wrapped around his neck. Dark Ray Ban sunglasses are resting in his front shirt pocket. He also was wearing on his right wrist a sixteen thousand dollar Cartier Ballon Bleu wristwatch. Our entire team is familiar with all types of watches and jewelry; we have gained experience over the years working for insurance corporations with significant theft and losses. Miss Bethany was standing to the left of Brian Regan and the right of Chancellor Wright. She was as bright as a summer sunflower, wearing a yellow sundress, a small string of large white pearls resting around her neck, and white sandals laced up to the back of her kneecaps, Roman Gladiator-style. Her makeup had indistinct yellow glitter sparkles on her face and arms. The glitter reflected the room's natural light when she shifted. The three of them each held a large cup of beer in university clear plastic cups. The Chancellor saw us and stood, and rushed his considerable girth over to Kat and me, "Mr. Jeanette, great to have you with us today."

"Thank you for the passes, and again, call me Scooter,"

William Wright would not let a pesky seventy-eight-degree September college football game interfere with his archaic and stuffy wardrobe. Today he was showcasing a slightly different version of his Scottish educator garb. My recent experiences and interactions on this particular university campus have revealed much clownish behavior from the staff; the relatively large Chancellor was no different. I knew he was born and raised in Orlando, Florida, and probably had never even visited the UK. But today, he sported a dark brown, fall tweed sport coat with light brown patches on the elbows, a light-blue dress shirt, and dark brown corduroy slacks. At least they were ill-fitting and not recently pressed, and tan oxford leather shoes that needed proper polishing on his feet.

"Holy God, you are beautiful," William Wright suddenly called out.

Kat smiled her number seven smile and said, "Thank you but no need to bring God into this."

William Wright tilted his head back and laughed loudly and then said, "Come, come make yourself at home. There are assorted appetizers as well as hot dogs, corn dogs, cheeseburgers, chicken sandwiches, onion rings, and French fries, and everything is buffet style. Scooter and Kat there are assorted beers, wine and selected liquors, unfortunately none of my special port is available," and the rotund educator winked at me. He left us and began working the room, slapping backs, shaking hands, and just being jolly.

One of my most essential goals in early clue gathering is always to grab a beer if the opportunity presents itself. Kat and

I walked up to one of the small bars, and true to past forms, the bartender was young and athletic. Kat and I selected a *'Thirsty Dog Irish Setter Red Ale'* draft beer; they were poured from a portable tap system into twelve-ounce plastic cups with the blue university logo on both sides. The Thirsty Dog Brewery is located on Grant Street, a half a mile from where we stood. I sipped my beer and being a grade-A detective, I deduced it was excellent. I was also quite sure it wouldn't be my only one of the day.

Out of the corner of my eye, I spotted Milton Haft, the university attorney; he was standing in the corner of the room closest to the football field, next to a long counter featuring hot appetizers and assorted chips and dips. His attire was bright, loud, and golf-ish. He was talking to an attractive and petite woman with strawberry-colored hair who exhibited body language that talking to the attorney was an unpleasant affair. I recognized her as Gunner Thompson's mother from the videotape I had watched.

I nodded toward both of them and said, "Babe, that's the university legal beagle who was upset when the Chancellor did a total end-around override on our contract. And that is Gunner Thompson's mother."

Kat looked over and said, "She does not like him. She is uncomfortable, and did you use a football metaphor? Anyway, I may mosey over there and modify his ugly behavior by deviating his septum."

After pleading with Kat not to intervene, we watched for a minute until Gunner's mother extracted herself from the situation by walking away. Kat and I walked around sipping our beers while continuing to people-watch. It would make sense that William Wright's suite would be the number one suite in the university hierarchy. large piece of expensive leather furniture and expensive decor, The suite to end all suites, I wondered what the employee ranking was to receive a game-day invitation into this domain. The testosterone and estrogen levels were off the charts. I wanted to find a shower. Everybody was competing to say the right things, the husbands and wives trying to blend in with the work wives and husbands. "Did I wear the right university fan gear? Am I drinking the right beverage?" It was palpable and exhausting. Kat and I went through the glass door and down three small concrete steps and chose two seats on the right. There were nine other fans occupying seats.

Our team won the ceremonial coin toss and elected to receive the opening kick and the football first rather than deferring to receive the ball at the start of the second half. Kat and I settled in and began to watch the game. Gunner Thompson was good, really good. He directed a seven-play, seven-two-yard touchdown drive with four completed passes, including one in the back of the end-zone to a medium-sized running back wearing number thirty-two. There was a game-day program sitting on the empty chair next to me. It was in full color and contained every player's statistics, along with biographies of all the players and coaches. It looked like a coffee table book; if they toned these football programs down, they could lower overall tuition by ten percent at a minimum.

"Our quarterback is much better than the other players, "Kat announced.

"Gunner, Gunner Thompson, and he is our client, well, our client, through our paying client, but the main reason we were hired. Do you know what's bothering me?"

She smiled intensely and replied, "I can only imagine we were only in the suite for a few minutes, and the asshole quotient was chart-topping."

"I expected that, but no, that's not it. The quarterback for this university is a three-year starter, an All-American headed for the pros, an all-around decent human being and there is no immediate concern about the death threats, none. Especially from the guy who wrote us the check. He's in there acting like it's an all-day frat party."

Kat stood, kissed me lightly, and said, "I will let you obsess over that like I know you will. I must use the lady's room."

While Kat was gone, we intercepted a pass from the Bowling Green quarterback and returned it thirty-nine yards to set up another Gunner Thompson touchdown pass. That made the score 14-0, and our guys were on the good side of the tally sheet. I scanned the roster and found the three players from Cuyahoga Falls High School who Principal Ann Runkle Ritchie had spoken of in her office: Todd Caruthers, number 72; Steve Kapusinski, number 40; and Darris Blackford, number 44. I sat back and finished my beer, and thought about this for a moment.

Kat returned with two more cold beers and a small white cardboard boat of popcorn.

"That's it? The suite is crammed with the holy grail of pigskin-watching food, and we settle for popcorn?" I asked.

Kat sat, placed the popcorn in my lap, grabbed a large handful, and said, "First of all, shut it, and second, after the game, you are taking me to Luigi's for a #9 and a house salad."

I smiled because I knew Kat took her Luigi's very seriously and never strayed from her favorites, a large pepperoni, sausage, mushroom pizza, and the house salad with chopped lettuce, tomatoes, special dressing, and an obscene amount of shredded mozzarella cheese on top. Luigi's has been in the exact location since 1949 and is a tasty Akron mainstay. The Northside neighborhood where Luigi's sits has seen an economic boom, economic despair, and now another economic boom thanks to art galleries, small shops, a nationally branded hotel, a popular music bar, and the resurgence of downtown Akron just down the street.

"If you're good," I said.

Kat rolled her eyes so far in the back of her head that I feared they may not come back this time.

Gunner's mother walked down the three small steps next to Kat and me and sat in the row and a seat directly in front of us. She wore stretch blue jeans and a blue and white Gunner Thompson number '19' jersey. Her strawberry blond hair was pulled back and held in place by a big blue bow. She was drinking a small beer in a university plastic cup.

I wanted to talk to her, and as I considered a way to do just that, Kat leaned forward and tapped her on the right shoulder. Gunner's mom turned to her left side, and Kat asked, "Are you Gunner Thompson's mother?"

"Yes, I am."

"He is quite good," Kat said.

I glimpsed at her hands; they were slender with small but noticeable freckles, and her nails were neat with shiny blue polish and silver specks. She wore a silver Irish Claddagh ring on her right pinky finger. We were fans of these rings; Kat and I each wore one.

"Come up and sit with us," Kat said as she moved her football program and the popcorn boat from the seat next to her. Gunner's mom stood, ascended one step and hurried between the empty seats, and sat on Kat's left. It always amazed me the sheer amount of times and the staggering number of people that listen to Kat. There was a sense of steady collectedness and confidence in her voice and body language. She taught me how to stay in the present always. Kat caught my eye and slyly winked at me.

"Hi, I am Kat, and this is my husband, Scooter Jeanette; I love your Claddagh ring," Kat smiled and held up her hand to display her Irish ring.

We all shook hands, and Gunner's mom turned to me and said, "Hi, I'm Taylor Thompson."

"Nice to meet you, and as a football fan, Gunner is a man among boys."

She smiled and said, "Thank you."

I handed her one of my business cards and one of The Chancellors. She glanced at them, peeked at me, and put both in her small purse. It made sense for me to let Kat talk with Taylor Thompson for now. I handed her the business cards to get a reaction. But I didn't see one.

I excused myself, stood up, and headed into the suite to make a beer run. I also wanted to get another quick look at the attendees in the Chancellor's private suite. William Wright was taking up a sizable portion of his table and speaking with animation on his subject manner, which most likely had nothing to do with football. There were three other people at his table, two older males I didn't know and Miss Bethany, who sat with her hands folded on each other, a plastic cup of beer in front of her now halfway gone. I watched them for a moment. Miss Bethany looked content watching her boss speak, laughing at the correct times and nodding when required. Brian Regan was not present. The football game was being telecast on six large television screens throughout the suite. After a moment I retrieved three beers. Getting back to my seat and delivering the other two beers, I began drinking mine. We watched the game; Kat and Taylor Thompson talked about clothing, television shows, and decorating spaces by water. I pondered. Kat and Taylor shopped in the team shop at halftime. I pondered some more and drank some more outstanding draft beer. The females returned with bags of clothing, and towards the end of the game, Gunner threw a rare interception in the fourth quarter, which led to a Bowling Green State University touchdown—making the score 28-14 in favor of our favorites.

I took the last sip of my beer and watched the last few seconds of the game wind down when a text message came onto my phone, shaking me from my contemplations. It was from Sully: *Joseph Votto Senior has eyes on you, Kat, and your female guest. Joseph, Buster, and two other bodyguards are sitting on the other side of the field from you and are using binoculars.'* I scanned the other side of the stadium and spotted them seated on the second level, three sections from the end zone.

With the game over, Taylor Thompson stood and said, "It was nice meeting you; it's time to take Gunner out to eat."

"What's his go-to post-game meal?" Kat asked.

"Mike's Place in Kent, Gunner loves the food, especially the cheeseburgers and fries."

"We love Mike and his food, and actually, we used to play in a mixed darts league on Sunday nights there," Kat said.

Chapter 22

KAT AND I watched a few minutes of the post-game handshakes on the field, waiting for the suite and outdoor seats to vacate. As we entered the suite through the glass doors, it was mostly empty except for the Chancellor. He was standing at the bar holding court in front of Brian Regan, Miss Bethany, and three or four other subordinates whom neither seemed to be enjoying their time with the Chancellor any longer. William Wright was drunk, red-faced, and loud, really loud, talking about the future of brick-and-mortar colleges. I nudged Kat forward; I did not want to be roped into that boozy sermon.

"So, what did the text say that rocked you a bit at the end up there?" Kat asked as we walked. I carried the two large team shop bags.

"Oh, you saw that?" I asked.

Kat's eye roll was so impressive because she kept right on walking. I would have fallen over backward trying that kind of maneuver.

"You will see very soon," I replied.

We took the elevator to the stadium's main concourse and headed to the main exit, and as we did, we saw Buster, Joey Votto Senior's right-hand man for three decades. Buster was standing just outside the metal gates, leaning against a wall with his feet crossed, Mr. Casual. 'Buster' is a nickname he acquired years ago from a rival thug because his wardrobe consists of brown, brown and more brown, including his hats, shirts, belts, socks, and shoes. Get it? 'Buster Brown.' Also, I know his gun a Glock 19 to be brown, it has been pointed at me on more than one occasion. We weren't friends, but his word was good, and in our business, that sometimes is enough.

Catching a glimpse of Buster, I tapped my right side for my gun; hunkering down in its holster, I held the team shop bags in my left hand, and I felt reassured. I looked over at Kat; she had a three-inch knife that came from her belt tucked in her right hand. Her fingers were coiled inside the square end, and she had it palmed so the casual college football fan, with or without a few alcoholic pops, wouldn't notice.

Buster pushed himself away from the wall and put his hands up and out in front of himself and said, "I come in peace. I have a small request from Mr. Votto."

I nodded, and Kat and I continued walking, with Buster tagging along behind us. My wife was humming 'Tomorrow Never Dies' by Sheryl Crow from the famous James Bond movie.

Bam-Bam suddenly appeared wearing blue jeans, a black tank top, a plain black baseball cap, and black combat boots. He had his gun visible on his right hip, not bothered by the optics it may cause, and walked directly behind Buster. If Buster saw Bam-Bam and his weapon, he didn't show it. We all turned onto a side street dubbed 'Celebration Alley' now with post-game victory revelers. At the center of the block was a large sound stage where Jeff Miner and his band, DT and the Shakes, were jamming loud. The band is a local favorite; the drummer, Jeff, is our great friend. Frankly, his drumming makes the band so good that if they didn't enjoy local gigs, they could be big time at least, that is my opinion. The '*Shakes*' were on point, playing some great rock and roll music. Scanning the multitude of people, I spotted Jim and Tracy Long, along with Jeff's beautiful and thoughtful wife, Christina, whom I have known for years. Jeff, Christina, Jim, and I all went to high school together, and if we weren't presently trying to ascertain why a mafia boss was requesting a meeting with us, Kat and I would have enjoyed sliding up to these fine folks and enjoy the music.

Instead, Kat, Bam-Bam, and I found a semi-private area down the block towards Exchange Street next to a large orange generator that was powering the band. My wife was on full alert - her face was sharp, her eyes bright, and her body language and movements cautious but semi-aggressive. The knife remained in her right hand. I knew Sully was also near, but we wouldn't see him until he chose to be seen. Buster showed no emotion. The air was robust with the rock and roll music of *DT and the Shakes*.

"Mr. Votto would like to speak to you concerning a current situation that involves your entire team."

I tapped my compact iron on my right hip again for confidence. Buster was an evil man, the man you send to get Michael Myers, the man you send to annoy the boogyman.

"Sure," I replied. "Where and when?"

Chapter 23

THIS EVENING ENDED the Lock 3 summer concert series with a tribute band that played Dean Martin, Frank Sinatra, and Sammy Davis Junior. And proved to be year in and year the most popular evening of outdoor music. Lock 3 is the third lock of the 21-lock Ohio-Erie canal system, a primary transportation mode for trade in the Midwest. In the early 1800s. The 308-mile canal ran through the Buckeye State and moved passengers and commercial goods between Portsmouth, Ohio, to Cleveland and Lake Erie. Now an entertainment gem for Summit County.

Kat and I followed Buster's Lincoln Navigator into the empty parking garage, driving to the top level. The parking garage wouldn't start to fill up with Lock 3 concert-goers for another two hours or so. Winding upwards in the dimly lit garage to the top floor, our tires made loud squeaking noises in the quiet parking deck. Joseph Votto Senior and his six vehicles commandeered six parking spots in a half-square pattern. Kat and I parked next to Busters Navigator.

"You think this is payback for putting Joey Junior in prison just a few months ago?" Kat asked.

"Not sure, I thought we were good on that, and it's not in Joseph Votto's make-up to change; his word has always been good," I replied. I still wasn't ready to divulge seeing Joseph

Votto Senior on Gunner's senior night tape. We would know soon enough.

The aging gangster was leaning on the half-cement wall overlooking parts of downtown Akron and the Lock 3 Amphitheater. From this spot, a person could see for at least a mile toward Cuyahoga Falls. If the view were reversed, we would be looking at Canal Park, the home of the Akron RubberDucks, The Peanut Shoppe, and the newly constructed Main Street.

Below us, roadies were busily setting up the Lock 3 Amphitheater for a *'Rat Pack'* tribute band that would be taking the stage later in the evening. They set the stage with instruments and prominent black speakers and began multiple sound checks: "One, Two, Check, Check..."

Joseph Votto Senior had his white Maserati Levante Trofeo parked perpendicular to where he was standing, creating a barrier and a lovely square with the garage's half wall, Buster's SUV, the yellow lines of two parking spots, and his $185,000 luxury vehicle. In a Cadillac Escalade parked twenty yards away, I saw two other bodyguards; Buster got out of his Lincoln and leaned against his Lincoln Navigator.

Kat and I exited our Corvette and just I cautiously walked up to Joseph Votto; Kat leaned against the passenger side door of the Corvette, her gun drawn and hanging to her side. It was her favorite small .22, Sully, Tilly, and Bam-Bam would be close, somewhere in the dark parking deck.

Suddenly Joseph spoke, "My grandfather used to let me tag along when I was a very young man when he would sing with 'Phil Palumbo and Pals' at his supper club on State Road in

Cuyahoga Falls back in the day. Damn, that was good music; the second the big horns jumped in, I fell in love with that music."

He did not start with hello, and no, thank you for getting my dirtbag son an exceptionally reduced sentence for his multiple felonies. Then again, it was usually all about him anyways. But this time, Joseph Votto Senior looked drained; the good-looking, cultivated mobster looked tired and older than the last time I saw him. And that was only five weeks ago.

This evening, Joseph Votto Senior wore gray slacks and an Italian linen long-sleeved blue dress shirt with subtle white stripes. His collar was open, and he wore no tie and no suit jacket; this was as lenient regarding his dress style as I had seen. He looked human, a casual, harmless grandfather. Well almost. That's like saying a wild badger would make a good pet. I peered over the parking deck wall at the scene below us and peered at the vendors preparing their spaces for the night's sales. I would be patient; Joseph Votto Senior wouldn't be rushed. He would get to the specific reason for this meeting. He was not one to prattle on but was always careful and calculating before he spoke. Below us, the musicians had joined the roadies and were now performing their sound checks again, repeating the 'check, check, one, two' an annoying amount of times. I remained quiet, patient, and attentive.

As he stood with me, Mr. Votto smoked a cigarette, and watching Joseph smoke a cigarette was extraordinary; in all my dealings with the man over the years, I had never seen him smoke a cigarette. Cigar's quite frequently, but never a cigarette. My interest was piqued; something was bothering him.

"You're working on a thing over at the university," It was a statement, not a question.

And there it was, the reason we were summoned.

"We are," I replied.

"Enzo Barra sent a couple of goons to warn you off."

"Yes, they threatened to shoot our dog, Sabaka."

Joseph shook his head, then asked, "What happened with his two men?"

"Sully and Bam-Bam shot both of them in the back with darts containing a very powerful hallucinogenic."

The aged mafia boss turned his head and gazed at me in either amazement or disbelief, I couldn't tell which one. His gaze encompassed a full minute before asking, "What did the two goons look like?"

I described the wise guys in detail, and Joseph Votto responded, "That would be Nagurski in the wool coat and his mentally challenged sidekick, Frank, or Big Waddles. Both carry trademark .44 magnums."

"Big Waddles?" I asked.

"Yeah, he waddles like a two hundred and eighty-pound duck. Jesus Christ, these two love their work and are psychotic," Joseph then took a significant drag from his cigarette.

"Good to know. Next time I will be sure to kill them," I said.

"Yes, probably a requirement shortly."

There was something in the way Joseph Votto Senior said 'shortly' just then. There was a massive meaning behind it, and I couldn't grab it. But I would.

After a minute, I replied, "And you already know that we are investigating the alleged death threats involving Gunner."

The parking deck was silent except for the occasional tire squeal a couple of levels below us or a roadie's voice wafting up from below. It was comfortable up here as the Northeast Ohio evening sun flexed some muscle before she departed for the evening. Watching Joseph Votto stare into space and fidget with the cigarette was captivating; I didn't know anybody in my orbit who still smoked, especially Joseph Votto Senior. He was in fear of something.

"Tell me what you have found so far," He demanded.

"Nope, what's your interest?" I asked.

Out of the corner of my eye, I saw Buster shift his body a little. I also felt Joseph Votto Senior's body language change as he straightened.

While I considered these movements borderline hostile, I didn't like anyone demanding anything from me, especially while on a case. Joseph Votto Senior was a lethal man to be feared, but a significant factor in hiring our team was our brains, gonads, determination, and experience. Besides the guys on our team, we also had the two most formidable women on the planet. Lose those features, and our phone stops ringing.

My shoulders instantly became tense and knotted. I continued to lean on the wall, but now acutely aware of the weight of my Sig Sauer P320 on my right hip, I had switched firepower in the car on the ride to the garage. I was also aware of exactly where Buster was standing, although that didn't help with my tenseness.

"Mr. Votto, it's still early in our investigation, but it's not our practice to share private client information with anyone. Our reputation kind of depends on it."

"I could insist." The mobster said, taking a short puff off of his cigarette.

I gave him a look like, '*What else you got?*'

"Yeah, shit, you guys are pretty hard to insist; that's not going to work," he said in resignation before taking a long drag on his cigarette. He then held up his long and bony right hand and said, "I need your help."

He said this so softly that I had to stop watching the setup in the amphitheater to focus and concentrate on the aging mob boss's words. He continued, "Gunner Thompson is my son, my biological son, and he is being blackmailed into shaving points; there are no death threats, those are phony."

I let this admission from Joseph Votto Senior sink in. The air suddenly became thick and heavy, and the questions began piling up in my head in a rapid fashion.

The roadies below us continued to prepare the stage, and they reminded me of worker ants. From above, it was organized chaos, each crisscrossing around the other, electric cables snaking in different directions, all knowing there was a timeline. Kind of like my line of work. A few of the singers continued with their sound checks.

"We were hired under the pretense that your son was getting death threats, but you're telling us this is not true?" I asked.

"Yes, it's a way bigger and more dangerous game."

I blew out some of the hot air I had been holding in; this was not the road I wanted to go down today or any other day: Cheese and Crackers, point-shaving in college athletics. In our backyard.

"There would be a lot of money involved with Gunner's talent in covering point spreads and being manipulated on the professional level. And there are probably more than a couple of scumbags in this woodpile." Joseph said.

He raised his head and looked directly at me. At that moment, he wasn't an aging mob boss at the end of a long career but a glimpse of the once young Joseph Votto Senior, the feared and respected gangster. A man driven to save his son. His eyes became sharp, and his face grew tight. We looked at each other for a few seconds in silence. I was exceptionally pissed off that we were nothing more than pawns in a game I didn't understand. But we were going to find out, soon.

He motioned for Buster to come over as he said, "Call your team over; time for a cocktail."

While I texted Sully, even though we all had our earbuds in, Joseph's accomplices opened the back of the Escalade and began removing items, including a fold-out table. A large silver YETI cooler, of course, Joseph would own a twenty-seven hundred dollar ice chest instead of a Coleman or Igloo brand. By the time Bam-Bam, Tilly, and Sully walked over to us, our entertainment district was assembled. Four high-back wooden director's chairs with red canvas seats and canvas backs were set up next to a metal table with a thick red and black checkered linen tablecloth. There was a silver bucket being filled full of ice and a set of silver tongs, black paper napkins, eight unopened bottles of water, and a just-opened bottle of 19-year-old Balvenie Scotch whisky. I couldn't speak on anyone else's behalf, but I was a fan of this expensive and exceptionally luxurious liquor from Scotland. Kat, Tilly, Sully, and Joseph each took a seat in the director's chairs; Bam-Bam and I stood while Buster mixed seven scotch and sodas with limes, then handed each of us a drink and a napkin.

"Salute," Joseph said as he raised his drink.

"Cin Cin." Tilly replied with the Italian equivalent of 'cheers.'

"Do you always travel with a full bar set up, table, and chairs?" Kat asked.

Joseph took a large gulp of his drink, held it in his mouth, then slowly swallowed and said, "No, not usually. But this is my favorite night of music every year, and this is the best vantage point."

"This is premium parking, doesn't the parking authority or APD say anything about all of this?" I questioned.

Joseph Votto smiled a cryptic and creepy smile and said, "No, they do not."

Because we all were wearing our earbuds, the team was up to speed on the evening's events so far.

"Tilly, Kat, you both look splendid as usual this evening," Joseph Votto Senior said while tipping his glass.

Kat nodded without comment; she was always on full Defcon One when Joseph Votto Senior and Buster were in our general vicinity.

Sully and Bam-Bam remained quiet; they were focused on Buster and every place Buster's right hand went. Now and then, BamBam would glance at the other thugs sitting in the Cadillac.

It was quiet, almost peaceful, almost relaxing, as we all partook in the five hundred-dollar bottle of imported scotch.

"I assume you guys are up to speed," Joseph said to the rest of the team.

Sully pulled out his earbud for Joseph Votto to acknowledge.

Joseph Votto blew out a big breath and said, "I owned a small restaurant and bar on State Road in Cuyahoga Falls called Art's Place years ago. Gunner's mother worked for me as a young waitress, and we became friends. One night, and one night only, we, as the kids say, hooked up. She got pregnant with Gunner, but when she found out who I was and what I did for a living, she cut me from her life and, consequently, from Gunner's life forever. She wouldn't take any money from me, but as a saving grace, she began accepting a box of essential items from me monthly. Diapers, baby clothes, gift cards, damn, she is a strong woman, but even she realized she needed help. Over the years, I added a few luxury items for her: wines, dresses, school clothes, and earrings; a man should be allowed to provide for the mother of his child and, most importantly, his flesh and blood."

Kat raised her eyebrows at me, and I nodded yes; then she said, "Joseph, what do you need from us? Why not go to war with Enzo Barra? What's stopping you?"

The mood and the spirit shifted around us; the parking deck seemed to get darker and colder. Everybody felt it and casually moved into stances to easily retrieve their weapons if necessary.

Tilly's hand was in her handbag, reaching for Delores. Not many people ask Joseph Votto Senior personal questions especially one that challenges his manhood. Well, few who lived afterward, anyway.

"Everybody stand down. I respect Kat; I asked for this meeting, and honestly, she terrifies this older man a little these days."

Joseph nodded to Buster, and Buster began passing out cigars from a medium-sized wooden box of Partagas cigars sitting on the table. Everyone partook, and Buster produced a high butane cigar lighter and a heavy silver cigar cutter.

Everybody relaxed, but Tilly took Delores's deadly .22 handgun out of her large handbag and said, "I think I will keep Delores on my lap until I feel a little more relaxed with this conversation. Trust, but verify that trust."

Joseph Votto Senior nodded his head in agreement. He then raised his right hand and made a twirling motion with his right index finger. Buster began making the rounds and filling our glasses with ice, but Tilly and Kat covered theirs with their hands. I knew they wanted another drink, but they also knew that they needed to be the ones sober and ready if the balloon popped. We also knew it would have been a sign of disrespect for the rest of us to decline another drink from Joseph Votto Senior. But for me, I didn't give a crap about any respect or disrespect. I wanted another taste of the five hundred-dollar bottle of scotch. Buster made the rest of us another drink, and his drinking with us was an unwritten code for peace and respect. Our world was full of verbal signs and unwritten codes for many situations; I liked these because they kept me holding safely onto the monkey bars.

"Kat," Joseph Votto Senior spoke, "It's a fact that maybe I don't have the firepower anymore. It's a younger man's game, and Enzo is a sociopath with no distinction between right or wrong, good or bad, peace or chaos. He is also hell-bent on invading and taking over other established territories. Buster wants to go at him, but I am tired, just tired. But the main reason I don't take that piece of crap on right now is he will kill Gunner's mother and ruin Gunner's career forever if I get involved."

This admission sent ripples of a surprise to all of us.

"Again, Joseph, what are you wanting from us?" Sully said with a bit of starch behind it.

"I need you to make Enzo Barra leave my son alone so that the point-shaving never comes to see the light. But, now he has my son's hopes and dreams in the palm of his hand. But again, the worst is that Enzo will not hesitate to kill Gunner's mother."

Joseph Votto Senior asking for help and admitting he wasn't tough enough anymore was akin to playing gin rummy with Big Foot. His voice confirmed that he was indeed on shaky ground. I was going to tell the somewhat embarrassed gangster that we needed to think about it for a while, but Sully suddenly cut me off before I could say anything else.

"We will help you, Joseph; you have my word on it, and we will get Gunner out from under this mess," Sully declared.

We all looked at Sully, astonished, as he had never done this before, ever. Sully looked each of us in the eye, and I took a sip of my drink just to be doing something. I had hoped he would have hedged his bet a tad. The Rat Pack Tribute band began to play, and the first song they sang was '*Aint that a kick in the head.*'

The air was cooling down, but Joseph Votto had a few blankets in his trunk that he gave to the females. We decided to have a few more drinks and another cigar. Just a few private detectives, two of the most dangerous senior citizens that ever lived, an aging mob boss that was still very dangerous, and his hired killer singing to songs of days long ago. Music truly is the universal language.

Chapter 24

MY CELL PHONE ringing and vibrating jarred me from a profound sleep, and it also got all three dogs in a frenzy. After fumbling around, I finally found my cell phone on the nightstand and looked at the person's name, and said, "This better be important." I whispered, trying to calm the dogs down. It was two-thirty-seven a.m. Kat leaned on her right elbow and listened; I put the phone on speaker mode so Kat could hear in case I needed a second opinion later. Late-night or early-morning phone calls are usually nefarious.

The caller on the other end was Billy Cunningham, and I could hear that cop hardness in his voice, which meant someone was dead. He told me who and where. I slipped out of bed and began foraging for clothing in the dark. As I was getting dressed, I told Kat who exactly was murdered.

"Holy mackerel, already?" Kat said.

It took me twenty-five minutes to reach the university campus and Squirrel Hill. There were so many cops and first responder vehicles I couldn't count them all. The flashing, multi-colored lights were so bright I was afraid an airplane from the Akron Canton Airport would get confused and try to land in this very spot. I had to park three blocks from William Wrights's office. It was chilly, and without the moon and stars, it was dark. I walked slowly, and the Chancellor was in no hurry now; he had just recently taken three slugs into his body. There was a bright yellow tape line scissoring through the black wrought iron fence that I admired on my first visit, and now it was part of a brutal crime scene. There were Akron police officers, Summit County sheriffs, and plainclothes detectives taking statements from what I assume were university employees and nearby fraternity and sorority members. There were three television trucks with massive round antennas mounted on the roof of each. I spotted channel 8-WJW, Channel 3-WKYC, and channel 5-WEWS.

Off to the side were a couple of female EMS responders drinking bottled water. None of the police officers were smoking. That meant the Chief of Police was on the property, and all had their caps on and perfectly straight.

An Akron police officer was standing at the entrance to the building. His name is Cole Bassett, and I knew him from Canal Park from doing security for home RubberDucks games. He nodded towards the open door while saying, "Summit County Inspector Cunningham is waiting for you."

"Thank you, Officer Bassett," I replied.

It was the same lobby area that I had been in previously, with the glaring exception of the number of people occupying it at this moment. There were two plainclothes detectives, seven Akron police officers, the summit county medical examiner, Billy Cunningham, and Police Chief Jake Lann. Also, lying on his back in the center of the circular lobby was Chancellor William Wright. His right arm by his side and at a very odd angle. Chancellor William Wright's body was surrounded by thick puddles of purple and reddish blood already soaking into the plush carpeting. The blood smelled like iron and copper, which was a strong smell.

I moved a couple of steps to my left to allow a crime scene photographer to lean in and begin taking photographs of the gruesome scene. My movement caught Police Chief Jake Lann's attention, and he walked briskly over to me.

"What are you doing here?"

"I asked him to join us," Billy Cunningham said without turning from the very dead William Wright.

The Chief snapped, "What the hell for Billy?"

"Well, for starters, the recently deceased is holding a Scooter Jeanette private investigators business card in his left hand. Mr. Jeanette is currently under Chancellor Wrights's employ, which I would think the university's employ as well."

"What the hell is it with you and this university?"

"Chief, are you at the same address?" I asked.

Exasperated, the Chief said, "Yes, why?

"I want to ensure my Christmas card makes it safely this year."

The Chief of Police looked at one of the nearest plain clothes detectives and barked, "Detective Daniels give him fifteen minutes and watch every move he makes while he is here."

Chief Lann turned and left in a huff. I looked over, and Billy Cunningham stared at me in disbelief before he said, "Now, was that helpful?"

"Yes, very much so, but who found William Wright, and do we have a time of death?" I asked Billy.

"The Medical Examiner estimates between nine o'clock and midnight. His wife tried calling him numerous times between ten and eleven o'clock, but he wouldn't pick up, so she used his find my phone option. It led her here, and she's in an empty office across the hall from us."

"She a suspect?" I asked Bam-Bam.

"Of course, you were in the Chancellor's office; look around and see if anything sticks out," Billy said.

Detective Daniels followed me but stood in the doorway as I roamed into the Chancellor's office. I turned and said, "Chief Lann is my biggest fan."

"Sure sounds like it," the detective replied with a smile.

The office was lit dimly by the lobby lights. I turned to my private guard and said, "Can I turn on the lights here?"

"Yes." He replied.

I used my shirt sleeve to turn on the light and looked around. The blue and red flashing lights from the emergency vehicles outside cast colorful shadows that danced on the walls, ceilings, bookcases, and assorted furniture. The suit of armor looked Monty Python-esque, with the blue and red lights playing a disco dance upon its metal shell. Tonight the statue appeared larger, not overshadowed by the substantial William Wright. The laptop was missing, just an untethered white power cord lying on the tidy desk. I have looked at many crime scenes, and the key is to clear the mind and scan the room, not looking at what is there but what might not be there. I sat in the same chair as my previous visit. I crossed my legs and began looking slowly to my left. There were four diplomas on the wall hung neatly; a bachelor's degree from Case Western Reserve, a

Masters's degree from Case Western Reserve, a Doctorate in education, and a Ph.D. From Case Western Reserve. I hoped William Wright's family would be allowed access soon to retrieve these educational milestones.

The dark oak credenza mini-bar with the disgusting port beside the expensive clock looked the same. The credenza where the journal's daily planners were sitting was now closed. I walked over and opened the door. Instead of looking at numerous worn leather journals, now I was looking at two shoddy cylindrical glass vases, a small stack of university undergraduate brochures, and a small clock. But no journals. I peeked in but didn't touch anything, and the twofold color brochures were an advertisement for the university's school of business. The booklet was dated three years ago. The clock was displaying the wrong time and needed batteries. Whoever removed the small leather journals hastily added these items in a mock cover-up.

Chapter 25

BILLY FOLLOWED ME back to the marina for an early morning bite to eat after we met with Detective Daniels. And after drinking rancid coffee for two hours and forty minutes at the crimes against persons-major crimes unit within the Harold K. Stubbs Justice Center in downtown Akron.

I opened the marina refrigerator and began foraging for food and drink while Billy sat at our large kitchen island. We were in luck, Tilly had stocked fresh orange and tomato juices in large glass pitchers, and I grabbed both. I found the portioned honey ham in large Tupperware containers. I grabbed a jar of mayonnaise, hot mustard, slices of sharp cheddar cheese, a bag of shredded lettuce, a large tomato, and six hard-boiled eggs. I placed it all on the kitchen island. In the pantry, I found a homemade jar of unopened hot Hungarian peppers we had canned last year, a large bag of potato chips, and a half loaf of thick artisan bread we bought at Sarah Janes Bread Company in Monroe Falls just outside of Stow and Cuyahoga Falls.

I collected the appropriate utensils and glassware and placed them in the middle of the table. We assembled our versions of large Dagwood sandwiches and ate in silence. Billy and I were relaxed and comfortable being around each other without speaking. We have been in more than a few urban firefights and many great times together. The truth was Billy insisted on my silence frequently.

Billy finished his sandwich but left a few chips on his plate and said, "Damn, that was terrific; how do you not weigh three hundred pounds, Scooter?"

"I will relay your compliments to Tilly. She boldly contends that her ham is superior to that famous spiral sliced ham company, and I have good genes, my friend."

"I agree with her."

Billy leaned back in his chair and looked towards the ceiling, and said, "I should have recognized that I would be dragged into this university mess after our happy hour session at Leo's."

"I can't have all the fun."

Some years ago, when I was in college, Billy Cunningham was introduced into my life through chance. I was a junior studying business administration, and not I was not enthused. One drizzly morning the deputy governor of Ohio, Laura Pierce, was laying her mother to rest at Oakwood Cemetery in Cuyahoga Falls, eight miles from my university apartment. Her young daughter was abducted during the service, which resulted in a massive hunt for her. For some reason, I knew I could find that little girl. I studied all footage from the three main television news channels, found missing paint on one of the funeral home limousines, and it led me to her. But not after I killed both of her abductors with a crossbow that I had never fired before, ever. A grateful mother in a unique position sent a younger Billy Cunningham with the Summit County Sheriffs' department to my apartment. He brought two handguns and a State of Ohio private investigators license. Billy taught me everything he knew about firearms which represented almost everything there was to know concerning guns and safety.

"You didn't give Detective Daniels much information," Billy said.

"I didn't have much to give," I replied.

"Bullshit."

"Ok, when I met William Wright, the credenza was full of small leather journals. But tonight, they were gone, and in their place was a small clock that needed batteries and outdated university brochures.

"Did the Chancellor appear to have enemies?"

I sat my mostly eaten sandwich on my plate and replied, "At least one."

Billy gave me the cop stare.

"No forced entry," Billy said.

"The Chancellor knew his killer," I said.

"Female?" Billy asked.

"Maybe, we know that he was shot underneath the chin at close range with a .22, so someone was able to get close to him."

"You going to the funeral?" I asked.

"Probably going to have a couple of guys outside checking things out and running plates."

"Is that legal?"

"I think," Billy replied.

Chapter 26

IN THE EARLY afternoon, just after two-thirty and after a brief nap, Kat, Bam-Bam, and I were in the fitness room doing fitness things. I was taking a stroll on the treadmill, thinking that on this team of opposites, I was the planner and the shooter. Kat and Bam-Bam are the hitters and the muscle and the demolition team members. Tilly and Sully, we're freelance operatives.

The rain outside was so intense it cascaded sideways down our fitness room windows. Kat and Bam-Bam were taking turns boxing on an apparatus called a body action system. It was incredible how Kat and Bam-Bam mirrored each other, not just in physical appearance but in how they walked, ran, punched, kicked, and boxed. The boxing machine looked like a large robot with arms and legs. I deduced after a few rounds that the objective was to punch and kick these padded arms and legs with equal speed and force. Each strike was rewarded with a loud slot machine-like sound and a burst of ensuing blue and red flashing lights. Kat was wearing a purple backless and sleeveless bodysuit with purple cross-trainers. Her trapezoid muscles looked strong, and her toned and fit arms were shiny with sweat. Bam-Bam wore black Nike workout pants, a black t-shirt with the sleeves cut off, and black Nike slip-on exercise shoes. His arms were like massive steel cables. While one twin was performing this grueling exercise, the other screamed encouragement to dismantle the expensive padded robot we had just recently purchased. I, on the other hand, was taking a stroll on one of our treadmills and the video screen showed me trekking a steamy trail somewhere in Uganda.

After another half hour, I shut my machine off, grabbed my towel to wipe my face, and then shook my head at those two twin maniacs and searched for Tilly and her kitchen. Upon entering Tilly's kitchen, all three dogs were lying on the tile floor, each catching a piece of the emerging sunlight coming through the overhead skylight. In Ohio, you can count on the weather changing every hour. They did not get up, but in unison, they slapped their tails against the tile floor. I'll take what I can sometimes. Elvis was piping beautifully from our hidden speakers.

"Hi, Scooter," Tilly said in my general direction as she looked up from washing an alarming amount of green beans in the large sink. Next to the sink, in large wicker baskets, were mounds of tomatoes, potatoes, carrots, and shucked corn on the cob. This would probably be our last bounty from our garden for the year. Tilly's domain was the ultimate dream country kitchen with large hanging copper pots and sizeable stainless steel industrial appliances; the stove had eight burner tops and two induction ovens. The rest of Tilly's habitat had considerable airy windows, acres of counter space, a wood-burning fireplace, and two large flat-screen televisions with a dynamite audio system. The sassy women that ruled this kitchen had on an Elvis Presley cooking apron and had at least seven deadly weapons within arms reach.

"Good morning Tilly." And I grabbed a coffee cup from the overhead cabinet above the coffee maker, poured a cup, refilled Tilly's cup, and proceeded to make a fresh pot for Kat and Bam-Bam. We drank a lot of coffee in this house, the time of day was inconsequential.

I leaned against the counter and sipped my coffee and watched Tilly wash her vegetables, and listened to Mr. Presley sing '*Amazing Grace.*'

"Darling, I don't even have to look at you to know that your squirrel cage is spinning up a storm this early afternoon," Tilly said.

I sipped my coffee and thought for a second before I responded, "We just started this, and we have been told an untruth, and with Joseph Votto's alarming admission of being Gunner's father, there is an enormous amount of individual lives and freedoms at stake here for Gunner and, in turn, for his mother, Taylor Thompson. This one must be mistake-free."

Tilly grabbed a dish towel and wiped her hands, and grabbed water from the refrigerator. She opened it and took a sip, then turned to me and said, "Let's make it mistake-free, Scooter."

I took a sip of my coffee and said, "Okay."

Tilly was holding her bottle of water with both hands while staring directly at me, and after a moment, "Scooter, you are the best we have ever worked with, ever. You are kind, intelligent, crafty, passionate, and an utterly nasty dude when one of us or one of our clients has been wronged. Let's save that young man and his mother, mistake-free."

Chapter 27

I KNEW THE exact locations of those missing journals. In our experience, most people hid items in accessible and easy to get to places at a moment's notice. It was two thirty in the evening, and Bam-Bam, Kat, and I was watching Smoke and Gigabyte examining the security system, or rather the keypad for the security system for the executive offices located on squirrel hill. Smoke is referred to as Smoke because on an assignment he is wispy and silent. There isn't a lock or security system he can't break. Gigabyte is a hacker extraordinaire. We were all dressed in black from head to toe, including black leather gloves. Gigabyte was studying the electronic keypad to the right of the door. Smoke had a pair of wire cutters with red rubber grips in his right hand while examining a gray wire that ran vertically to the front entrance.

"Ok, Smoke, I will press a couple of keys on this keypad, and when I say, "Go, cut that wire, the rest of you, my guess is fifty-fifty that this will work. If it doesn't, run like hell because this alarm system is loud," Gigabyte said quietly.

Right before Gigabyte began pressing buttons I brushed his hand away and touched 1-8-9-0 and opened the front door. No loud sounds, no lights.

"What the Hell Scooter?" Bam-Bam asked.

"I got the security code from Billy Cunningham; let's go in before we are spotted."

"You're an idiot, Scooter; smoke you and Gigabyte, keep a lookout." Bam-Bam said.

Bam-Bam walked passed me, scowling, I think, but I wasn't sure the offices were very dark. But I could hear Kat giggling. Bam-Bam strongly loathes when I prank him and his men. We all retrieved small mag lights from our pockets and switched them on, and kept them trained on the floor as much as we possibly could.

"Hey, funny man do you know what you are looking for and possibly where to look?" Bam-Bam whispered through clenched teeth.

"Yep." And I pulled a small rubber mallet with a wooden handle from my cargo pants and walked directly into William Wrights's former office.

Kat and Bam-Bam both followed me, with the three of us using the small mag lights to guide us directly to the tall armored statue. I gently tapped the right thigh, then the left thigh, then the arms and legs, and then the lower chest, and the last tap made a different sound. I looked up at Kat, and she was leaning down with her hands on her knees, smiling. The illumination from the mag lights highlighted her new almond edges, gorgeous. Again, Men are from Mars and women are from Venus.

"There's something in there, isn't there, Scooter?" Bam-Bam asked.

Kat giggled again while I ran my gloved right hand over the armored crotch area of the statue, and after a few seconds, I found the hidden latch that sat under and behind the statue's right kneecap. The latch was small, and the opening was approximately twenty-four inches by six inches. The three of us directed our mag lights into the small entrance. The space wasn't vast but was as high as the statue's entire chest plate, and it was comprised of many leather journals, a small stainless steel revolver that looked like a .22 caliber, and six bundles of large denomination bills. I began retrieving the bills and the journals.

Chapter 28

BACK AT THE marina, we were all gathered in Graceland, reviewing the journals we had just liberated from the tarnished chrome belly of the centuries-old metal guard in what was once Chancellor William Wrights's office. There were seventeen small leather journals in all.

Sully was standing behind the bar, and Kat, Bam-Bam, Tilly, and I were sitting on bar stools. Sully was drinking a draft beer in a tall pilsner glass, Tilly was drinking tea with a shot of peach brandy in a thick white china mug, Kat was drinking plain green tea, I was drinking a cup of hazelnut coffee, and Bam-Bam was ingesting some green and purple protein shake in a thick glass.

In the middle of the bar sat a pile of gruyere herb and onion grilled cheese sandwiches cut in halves with a big basket of tater tots. Everybody grabbed some food.

"So you think the Chancellor's killer resides somewhere in these voluminous pages?" Sully asked while looking at me over his cheaters.

"I do, and I think the Chancellor got mixed up in this point-shaving scheme that got him dead. Hopefully, these journals will lead us to the other players involved in the blackmail scheme besides Enzo Barra."

We each took four journals and started with the most recent dates entered, and we worked back. We all had notepads and pens. I wanted us to look at names, dates, or places that occurred more than once. After thirty minutes, we would compare notes. The Chancellor was a gregarious and colorful person, but that's not why he was murdered; his life was taken because he hired us; this I knew in my soul as fact. Why he hired us is still very unclear.

The first journal I reviewed was an employee demerit list; Chancellor William Wright was a serious grudge holder.

After thirty minutes, I said, "Ok, students, pens down and eyes forward."

"Don't be an asshole," Bam-Bam said.

"What would that even look like?" Tilly added, and the group, minus myself, had a nice little chuckle.

"You done?" I asked the cackling adults.

We went around comparing notes, and when it came to Kat's journal, we scored a touchdown. In her journal, four names were repeated with dates, specific times, and numbers.

Those four names were neatly organized in columns. Those names were; Gunner Thompson, Darris Blackford, Steve Kapusinski, and Todd Caruthers.

Sully's journal was a close second to Kat's. In the journal he reviewed and took notes, there were over eighty-five references to E. B. and B. R. with monetary denominations and dates. A quick estimation showed approximately nine hundred and fifty thousand dollars from those entries. A brief review of the other journals had the same type of entries, also with large sums of money.

The inside of Graceland was cast in a cozy yellow glow from the outdoor dock lights and the muted recessed ceiling lighting. Tilly had 'Blue Hawaii' and Elvis the Pelvis on the four flatscreen television sets on low volume.

"Sully, can I get a Portage Lakes Pontoon Amber?"

Sully set his journal aside and said, "Coming up, Columbo."

Sully placed it in front of me, a perfectly poured draught beer with a two-inch head of foam in a tall eighteen-ounce pilsner glass. I took it and walked over to Graceland's floor-to-ceiling windows and took a big sip, and admired the full-bodied taste. I thought about some things and then an about some other things. The water was murky and black, the sky dark with no moon or stars. I sipped more of my beer. I thought some more. I sipped some more Portage Lakes Pontoon Amber Ale. I thought some more. I finished my beer and turned around.

"You have that look, babe; you know something; what is it?" Kat asked softly.

"So, those numbers can only be one thing, the roadmap to the actual game, the same play, the exact player that committed the actual point-shaving event in real-time. All are documented on film and paper. So they either included his three childhood friends or they are part of blackmailing Gunner."

"Also, Sully, can you locate a copy of the canceled check that the Chancellor paid our retainer fee?" I asked.

"Will do."

After a few keystrokes, the check was visible on our seventy-five-inch flat-screen TV.

"The check is drawn on a university charities account that the Chancellor referred to as 'This one will work.' I am assuming this because he controls it completely with no oversight. The Chancellor was in on the point-shaving scheme and contributed to why he was murdered."

"But why hire us?" Tilly said.

"I am betting a game of chicken between the participants."

"Now what?" Tilly asked.

"First step is confirming the point-shaving players being blackmailed, knowing Gunner is number one on the list. And then we figure out who is making local bets to get to those staggering amounts of money, assuming those sums are profit gained from Gunner controlling the games and, in turn, manipulating the score.

Later that evening, Kat and I were in bed with all three dogs, lying in varied and unique sleeping positions. It was dark in our bedroom except for the dock lights casting a soft glow.

"Kinda hard to make love with these three taking up most of the hopefully soon-to-be adult playground."

"Shush, you will wake them up and never call our marital bed that again," Kat said.

"Sometimes, I hate them."

"Shhh, and no, you don't; go to sleep, goofball," Kat replied while kicking me lightly.

Chapter 29

FEDERAL STREET IS one of the main parkways through downtown Youngstown Ohio. It has always been a steel city's rust belt community like other cities similar to Chicago, Buffalo, Detroit, and Pittsburgh. And Federal street is where we found Smokey's Cigar Den and where we went to roust a dangerous gangster. Enzo's cigar bar sits between a trendy coffee shop called *'Hut with the Java'* and a small barbershop with an authentic red candy-striped barber pole opposite the entrance.

It was eleven-fifteen a.m., and Bam-Bam, Kat and I were sitting in Kat's 1977 classic Pontiac black Bandit Trans Am with the enormous gold bird on the hood. Having just arrived in thirty terrifying minutes of what is usually a gentler fifty-minute drive from our home in Franklin Township, Bam-Bam and I were a little rattled, but to convey that to Kat in any way, shape, or form would not be ideal.

Bam-Bam cleared his voice by fake coughing in his hand as a cover-up said, "So we are going to brace a psycho madman that runs most of the rackets on the East Coast, and that same psycho sent two enforcers for lack of a better word, to enforce us just recently. And whose employees we recently darted in the back? Who may recognize us on entry?"

"All may be true, but Yes, and I guarantee that this self-important putz has no clue; he is way, way forever caught up being Enzo Barra. However, today he gets to meet us." I said.

"Scoot, my man, you are many things, but you are not boring," Bam said, chuckling.

"Freaking A, my hubby is fun." Kat chimed in.

We verified twice that our firearms were loaded and that extra weapons like knives and mini taser guns were all accessible if Enzo Barra was, well, Enzo Barra. We walked under the black awning, up the three concrete steps, and through the glass door. We were quickly met with an assortment of different and wonderful-smelling tobacco leaves. The interior was gloomy and dim, and the morning management hadn't turned on all the lights opting to use the large front windows for illumination. There was a long, polished mahogany bar the entire length of the left-hand wall. There were fourteen black oak barstools sitting in formation against the long bar. Behind the bar sat a massive credenza stocked with liquor bottles in front of the wall-to-wall mirrors on the back wall. A square-shaped leather pit of couches overpowered the middle of the room, and against the back wall was a full-length wooden seating bench with six small tables and one chair evenly spaced for each table. In the rear was a substantial glass-enclosed walk-in humidor. I counted ten large televisions in strategic positions. Six of them were playing a NASCAR rerun from the weekend, two had news channels, and the remaining two were live security video feeds from the front and rear of the building. I counted at least six security cameras through the front room.

The place was empty, and our intel had verified it would likely be open or primarily empty this time of day. Still, most importantly, our target, the owner Enzo Barra arrives promptly every morning at eleven thirty.

A mature and less than enthusiastic male bartender was wiping down bottles and wiping down the bar, all while smoking a large torpedo cigar. It smelled Nicaraguan and expensive. I read the blue and gold band on the cigar. He wore black slacks, a worn black leather belt, and a faded, dingy white long-sleeve button-down dress shirt. The collar was filthy, he was getting older as I watched him.

We entered the walk-in humidor, and I spotted four additional security cameras.

"A lot of security for some cigars and liquor," Kat said.

"I counted twelve but dollars to donuts. There is a counting room in the back; this is a cash stash place." Bam-Bam said.

That's why I am a shooter, and he is our demolition man. We each chose a cigar, actually, we three chose the same brand of a cigar; Toro Blue Sapphires.

Grabbing seats at the bar, the sluggish bartender noticed and placed three cardboard drink coasters in front of each of us very slowly. I was concerned I would need a shave before we even got our beers. The drink coasters were advertising for an expensive Tequila, Don Julio 1942. We ordered three Samual Adams Wicked & Easy ales in the bottle. Then three large ashtrays, a cigar cutter, and an electric torch cigar lighter were placed in front of us. We had just finished the pre-perfunctory tasks before actually smoking the cigar when our beers arrived. Up close, the elderly bartender's face and neck were wrinkled and dry looking, like most long-time smokers acquire. His face looked like a discarded catcher's mitt.

At eleven twenty-nine, the front door opened, and Enzo Barra slithered through the opening. He was wearing black trousers, a black polo shirt, and black loafers. He was followed in the door by two large middle age-wise guys who wore dark slacks and dark short-sleeve button-up shirts with intricate stitching on the sides. I think they are called bowling shirts. Neither men were Waddles or Frank Nagurski or as I called them fatty wool and Frank. Because of television and film, everyone assumes mafioso characters look like Marlon Brando or Tony Soprano; Enzo Barra does not. Enzo resembled a greasy, scaly reptile. He stood about five foot ten inches and weighed about one hundred and fifty pounds with rocks in his pockets. He had wispy black hair combed straight back. His forehead was hooded, and his pointy nose and weak chin made his false teeth look too big for his mouth. I wanted to take his temperature and see if he was human or reptilian.

He walked past us with his two wise guys in tow. As they passed us, I smelled cheap cologne, sausage, and a lot of body odor. As they whisked passed us, they appeared not to notice us; that would turn out to be a colossal mistake. They entered an unmarked wood-paneled door in the rear and to the room's right.

"What now?" Kat asked.

I smiled and replied, "We enjoy our pleasant cigars, we drink our beers, and we wait."

"That's your entire plan?" Bam-Bam asked, leaning forward and around Kat.

"Have I ever let you down?"

Kat made a noise similar to a snorting sound but I knew her to be more elegant than that. Well, most of the time.

I took a delightful puff from my Toro Blue Sapphire, held it up to the subtle light, looked at it, and asked, "Do you know where the meaning of 'Close but no cigar' originated?"

"No, Poindexter, but I have a strong feeling that you do and are chomping at the bit to inform us, Bam-Bam replied while scanning the room using the big mirror behind the bar.

"In the early twentieth century, the cigar was the Cadillac of carnival prizes, so when the contestants just missed winning a prize the carnival barker would shout out *'Close, but no cigar'* to the crowd."

Bam-Bam silently stared at me in the large mirror; Kat smiled her mischievous smile and kissed me on the mouth. I asked her "What was that for Babe?"

"A reminder of things to come later tonight if you don't expound on the 'Cadillac' reference in your definition; I mean, you teed it up on a tee for another one of your fun facts."

As Bam-Bam and Kat began laughing more than required, I drank my beer and smoked my cigar. After a few moments, the door in the back opened, and Enzo emerged with the two large wise guys. The reptilian gangster walked the distance of the room and took a seat at one of the tables set against the wall. The two bodyguards took seats at the bar three stools from Kat and Bam-Bam. Never even glancing at them, that was a mistake.

The bartender took a large cigar from a small humidor on the back counter. Then he grabbed a large rocks glass from the credenza and filled it with ice with a clear plastic ice scoop. He then grabbed a bottle of Crown Royal and filled the rocks glass three-quarters of the way, and then the bartender watched the ice and whiskey settle into the glass, adding a few more cubes of ice into the whiskey. On a small circular black serving tray, he placed the drink, cocktail napkins, an expensive cigar lighter, a giant orange glass ashtray, and a black cigar cutter. He then inserted a folded newspaper into the crook of his right arm along his right side. Then he walked across the room and delivered all to his boss in a slow, prolonged mode.

After a few minutes, I took a sip of my beer, savored another long and enjoyable drag from my Blue Sapphire, and stood.

"Time to annoy a dangerous gangster," I said in a whisper.

"Don't let him bite you; I don't have anti-venom on me," Kat said.

Enzo was clipping his cigar when I took the single seat in front of him. I placed my beer next to me on the right and knocked the minor ash off of my cigar in his ashtray. He kept his focus on the cigar task. He had a large diamond ring on his right pinky finger and a silver Rolex on his wrist. I watched him as he carefully clipped his cigar methodically like he was pruning a bonsai tree. His face wore the years of alcohol, stress, betrayal, dishonesty, and childhood measles. Enzo's dark and thick eyebrows were a fraction away from being a unibrow. His opaque eyes were suspicious, cautious, and without life.

"Can I help you, pal?" the gangster asked when the cigar was lit. His voice was higher than expected. Probably had a voice stand-in when he yelled at people.

"Ah, there it is. I heard you were a charmer, Enzo; my name is Scooter Jeanette, and I need a few minutes of your time."

His eyes darted to his two giant, personal body sentries, but they were at the bar unmoving, and at this moment, Kat and Bam-Bam were each pointing .9mm handguns, sixteen rounds to a clip at their respective midsections. The guns were underneath the eye level of the bar, and their bodies shielded them. Enzo sensed something was not kosher but was too used to be scary, so he plowed forward with me. Besides, there would be more bodyguards in the back room.

"Before I throw you out or worse, what the fuck do you want?"

"Debatable at this point on both but we will cross that certain bridge together in a little bit. I am here to discuss an important business matter with you." I replied.

"People don't just walk into my bar and start discussing shit with me," Enzo said.

"Well, you can't say that anymore, Enzo, old pal. I am thinking of doing it weekly."

His face momentarily showed anger than surprise; the gangster was confused. There were white droplets of saliva in the corners of his mouth. It was inevitable that I would be hit randomly by gangster spit, the hazard of the job. Enzo was so used to getting respect everywhere he went or from anyone he talked with. His eyes softened, and in a quick, firm decision, he wanted to find out who I was; he was losing and needed more information.

"Ok, you got my attention. What do you want to discuss?"

I took a long puff of my cigar and said, "You sent a couple of out-of-shape and out-of-their-league toughies to shoot my dog and to get me off the case that I am currently working. Also, a long-running feud with a local mafia boss that has unfortunately spilled over to a young man I am trying to help on this very case, and we would like it to stop immediately."

Enzo took a big pull from his whiskey, he was stalling for time. He wondered why the guys in the backroom hadn't glanced at the security cameras and come out to investigate. He was also surprised that he was being fucked with on his turf and that I knew his business, and he didn't know much of mine.

"I have no idea what you are talking about."

"C'mon Enzo, let's not insult each other here, I know there is a grudge with Joseph Votto Senior, but I am trying to save a young man's life and career."

Enzo smirked at me and said, "I don't give a fuck what you little piss ant thinks." And he took a sip of his whiskey.

"Well, this little piss ant is going to crawl into every aspect of your filthy and slimy life."

"You're going to pay for this asshole." Enzo said and I was showered with saliva.

I handed him a napkin sitting next to him, and said, "Spit on me again, and I will shoot you in the lip."

His face erupted in rage while he said, "Do you know who I am, you stupid fucker?"

I sighed heavily, "Yes, and I just warned that if you spit on me again, I will shoot in the lip."

Kat and Bam-Bam laughed through the earbuds.

Enzo's right hand had been slowly sliding towards his right pant pocket.

"If your right-hand moves another millimeter, my beautiful wife will put a bullet in your forehead from across the bar."

Kat waved at him with just her fingers on her left hand and showed her .9mm to Enzo.

"You are blackmailing a young athlete to throw college football games for you and others, and I want it to stop right now."

Enzo's eyes tightened, his facial features became meaner, and he said, "In a few seconds, I guarantee a handful of certified toughness is going to come through that back door, and then you, my new enemy, are screwed."

On cue, the back office door opened with an aggressive thud against the wall, with four of Enzo's wise guy buddies entering the room slowly. Bam-Bam's men, Rhino, Snake, Mongoose, Dozer, Gator, and Sully, 're directly behind them. Our guys each carried a firearm, Enzo's guys did not. The wise guy in front of Rhino had an impressive red welt emerging quickly underneath his right eye, and it appeared he was bleeding from his left ear. The guy being directed by Mongoose was holding his right arm at a ninety-degree angle against his body and appeared to be in a state of shock, with blood running swiftly from his nose. The pain would come in a few moments. Further in the back of the room, six of BamBam's Army comrades dramatically entered the room with equally dramatic wardrobes. All full commando combatant Gear. Head-to-toe black and grey camouflage, high-top black Nike nylon tactical Army boots. But most extravagantly, they each carried M249 lightweight machine guns; this was not the firearm to mess with. They all wore black face coverings. Each man took a varied and strategic position inside the cigar bar. If I had known them not to be on my side, I might have thrown up; they were frightening. I also knew even with this show of force; there were two of Bam-Bam's men ever vigilant with Gunner back home.

"You had the first part correct but a swing and a miss on the second prediction; I like our chances," I replied while taking a showy drag from my cigar.

"What the hell," was all Enzo could sputter.

We all remained quiet, and there was a rustling in the back; the goon in front of Snake tried to break from Snake's grip. He failed miserably and was now flat on his back and not moving; Snake had his right tactical booth on the stupid thug's neck.

"Before one of your goons again tries something foolish and gets killed over it, let us get back to the matter at hand," I said.

"Sully, what the fuck are you doing? "Enzo replied as he had just noticed him in the crowd. Enzo was beginning to comprehend the totality and fullness of his current situation.

"We are the one's that shot your goons with dart guns, do as we say. Drop this young man and let him live his life," Sully replied.

"My men had to be hospitalized; that bill cost me six large greenbacks." Enzo said firmly but with little enthusiasm.

"Shop around for better health insurance; Cobra prices are coming down," Sully said.

And while we had been sitting there, I had been slowly moving the wooden table toward Enzo and the back wall. The brutal mobster was so caught up in being Enzo Barra he didn't realize it until I had him pinned against the wall.

"Now, we want you to walk away from the university football program, no more contact with Gunner Thompson, his mother, or any teammates, zip, none," Sully said.

Enzo leaned back and said," Nobody tells Enzo Barra what to do, not even you, Sully. You have just signed your death warrants, and Enzo spits in my direction.

I stood very quickly and grabbed the reptilian gangster by the nose between my two fingers and shook his head back and forth. Then up and down and said, "Enzo, you are pathetic and now completely helpless. We can do whatever we want to you right now and anytime we want. Your crew is watching and losing all respect for you. You got bullied in your own bar. Jesus Christ, pathetic, what's your answer?" I asked.

He shook his head no, and "You are fucking dead."

"Enzo, if we keep score by blood spilled, it's us one, and you zero."

Chapter 30

IT WAS ONLY one-thirty in the afternoon, but it now was growing darker, and the underside of the clouds up above was a couple of different shades of gray; the threat of rain increased by the minute. It had dropped four degrees during my short drive from Portage Lakes to Cuyahoga Falls. It was two days after my less than agreeable meeting with Enzo Barra and I was sitting on Front Street in downtown Cuyahoga Falls in the SUV listening to a local talk sports radio station. I was eyeing the Cuyahoga River Condominiums, Taylor Thompson's residence. The condos sat directly on the Cuyahoga Rivers's edge in downtown Cuyahoga Falls. I was parked in a metered spot on the East side of Front Street in front of a great bookstore called *'Shelf Life.'* Kat, Tilly, Sully, and I enjoyed this unique bookstore designed with love and respect and expertise by the highly energetic owner Danielle Sawat. The painted deep purple stone walls and comfortable and satisfying small seating could make you lose an entire day reading in this small zen paradise; we love *'Shelf Life.'*

Mayor Don Walters has done a fantastic job revitalizing the downtown area. The resurgence has brought many great restaurants, bars, and a fantastic open-air concert venue with indoor meeting facilities. But the star of this downtown is and always will be the Cuyahoga River that was once burdened by a massive dam. The dam was removed and now the river flourishes actively and chastely. Now it embodies the city of Cuyahoga Falls proudly, and it is a kayaker's dream.

The condominiums were synonymous in appearance with Cape Cod homes. The condos were a mishmash of angled dormers, varied roof pitches, large skylights, and enormous bay windows. The exterior color was sky or cobalt blue. I liked them, Kat and Tilly would love them. I was sipping coffee in my orange RubberDucks travel mug, and my wing-dog today was Iggy; he would have the unceremoniously but not thankless job of watching my back today. I had a ziplock bag of bacon-flavored doggy treats. However, at this very moment, Iggy was methodically studying the insides of his eyelids for possible clues. He didn't like coffee. In her kitchen, Tilly was experimenting with a relatively strong roast from Jamaica, and I did not object; it smelled like rum, with deep rich cinnamon flavors, just fabulous. The entire team has recently migrated to being coffee snobs, and before Tilly began her current coffee inquisition, Folgers was our go-to brand.

I watched an older gentleman walking a big beautiful brown and white Saint Bernard dog, complete with a small brown keg underneath his massive jowls. While his dog suddenly hunched over and did his business, the beautiful dog's owner looked around as a reflex and tried to morsel up just a shred of dignity, picking up the doggy doo-doo as a dog power; this was not an easy endeavor. I placed my mug of coffee in the beverage holder and told Iggy and my new favorite Jamaican roast coffee, "I will return shortly." And Iggy opened his eyes for a short period and correctly ascertained no prospect of any food being offered, so he went back to sleep. My coffee rudely ignored me.

I was wearing a pair of Turnbull and Asser eggshell-colored slacks and a light blue short sleeve polo shirt with the hand-stitched whale in white on the left breast, and a lightweight, waterproof blue FootJoy windbreaker. I had on comfortable brown retro penny loafer dress shoes. All in all, I thought I enhanced the neighborhood or at the very, very least didn't taint it.

So now that we have attracted the attention of some heinous people again, I was wearing my Glock 19 on my right hip in a leather holster, it's the same gun that the Navy Seals use, and that comforts me. I also had a small Browning .22 pistol in a small leather holster on my right ankle; a mini taser and earbuds were mandatory for the team now that we picked a fight with Enzo Barro.

Taylor Thompson answered the front door after one doorbell ring and twenty seconds. I felt she was a little guarded by only opening the door a quarter of the way, Cuyahoga Falls is exceptionally safe, and I was an expert on body language. I filed that away. She recognized me and opened the door to allow me to enter; as she closed the door, she looked up and down the street and then double-locked her door with her left hand. Her right hand was immersed in bright white bandages; the bandages were wrapped professionally. Her right eye was black and blue, and it was fresh.

A large yellow Labrador stood at Taylor's side; Taylor inadvertently placed her left hand on the Labrador's back. Points for Taylor being a dog lover. The Labrador Retriever was growling a low, gravelly protective growl. I have been around a lot of dogs especially Labrador Retrievers and this type of behavior was odd.

"Bernie, hush." And she patted the dog affectionately on its head.

"Bernie?" I said.

"Yes, Gunner named him after Bernie Kosar from the Cleveland Browns.

Gunner's mother wore a matching peach designer tracksuit and white university ball cap; her hair was in a ponytail and hanging down her back and looped through the hole in the back of her hat. Her eyes were puffy, she had recently been crying a lot and for a long period.

"Of course, I almost forgot about our appointment; hello, Mr. Jeanette."

I didn't believe this for a moment; through years of experience, her body language suggested that this woman had recently been hurt or had reason to be cautious. In my business, I knew bandages and wraps, which were highly new due to their cleanliness. No dirt or accidental food stains.

Chapter **31**

WE ENTERED A great room by walking through the kitchen, and the large room was wall-to-wall windows and large glass sliding doors that were wet from the damp river spray. The carpeting was a light gray with hints of ocean blue. The Cuyahoga River view was incredible, and the massive windows showed the rushing water was at its core top speed due to the recent rain. There was a large flatscreen television in the right corner, a small wet bar sat adjacent, and on the other side of the room was a large Yamaha upright piano. The piano was black with the word 'Yamaha' in yellow stenciling centered on the front. An assortment of gray and cream-colored living room furniture was spaced strategically to enjoy the gorgeous view. On the other wall, there was a mirrored wet bar with a black and gray marble granite top, a single stainless steel sink, and a small cabinet with two blond oak doors. Three shelves with assorted glasses and stir sticks sat on the wall behind the mini bar's countertop.

Taylor had taken small and slow strides down the hallway like she or her body were acting together and concentrating on hiding physical pain. Bernie walked with a sideways gait akin to injured ribs. It was apparent both Taylor and Bernie had been recently hurt, most likely last night. I felt the weight of my handgun and went into full alert mode. I took out my cell phone and quickly texted three symbols and numbers to Bam-Bam, Kat, Tilly, and Sully; #1, $, #4. Our code for immediate security emergency protocol.

There was a massive picture of Gunner in his high school football uniform on the wall behind the elegant piano. He had his Black Tiger football uniform and his helmet under his right arm, and his blond hair was messy and sweat-soaked. There were two black chalk lines underneath his eyes. His smile looked genuine and earned.

"Ahh, hence the reason for the jersey number of nineteen. I was a huge fan of Bernie Kosar, but Gunner wasn't even born when Bernie played in the old Municipal Stadium in the late eighties and early nineties. Our good friend Frank Stams, grew up here and played locally at St. Vincent St Mary High School and The University of Notre Dame."

"Correct, but as Gunner studied the history of the Browns, he just latched onto Bernie Kosar and Frank Stams as another. Do you know how often I heard about Frank being a consensus All-American and winning a National Title?"

"Ha, ha, I'll bet a lot, and he is my Aunt Tilly's favorite."

Bernie the Labrador kept eyeing me and staying on Taylor's hip. I know dogs, and this particular dog is in full protection mode. Someone has recently injured them on purpose. My shoulders got tight, and they turned warm and became severely knotted. When the team, especially Kat and Tilly, catches a glimpse of Taylor Thompson and her cherished family pet's injuries, someone's candle will be extinguished sooner rather than later.

"Your view is extraordinary," I said as I watched a female and a male in bright yellow kayaks paddle south down the river. Some possible life-changing thunder and lightning weren't going to disrupt these two sports enthusiasts' plans for today.

"Thank you, I love it, and believe it or not, it is prettier in the winter."

"I can believe it. I also live on the water, actually a lake."

"Oh, which one?" Taylor asked.

"On Mud Lake in Portage Lakes."

"I love the lakes," Taylor replied.

I smiled because most people referred to Portage lakes as the Lakes."

"Can I get you something to drink?" Taylor asked me.

"What are you having?"

"I was thinking a bloody Mary would hit the spot," she said in a failed attempt at a happy smile.

Taking her wounded hand into account, I said, "Sounds good, but if you give me the okay, I can assemble them."

"Sure, but I will help, or as much as possible," Taylor corroborated.

I stopped and looked around the living room and said, "Will Gunner and his friends join us in a bloody Mary?" I inquired. Taylor looked at me and said, "Why, no, he is in school."

"Ms. Thompson, there are five empty coffee mugs in the sink, you and Bernie have recently been physically hurt, and the two bodyguards that we have following Gunner are currently sitting across the street from us. I know about the blackmailing and point shaving. We are here to help, and we are the good ones."

After a minute of silence, Taylor turned and said, "Gunner, honey come on down. I do believe that Mr. Jeanette is here to help us."

On the wrap-around of the second-floor landing, Gunner appeared and stood for a second and then walked down the steps and put his arm around his mother. It was astonishing how big Gunner is in person.

"How about the other three?" I asked.

Reluctantly, the other three young men descended the stairs and took positions around Taylor Thompson.

"Steve Kapusinski, Darris Blackford, and Todd Caruthers, I presume."

All three nodded their heads up and down.

"We are crystal clear on the point-shaving blackmail scheme, and we are going to get you out from underneath this mess, but you need to understand these are nasty men that are extorting and blackmailing you," I said.

Gunner visibly winced at the words point-shaving, the game and rules he learned and loved were being attacked. The artificial turf and sometimes grass have shaped him into the man that is now standing in front of me. Also, the sidelines with his teammates when he isn't on the field provided direction, pride, and a sense of belonging to something bigger than a game.

There was a knock at the door, and Taylor Thompson jumped a foot.

I walked to the door and said, "That would be my wife and her aunt Tilly."

I let Kat and Tilly in the door, and when we arrived in the living room, the onlookers were visibly shocked at these two women holding firearms. Kat carried a sawed-off shotgun, and Tilly a stainless steel Colt .45 handgun.

I put my right hand on Kats's left shoulder and said, "This is my wife, Kat, and the other lovely female is her Aunt Tilly. And rest assured; there are no better hands to be in; these two could guard Lithuania alone."

"In ten minutes or so, the rest of our team will be joining us, and we are going to install state-of-the-art surveillance equipment, impenetrable locks, and barriers on the insides of all doors and windows," Kat said matter of factly.

With another knock on the door, Kat let the crew in through the front door, and the garage, then directed them to the living room. It was Bam-Bam, Sully, Rhino, Mongoose, Snake, Dozer, Gigabyte, and Gator. All layered with special ops black uniforms head to toe. Gator had a Heckler & Koch submachine gun strapped around his chest.

"This be the cavalry," Tilly spoke up.

The intimidation factor was evident on Taylor, Gunner's, and the three teammates' faces. Then the relief set in fast.

Bam-Bam's men immediately turned and went to work. Snake set his backpack on the living room floor. I peeked out the window, and the team was using our commercial work van with the removable advertising decals, thin one today read, '*All American WiFi Repair Services.*'

As all the equipment was brought in, Gator rolled out long plastic sheets to cover the floors and carpeting.

I said, "First things first, Bloody Mary time; Darris can you assist Taylor and me?"

Taylor Thompson pointed to a green ice bucket with a large white shamrock on the front, and I walked over and grabbed it. And then Darris, Taylor, and I went into the kitchen for ice. The kitchen was large and had white's, gray's, and friendly and bright colors. The appliances were stainless steel and new. There was a giant overhead ceiling fan with black metal blades centered between two rectangular side-by-side skylights above us. I filled the ice bucket with ice from the freezer, and Darris managed valiantly to procure and slice the lime and celery. I placed it on a serving tray and returned it to the wet bar.

Back at the wet bar, I filled nine large glasses with ice, and Taylor foraged in the wet bars bottom cabinets and found a large unopened bottle of bloody Mary mix, a small container of celery salt, hot sauce, Worcestershire sauce, and salt and pepper.

"Spicy?" I asked.

"Definitely."

The only vodka on the wet bar was Vavoom vodka with the one-of-a-kind glass bottle of a naked woman with long hair. I knew this vodka brand retails for around two large ones.

As I held the bottle with some admiration, Taylor saw me and said, "Have you ever had Vavoom vodka?"

"Actually, yes."

"It is costly; I googled it," Taylor said.

"Was it a gift?" I asked, reflecting on Joseph Votto's admission about the monthly boxes.

"Yes, something like that."

We took our stunning bloody Marys into the living room and handed one to Tilly, Bam-Bam, Sully, and Kat. Sully was supervising Bam-Bam's men, so he set his on a table with a coaster. The only time he ever encroached on Bam-Bam's turf was when the only option was total perfection.

We all sipped our drinks silently, and I thought this had gone fast. I wasn't sure what the others were thinking. And then there was a thunderous crunch; we all looked at Todd Caruthers as he held the remaining half of the celery stalk in his right hand and continued chewing loudly.

"Sorry."

"He does stuff like that, and we call him Crud, Steve said.

Everyone laughed; it broke the tension in the room.

I looked at Kat and said, "Ok, so no need to kidnap Crud."

Taylor Thompson pointed to the black backpack and said, "That bag is moving."

We all turned our heads and looked at the bag, and indeed it was moving. Bam-Bam stood and walked out of the room, and in thirty seconds, Bam-Bam returned with Snake. Snake walked over and unhooked the backpack's fasteners. In a few seconds, a large yellow and black rectangular head with small green diamonds slowly emerged.

The group stood and backed away in any direction they could from the backpack. Except for Crud, he remained seated and calm.

"Holy Hell, it's a freaking snake," Gunner exclaimed.

"Her name is Stella, and she is an invaluable resource in gathering information, more specifically to drill down to the truth quickly, besides Snake takes her everywhere," I said.

Stella is six feet of pure reptile. And now, about three feet of her was out of the backpack, her head moving back and forth methodically. Her red forked tongue darted in and out of her mouth, gathering intel by gathering chemicals in the air and the ground about her surroundings.

"Can I hold her?" Crud asked.

We all gawked at him in disbelief.

"She smells fear, man," Snake replied.

"Seriously, bring big momma over to me," Crud said.

Snake shook his head and pulled the massive Stella from her home away from home and walked Stella over to Crud, and held her close to Crud. Stella flicked her tongue rapidly toward him. After two minutes, Snake nodded his head in acceptance and gently placed the giant reptile in Crud's lap. Stella repositioned herself to look at Crud's face for a full nerve-racking minute. Then she turned back around and nestled into his lap, and went to sleep. There was a collective and vociferous sigh in the room.

Taylor, Gunner, Darris, and Kap found alternate seats as far away from Stella as they could and still be in the same room.

Bam-Bam reached into his black backpack and pulled out a first aid kit and, in minutes, gave Bernie a gentle going over with his hands and then wrapped Bernie's ribs with blue elastic bandages.

"Ok, Taylor, first things first, who hurt you and Bernie?" I asked.

Taylor Thompson stiffened and looked at the floor, and said, "I am scared."

"Don't be; when Bam-Bam's men are finished, the only place more secure on earth will be Fort Knox. And from this point forward, there will be two around-the-clock bodyguards outside, a rotation of those big mean scary men you just saw. Whoever hurt you is in on the blackmail scheme, and we need to start somewhere."

The bodyguards eased Taylor somewhat, "There were two of them, two fat guys that sounded and talked very threatening.

"Please tell us what they said and what they did," Kat said in an empathetic but forceful tone."

Taylor blew out a deep breath and began, "So I pulled into my garage last night, and they followed me in on foot and dragged me by the hair into the house."

Tears began to roll down her cheeks; Gunner stood and began pacing back and forth like an anxious lion in a cage.

"They began kicking Bernie in the ribs, then they grabbed my hand and held it on the kitchen counter and smashed my last two fingers with a large hammer. They knew what they were doing; they said good luck playing the piano now."

"Did they bring the hammer with them?" I asked.

"Excuse me." Taylor replied.

"If they brought the hammer with them, that shows they intended to smash your fingers before they showed up," I replied.

"Yes, it wasn't mine they must have brought it with them."

Kat's eyes became moist; she turned and walked over to the large window and gazed at the Cuyahoga River. The two thugs were not long for this earth.

"Gunner, Tell us how contact is made?" I asked. And he did. After receiving this information, Kat and I headed back to the marina; we had some planning to do and favors to cash in; Enzo had lied to us.

Chapter 32

STARK COUNTY, OHIO, is twenty-five minutes from our home in Portage Lakes. Stark County consists of five hundred and eighty-one square miles and is home to the cities of Massillon, Alliance, Louisville, Canton, North Canton, and Canal Fulton. If Stark County sounds familiar, it is home to the Professional Football Hall of Fame.

Today we were locked into a gated community called Glenmoor Estates and Country Club. What used to be a former monastery is now an elegant hotel and restaurant complex. Palatial homes surround an eighteen-hole golf course, but we were only interested in one hefty home inside the seven-foot black steel gates; it belonged to Enzo Barra. We were armed to the teeth, we had Kat, Bam-Bam, Sully, Tilly, Rhino, Dozer, and Mongoose in four lethal-looking and jacked-up pickup trucks. We also had four Federal Marshals, two female and two male, in a black SUV, and Ed Sutter, the charismatic owner of

Eddies Famous Cheesesteaks and Grille, with his incredible food truck. The final piece is a beat-up black minivan containing a three-piece band specializing in electronic rock music. I listened to a short online demo last night before hiring them; they were annoying and loud, and not good, which is probably why they were available. We were all idling on the street called Hills and Dales Northwest.

I got the go sign from Bam-Bam over the radio and said, "Ok, gates are open, let's roll," over an extensive network of two-way radios. We had a permit to perpetuate our activities and to host a block party from ten a.m. until three p.m. A major favor called

Within three minutes, we were all parked directly in front of Enzo Barra's stately home, purchased with unlawful criminal activities. The substantial house sat behind an enormous green, manicured lawn; the lawn was recently mowed in a cross-cut pattern. It looked like the outfield of Yankee Stadium, bordered by assorted colors of creeping myrtle and other bright and colorful flowers. The house was built with different muted brownstone bricks, and the roof was an expensive dark black shingled rooftop. A long concrete driveway wound towards the house, seemingly into three enormous garages. We all exited the vehicles and began implementing '*Code annoy a gangster today.*'

Bam-Bam's men began assembling a couple dozen metal folding chairs, and Eddies Famous Cheesesteaks and Grille's food truck parked and started prepping. The musician's minivan rolled up on us, and three young musicians tumbled out, dragging their prominent speakers and other musical equipment.

"Oh, I love the red carpet phlox and the yellow black-eyed Susans," Tilly exclaimed, looking at the gangster's manicured lawn.

"The blue and pink hydrangeas are flipping gorgeous, " Kat replied.

"I wonder who he uses for his landscaping," Tilly said.

I stared at them for a minute until saying, "This guy ordered his henchmen to maim a wonderful lady and devoted mother. He is ruining a young man's career. And they kicked the hell out of a defenseless family dog. Stay focused, ladies."

I rarely talked sternly to these women, so it got their attention quickly.

Tilly said, "Sorry, you are right, Scooter; we lost focus; all joking aside, I may injure him today anyway."

Kat was wearing tight blue jeans and an equally tight yellow stretchy short-sleeve shirt. An orange Akron RubberDucks headband held her hair back. Her eye mascara was thick and dark, her warrior mode. She wore black wolverine combat boots with her pant legs tucked in them. A compact black Glock .9mm pistol with ten rounds and a four-inch barrel sat proudly on her right hip. She was a foxy beast, and both male and female U.S. Marshals were sneaking peeks at her.

"I will put my guys on each side of the driveway entrance, and we can use our earbuds for communication," Bam-Bam said.

"That works," I replied.

Bam-Bam started to walk away, stopped, and said, "Scooter, The pink rhododendrons are to die for."

"You just might."

Sully walked over to me and handed me a diet coke in the bottle, and said, "So we sit here and eat cheesesteaks, listening to an annoying rock concert. And our goal is to bug Enzo Barra, a reputed and feared gangster with murder and violence on his resume under hobbies until he cracks?"

"Yes, that is the plan."

"Simple, annoying, and set up at the last minute, make him buckle first; I love it," and Sully gave me a low five with his right hand smiling.

Both male U.S. Marshals approached Sully, and me, both in dark slacks, dark sunglasses, and dark blue polo shirts with U.S. Marshals stitched on the left breast and highly recognizable dark windbreakers. The taller of the two addressed me and said, "I don't know what kind of connections you have, but I don't like this one damned bit."

The uptight lawman had the prerequisite short haircut, probably since his days as a youth and then in the army. He had thick, black dark eyebrows similar to Eugene Levy.

"Hey Morty, lighten up, we get to screw with a piece of crap mobster and do a favor for the big, big boss, and we aren't driving all-around Timbuktu serving warrants; it's a win; it's a good day. I am getting a large cheesesteak and fries." He was built like a fire hydrant but had the same haircut. He turned and walked briskly for the food truck.

I stared at Mr. Eyebrows for a few seconds and then said, "On this beauty of a day in Ohio in late September, I am standing here taking shit from a guy named Morty? Probably short for Mortimer, Jesus Christ." And I walked away, shaking my head; Sully laughed loudly while walking with me.

The band was set up on the street, we had barricaded both ends of the street, and a couple of vigorous phone calls got us a police cruiser at each end of the road directly in front of Enzo Barra's house. The band was loud and enthusiastic, but on the bright side, they were also horrible. After a few minutes, the neighbors on both sides of the street began to peek out of their windows, and a few overachievers came out for cheesesteak sandwiches and loud music. We had two huge chalkboards in front of the food truck announcing all food was free.

I positioned two chairs for Kat and me so that we crept close to Enzo's property but not actually on it. And to raise the stakes in *'Code annoy a gangster today,'* We also rented a six-foot by four-foot digital advertising board that Bam-Bam trailered with his pickup truck. Last night we programmed three messages on it. The first message on the large sign read 'Enzo Call Me...Before we show another message that reveals your true occupation:330-929-....'

As we sat there listening to a downright dreadful guitar player, a downright horrible drummer, and a downright disastrous lead singer, Enzo Barra would peek out of his front windows. Probably the living room or large dining room. The food truck's aroma permeated the surrounding air, and it smelled wonderful.

After forty-five minutes no phone call so I walked over to the electronic billboard and flipped a switch to revert to the other message. It read, "Your neighbor Enzo Barra is a gangster who has murdered people; he runs a stable of young underage prostitutes. He breaks legs over unpaid loans; he is an evil man."

Bam-Bam slowly drove the electronic sign up and down the street, and four minutes later, my cell rang, and I answered, "Scooter Jeanette and I excel at annoying assholes. Can I help you?"

Enzo Barra spoke for a moment and then hung up.

"Babe, he wants to talk in his garage," I said.

"You think he means you harm?" Kat asked me.

"Of course."

I stood and pulled my Glock from its holster and checked the clip to see that it was fully loaded and one in the chamber. I kissed Kat and said, "Chow Baby."

On the uphill walk up the long driveway, I noticed Bam-Bam had positioned his men in a semi-circle in front of the massive home. Three of his men had long gun's. I looked over at Morty, the uptight lawman, who looked constipated. Enzo Barra was standing in front of the garage closest to the street, and in the garage to the right, one held a metallic green Pininfarina Battista, the fastest production car ever made. I knew they were at least two million dollars, Jesus Christ. The last garage door was closed.

Enzo wore dark slacks and a white button-down shirt untucked, and brown leather loafers. He looked tired and pissed off at the same time.

"You got some type of connections and big brass balls rousting me twice on my property's, I should kill you right now."

"Again not likely." I said while I spread my right arm towards the end of the driveway and to Bam-Bam's men.

"You think that fucking scares me, I made my bones dusting punks like you." Enzo said with a little spit bubble on the right side of his upper lip.

"I do; I think deep, deep down you are terrified, but Enzo, you being a sociopath won't allow you to have feelings; now quit trying to be a tough guy for a minute. You asked me in the garage because you are way over your head, and now you know it. Now let's talk and see if we both can't come to a mutually beneficial understanding."

Enzo stared at me, and his eyes were like a cat in a carrier being led in an airport. He knew this was affecting his reputation and anonymity as a gangster scum bag in his neighborhood. He nodded his head and went over to the wall, and grabbed two wooden folding chairs from a stack of at least fifty, Probably throws a lot of parties in this mansion.

"Can you turn off that fucking sign?" Enzo asked.

I told Bam-Bam to kill the Billboard for now through the earbuds.

The jittery gangster and I stood in silence. Enzo pulled a cigar the approximate size of a baseball bat from his right front shirt pocket and began the laborious process of getting it lit. He didn't offer me one. Looking around the massive garage it contained two green and two blue plastic trash receptacles; all four on wheels. The single door leading to the backyard was open, and what I saw of the green-manicured lawn was expansive and similar to the front yard. There was a double green six-metal shelf unit on the west wall with the obligatory small garden tools and a couple of small red plastic gasoline cans. There were no oil stains on the concrete garage floor. A motorized vehicle has never been in this garage.

"Can you kill the music for Cripe's sakes?" He asked.

"No."

Enzo continued smoking his cigar, and I continued admiring Enzo Barra. The annoying music played on. I waited. We were on his nerves, I went to high alert, a nervous sociopath is dangerous.

"Ok, what do you want?"

"Why are you actively ruining this kid's possible pro football career? and why did you order your two thugs to smash his mother's two fingers?"

Enzo smoked and thought, finally saying, "Whoa, I never ordered any broads fingers to be smashed."

I thought on this for a moment. Enzo didn't respond to the first question but was genuinely surprised by the second question. I did and didn't believe him; I have witnessed liars.

"Did you shoot Chancellor William Wright?" I asked him.

"You listen to me you snotty piss ant, Enzo Barra don't shoot anyone he don't want to, and Enzo Barra, don't hurt women. I will deal with my now two ex-associates, and I will cut their nuts off."

I loved it when people referred to themselves in the third person. But I have been doing this along time, I knew liars and Enzo knew Sully or anyone associated with him wouldn't wear a wire. So if he did these things he would have told me, he would have been proud. He would have liked to stare me in the eyes and show me his power. I think his two thugs went rogue on this one.

"Better do it quickly because, after today, Sully's hunting for them," I said.

"I will."

"How did you know that Gunner is Joseph Votto's son?"

The music wailed on, Enzo puffed on his cigar and continued to mean mug through the thick cigar smoke. After a long moment, he said, "Screw this; it ain't worth the aggravation or hassle. With the Chancellor being murdered, too much heat. I will drop the kid; he made me a ton of money anyway."

I sat and stared at Enzo, "Okay, but you have never done one right thing in your life, and that takes a lot of skill. If you renege on this agreement, or if it gets leaked Gunner was in any way, shape, or form involved in point shaving, I will make your wife a widow by shooting you in your Adam's apple; I swear to God, Enzo."

"Don't push me. I can still wage war on your ass, you silly punk fuck."

There was little to say on that note, so I stood and exited the oversized garage and headed down the long and steep driveway. Hopefully not getting shot in the back.

Kat, Tilly, Sully, and Bam-Bam were grouped at the bottom of the driveway. Kat took a step closest to me when I reached them and she said, "Good job you silly punk fuck?"

"Yeppers."

"Atta boy Scooter," Bam-Bam said.

After getting the team's feedback from the entire conversation, we tackled dismantling this mobster block party. I gave Mortimer and fireplug the excellent news that they could leave. Kat sent the band packing, Bam-Bam shut down the electronic billboards, and Tilly paid the food truck another two thousand dollars to treat the neighborhood a little longer for our inconvenience and disturbance.

Sully looked at me and said, "You aren't done, are you?"

"I think we need to find out who killed Chancellor William Wright."

Chapter 33

LATER THAT EVENING, Kat and I were sitting at the bar inside The Diamond Grille on West Market Street, not far from the university and squirrel hill, where I last saw William Wright alive and the last time I saw him lay dead. We were meeting Milton Haft at his request, some pretext of a status update to our previous contract.

Kat and I were drinking Singapore Slings in tall glasses with orange and cherry garnish because Kat thought it would be fun to drink what they would have consumed in this place in the nineteen forties and nineteen fifties. This information was found from a quick google search on the short car ride to the restaurant. George Peters, the long-time mixologist, concocted Kat's fancy and throwback evening drink idea to perfect statuses. Judging by the contented smile on her gorgeous face, she was enjoying her choice of beverages. I looked around and decided that The Diamond Grille would always be Akron, Ohio.

Kat was wearing a black leather skirt, dark sheer stockings, black over-the-knee with pointy-toe leather boots, a red jean jacket, and a blue linen blouse. Her hair was pulled back to the left with a pewter Don Drumm hair beret made especially for her birthday last year. I wore my Michael Kors dress, black jeans, a brown corduroy vest with five large turquoise green buttons, and a light blue Giorgio Armani dress shirt. My feet were pleased, or at least I imagined they were in white and black snakeskin cowboy boots.

"I love it here, we should make it a point to come here more often," Kat said.

"Three times a month isn't enough?"

"No," she said with a seductive smile.

"Babe," I said and raised my reddish and pinkish-looking cocktail, and Kat clanked her cocktail glass softly against it.

Kat sipped her drink and said, "I love you, and it doesn't matter where we are; I just want it to be with you." She said; her eyes had that softness that made my heart skip a few beats; her lips were champagne-wet. I leaned over and kissed her and looked at her face for a long while. Then I looked around the bar, and there were ten other comfortable bar stools, eight large booths, and six tables. There was a backroom with eight tables, generally saved for VIP clients in the hopes they could eat their meals in peace. Last time we were here Tiger Woods was in town and had a bunch of executives with him.

I imagined this landmark in the nineteen fifties, the world in black and white, but a time when people left the house dressed to the nines, no grocery shopping in sweat pants. Men wore fedoras, suits and ties, women were clad in colorful dresses and matching hats. Smoke filled bar rooms, crowded pool halls, steakhouses with sultry singers and the unmistakable sounds of the big band era. I would have loved to have been a private sleuth in that iconic era.

"Do you think you have been summoned to be handed your walking papers, Babe?"

"Yep."

"He doesn't know that you won't quit?" Kat stated.

"Nope, and I think he is fishing, he doesn't know what we know, and there was as bad as an underlying nasty vibe between two human beings that I have ever felt. It would be natural for the Board of Directors to empower their in-house attorney with more power now, and he is looking for information."

"You're not usually wrong, at times annoying but not wrong," Kat said, and she bumped her head against my right shoulder affectionately.

"Babe, wait until you get a load of this Peacock."

Chapter 34

MILTON HAFT ENTERED the Diamond from the front door and stood on the platform studying the room. After a few long seconds, he nodded his head in my direction and walked down the short steps and straight over to Kat and me. Milton was wearing bright orange slacks, a white belt, blue slip-on loafers, a blue sweater vest with a black penguin, and a yellow short sleeve polo shirt underneath. His blondish hair was slicked back in a wavy style. He wore a white Apple watch on his left wrist.

When he arrived at our barstools Milton Haft the Esquire in-house counsel for the university, breezed past me and exclaimed, "Well, hello, who do we have here?"

"Kat, my name is Kat Jeanette."

Kat had used her icy and, at the same time, her tolerable voice. I was afraid Milton would try to kiss her hand, and his man marbles would end up right below his eyes, and with the footwear, Kat had chosen for tonight, it was quite possible. But she wouldn't like him disrespecting me; that made me nervous. In our first meeting back on Squirrel Hill, I warned him. Milton introduced himself and shook her hand. I blew out a deep breath and took in most of the rest of my Singapore Sling.

George drifted over and took Milton's drink order.

"I will have an Absolute martini up, dry, and get these two whatever they want."

We stuck with the same two drinks; Singapore Slings.

"Singapore Slings?" Might have to revoke your man card Scooter."

Kat squeezed my right hand. I thought it odd that this was the same meek and sheepish man I had met just two weeks before this evening. Most pertinently, his boss was murdered in cold blood in the office they both worked in appears to give Milton a new lease on life, for lack of a better word group. I glanced at Kat while I took a sip of my cocktail, and she was studying Milton Haft as if he were a fungal science experiment. She was analyzing his mannerisms, his sense of style, his body language, and his choice of alcoholic beverage. George Peters returned with our drinks, and Milton pulled a money clip from his right pocket and extracted a one hundred dollar bill, and placed it on the bar. He didn't hand it to George's waiting hand; I knew this just put Milton on notice with Kat; she did not tolerate rudeness to service industry employees.

Milton took a sip of his martini and said, "Jesus Christ, I said dry, dry. Is this grandpa new to this bartending thing?" Then Milton set the drink on the bar with enough starch to get Kat's hand reaching for her purse and her taser gun.

George returned with the change and Milton pushed the drink towards him and said "Dry, I said dry."

The seasoned bartender politely replied, "Yes, sir, my apologies." And George retrieved the martini and departed to make another. We knew George to be an excellent bartender of unequaled skill of forty-plus years. But a millennial wearing a children's belt probably knows better.

I put my hand on Kats's right thigh and squeezed softly to encourage her to pluck her hand from her small purse. I needed to know why Milton wanted to meet with me. Again I was pretty sure our investigative services were being terminated, but I was curious about his possible motives. Murder always brings the snakes out of their holes for a quick peek, and when that happened, we pounced. After all, we were in the business of grabbing them by the neck and shaking. But what threw me for a loop tonight was Milton Haft's demeanor. Granted, I had only met him one time before this moment, which was in the Chancellor's office, a business environment. Now he was different, a completely different persona. I have seen many chameleons over the years, and not one time did it turn out well for the chameleon.

The new martini arrived, and Milton took a tentative sip and said, "Better, not great, but better."

"Thank you, sir; I will try my best in the future; my forty-two years in the field must have been for naught," Philip winked at Kat and me and then slowly backed away.

Milt took another sip of his martini, a little larger than the first one and set the glass back on his coaster, and said, "So, is Kat short for something?"

"Yes, Mrs. Katrina Jeanette."

"Just asking." Milton said and reached over to the bar and palmed a handful of peanuts and cashews, even though there was a small silver scoop and small white dinner plates next to the peanut bowl.

I went to speak, and Kat nudged my leg and gave a slight, imperceptible nod of her head for me to be quiet. This wasn't easy; I had many questions before I punched him in his right eye.

The obtuse attorney rattled the nut's around in his hand while he leaned against the bar and surveilled the room. After some internal question was answered he popped the peanuts into his mouth. He finished the remaining dry martini and waved for George. My patience was waning, quickly.

"Are you a golfer, Scooter?" Milton asked.

"I am," I replied.

"Do you belong to a private club?" Milton asked.

"No."

"Why not?"

"Don't want too." I replied.

While performing this Laurel and Hardy skit, Kat ordered an appetizer of stuffed banana peppers, the best in town. Kat then went to the powder room but not before planting a wet kiss on my cheek with a slight giggle.

"What's the best course you have ever played?" Milton asked me.

Christ; he was relentless.

"I don't know about the best, but the course I enjoyed the most is Shadow Creek in Las Vegas.

"Shadow Creek, I am freaking impressed. That's where Phil and Tiger dueled it out in the first 'The Match, at Shadow Creek' and nis Steve Wynn's private playground. Man, you are connected, I am in Vegas just about every other weekend and try to play as many great courses as I can, but that's one I can't set foot on," Milton said.

This admission sent bells dinging through my system. Vegas is a gambler's paradise. And we were knee-deep in a case with a common denominator that equaled gambling. Philip set our drinks down, and Kat returned from the lady's room when our fresh beverages arrived.

Milton Haft took a much smaller sip of his martini and said, "You two get out to Vegas often?"

"No, catching criminals, especially murderers, keeps us pretty busy lately." I replied with just the right amount of starch."

Milton Haft reacted accordingly to my comment. If he murdered William Wright, his overreaction or under-reaction would show his hand. The pause approach was good.

After an awkward moment, he said, "I stay at the Alani Nu on the North end of the strip. It's a newer skyscraper boutique hotel casino with a mostly adult-themed vibe. Great nightclubs, hip bars, and the rooftop pool are topless if one chooses. My main bro bartender, Ethan, works in the main bar, and Ethan surely knows how to dry a martini."

His words were becoming thick, and his piggishness of himself was emerging; he couldn't stop it. He validated this when he talked about the Alani Nu being topless. I thought about shooting his left big toe off.

"Great, did you catch the perpetrator making the death threats or William Wrights's murderer."

I didn't want to tip our hand on the point-shaving scheme. But something was driving me crazy about his facial features and mannerisms.

Milton Haft tried to mean-mug me but couldn't quite pull it off and finally replied, "That is none of your concern the university no longer employs you."

"I can tell you that it will significantly concern Summit County Sheriff Inspector William Cunningham. Chancellor William Wright's murder could be related to the alleged death threats towards Gunner Thompson."

"I have given the Akron Police Department a copy of the original Gunner Thompson death threat letter, and we as a university are comfortable allowing them to investigate."

I took a sip of my drink and was just about to reach into my back pocket and retrieve a certified check for the amount of the original agreement. Still, I held my glass in my hand and twirled it a few times, watching the light filter through it, and then decided against handing him that check. What jigged around my mind was the semi-secretive checking account Chancellor Wright had drawn funds from.

The restaurant was quickly becoming full. The booths being taken and the barstools around us full. The atmosphere was becoming livelier and louder.

"Hey, Milt Baby, leave a hundred dollar bill for Phillip for you insulting him. And please argue with me so I have a reason to make you cry," Kat said.

Milton Haft looked at Kat and then me and then Phillip and then Kat again, cheese and crackers. It felt like when I first met him in William Wrights's office. Ultimately, he reached into his pocket and extracted a one hundred dollar bill from his money clip and set it on the bar.

Phillip accepted it and said, "Thank you."

Kat said, "Now, I want you to buy the entire bar a round of drinks for being, well, being you."

Milton Haft looked at me, I shrugged, he looked at Kat, she shrugged, he looked at Phillip, and he shrugged, and Milton extracted another one hundred dollar bill from his money clip. This crisp Benny Franklin he flung on the bar and walked up the steps and out of The Diamond Grille.

"Shall we take our seats with Sully and Tilly and enjoy a couple of Royal Filet Mignons?" I asked her.

"You bet your sweet patootie and Phillip, please send our stuffed peppers to our table and buy the bar a round." Kat said.

Chapter 35

THREE days after William Wright was buried, Miss Bethany visited me at the marina. We were sitting in Graceland by the windows in leather chairs facing each other. We were both drinking coffee in thick green mugs from a full tray service; there were also some tiny homemade pumpkin and chocolate whoopee pies courtesy of Tilly and her magical kitchen. Miss Bethany was dressed subdued, a white dress with pink flowers and a simple string of pearls hung from her neck. She wore white tights and flat black shoes. Her hair was tied back with a pink beret.

"Who was that enormous man at the front gate," She asked.

"That was Rhino."

"Rhino, do you have many of them?" She asked softly.

"We do."

She looked smaller today, more frail, more fragile. Her movements precise but not often. She held the hot coffee mug in both hands and looked out the window towards the docks, our pontoon boat, and further out, just water and even other houses on the other side.

"Your home is beautiful," She said.

"Its all of ours and it was formerly a marina for eighty years." I replied.

"All of yours?" Without taking her eyes off the water.

"My wife, her twin brother, her aunt, her uncle, three dogs, and a sour cat named Colonel Tom Parker whom we rarely see."

"Like Rhino?"

"Yes and no, all have different skill sets, sizes, and shapes," I replied.

Miss Bethany seemed to contemplate this for a minute and replied, "I still can't believe he is gone, Mr. Jeanette."

"Please call me Scooter."

Miss Bethany turned and looked directly at me and said, "I want to pay you to find the cruel people that killed him."

"No need we take it personally when a client is killed on our watch, and we haven't even begun investigating the Chancellor's death."

"Oh, I am relieved." And she started into her coffee cup.

"Miss Bethany, were you in an adult relationship with Chancellor William Wright?"

It has been a long time since anyone has blushed like that around me, but she did, and with the rosy cheeks came the tears. Way to go, Scooter; now let the air out of her car tires; really make her day. I stood and walked behind the bar and grabbed a box of tissues, and poured Miss Bethany a healthy shot of blackberry brandy in a rocks glass. And I placed both in front of her. I retook my seat and waited.

"Thank you for your candor, calling it an adult relationship and nothing more vulgar or crude." She replied.

And then she lifted the purple liquor to her nose and sniffed it, then raised her eyebrows.

"It's very high-powered blackberry brandy."

She took a big gulp and stifled a cough, and said, "Wow.

"Give it a second," I said.

"You must think poorly of me." She said, eventually.

"Nope, none of my business, not in the judgment business."

"No, you are not judging William or me, knowing full well that he was married, and in its essence and core, it's still adultery."

Miss Bethany's little face and large wet brown eyes were shiny and red from the tears, making her look much younger.

We sat, she cried, I sipped my coffee, and I thought quietly. As if on cue Colonel Tom Parker appeared on the armrest of my leather chair, and then he took refuge in my lap with a few soft purrs. I could count the number of times Colonel Tom had sat in my lap; it was a low number. I chose not to think of what this could mean and just scratched behind his ears and waited for Miss Bethany's tears to fade. I have seen many people cry over the years and have become an expert on the sincerity of each one. I have seen the shoulder-shaking cry, the waterworks of tears, and the moaning cry. In the legitimate crying episodes, I felt the pain, the loss, the emptiness, the exhaustion, and the lack of hope. Sitting here now with Miss Bethany, I watched her tears, and they were real; her words sounded authentic, but there wasn't a feeling of layered grief. Curious. Very curious.

Chapter 36

RAY BAE, NICKNAMED Pay Ray, has been hustling out of the same convenience store and beverage drive-thru combination named Pay Ray's on South Arlington Street as far as I can remember. Pay Ray's sits a block from Triplett Boulevard, an Akron semi-iconic street, because it was one of the main drags to get to one of the most recognized structures in Summit County and the city of Akron history. The Akron Rubber Bowl. The Bowl hosted famous rock concerts, a world championship boxing match and was the university's home football field for years.

Ray Bae was as shifty as a three-dollar bill or shifter than Mr. Haney on The Green Acres, but he could sell. Ray and I got along well. A few years back, his cousin Lonny was accused of raping a white girl. Lonny claimed it was consensual, and they had secretly been dating. Her family was old Summit County money, the old money arrived hereabout the same time as the Mayflower hit Boston Harbor. Bigotry was printed on every dollar bill they owned, stole and it was considerable.

Ray hired us, and we dove headfirst into years and years of racism, white privilege, political power, ethnic intimidation, ignorance, and pure unjustified hate. All of that was no match for Kat, Tilly, Sully, Bam-Bam, and his men. We applied so much pressure that their false impenetrable walls began to crack, small pieces of rock began to fall, and then piece by piece, the walls of deception and untruths from the witness stand fell to the ground for all to see. We made some enemies and some hostile opponents, but I had never witnessed my group fight for something, fight so hard for a person they had never met. I asked them to get real bad on this one, and along the path, the truth came out. Lonny was released from prison, and the accuser was whisked away to whereabouts unknown with Daddy's dark money to avoid prosecution for lying under oath. There seems to be a very low priority on locating this individual on the County's end. But we have found Miss little liar, a liar whose pants are on fire, and we have kept tabs on her every move. And when the time is right, a meaningful discussion will occur; one of Bam-Bam's men died in that particular case.

I parked the SUV in front of the convenience store next to Ray's shiny black Hummer, and his vanity plate gave him away. I pulled my Springfield Hellcat .9mm from its holster and ejected the magazine. Thirteen rounds, plus one in the chamber, when complete. I knew it would be loaded, but being cautious and prepared can keep you from dying. I snapped it back into the gun. I liked this gun, one pound with a three-inch barrel. Easily hidden. Besides, it would be alarmingly stupid to walk unarmed into a relatively small convenience store widely known as an adult playground for weapon-carrying felons, usually hopped up on illegal narcotics.

The outside of Pay Ray's hasn't changed much since my last visit here two years ago. The advertising on the glass doors and windows has changed to the billion-dollar vaping industry. I walked through the doors, and the wiring running down the sides of the door jamb let out a loud electronic bell announcing my arrival. Trinity, a skinny female second cousin of Ray's, walked from a small room to the right of the glass counter that held the cash registers, the small printer, and a large rectangular case that contained twenty-six different scratch-off instant lottery tickets. The last time I saw her, probably six years ago, she was a gangly and awkward teenager, but now a beautiful adult. Her hair was blue before, now fire engine red. She wore a pink velour two-piece tracksuit with white stripes on the legs and arms, and she wore shocking pink tennis shoes. Large silver hoop earrings bobbed from her ears as she walked. An expensive tennis bracelet with many diamonds hung loosely on her right wrist. Trinity was now a full-grown woman.

"Well, if it isn't the white detective Shaft," she said.

"Hi, Trinity; you are looking quite healthy."

"Mr. Private eye man, are you looking at my boobs?" Trinity asked.

"No, ma'am, is the boss in?"

"Yeah. Let me get him." She said

I looked around the store, and Ray's clientele was not in favor of me being in the store. The three African American young men sitting at the small table against the wall kept shooting glances at me, and then one of them would say something in a whisper, and the other two would start laughing uncontrollably. There was a strong, musky solid smell of marijuana in the atmosphere, and I was hoping I wouldn't get stoned. Six gambling machines were set against the far wall, and all six were occupied, four females and one male. There were three customers in line waiting to buy lottery tickets and cigarettes and to pay for their beer.

"Trinity informed me a real honky was standing in my store wanting to talk to me, I assumed you were the po-po, but here you are, my dude, my whiter-than-white Casper the Ghost."

"Hi, Ray. I was in the neighborhood and just thought I would stop by."

"Sheet boy, you up to something? You got a white boy problem a black boy can fix, right?"

"Can we talk in private, Ray?"

Ray stood six feet and was as skinny as a rail. His face was cleanly shaved, and he had two gold front teeth. His head was bald, and his white warm-up suit had so many letters on it I quit trying to read them all. I knew him to have at the very least a straight razor in his sock, Bad Bad Leroy Brown style.

"C'mon Casper, let's get you out of my main lobby; you scaring my clientele."

"The six people addicted to your illegal gambling machines and wasting their welfare money and the three coke heads in the corner are clientele? and I am offending them?."

"Yes, my dude, you are."

Ray's office sits on the northwest corner of the convenience store on an inside wall. There were two South Akron toughies sitting in folding chairs in various poses trying to appear so chill it looked like it hurt. However, their awareness stiffened as I came through the office door.

"Take a stroll, homies; my pasty dude and I need my office."

The two south-side tough guys eyed me a little on the way out, not so much on trying to intimidate me. But trying to decide who I was and what kind of juice I had.

Ray sat behind his desk, opened a small wooden case, and pulled out a pre-rolled doobie. He plucked a purple disposable lighter off of the desk and lit the stick of rolled weed, and inhaled until I couldn't see his face from the smoke, and I watched him begin coughing up a lung.

"Medicinal?" I asked.

"I got a medical card and everything."

I waited, Ray repeated puffing, I waited, and then Ray stood and retrieved us both coca colas in the bottle.

After handing me my soft drink, he said, " Ok, now I can listen to your bullshit because every time you walk through those doors, you cost me ten thousand dollars."

"Every time, Ray?" I asked.

"Every dam time, Scooter," He replied with that smile that helped you forget that Ray Bae is a very bad man in Summit County and Northeast Ohio.

"Who has the sports gambling over by the university? I asked.

This question was a real moment of truth, and it just rolled off my tongue before I could stop it. Ray excelled in illicit drug distribution, but he also dabbled in the numbers and parlay sheets, so I knew he would have an answer for me.

Ray stood and put his hands on his desk and leaned on them, thought, or that's what I assumed he was doing, and after a minute, he said, "Word around A-Burg and this I can confirm is that there is a fraternity house that is bookmaking hard and this same boys club has deep, deep pockets and deep deep connections from an association with a legitimate gangster psycho."

I sat back and looked at the ceiling, there was a water stain in the shape of fat Burt Reynolds. I pondered that for a moment and then I expelled three large breaths, and realized that the picture of everything in this case just arranged itself, and fell into place very similar to a kaleidoscope. Son of a biscuit, I should have known better, "Enzo Barra is his name." I confirmed.

Ray play-shot me with his right index finger and said, "Bingo."

I called Kat and had her take a picture of the note with the address JD had snuck into our cannoli box. When I received it back, I mapped it out. I got the image on my cell phone and showed it to Ray,

"Yep, that's it, Casper, the worst ghost."

Chapter 37

IT WAS FOUR fifty-five on a Tuesday afternoon, and it was warm enough to keep the SUV's windows down while Kat and I sat gazing at the fraternity house; the fraternity is named The Lone Sons. Brief research showed the Lone Sons as one hundred and seventeen years old and the reigning misbehaving and immoral boy fraternity on the university campus. Multiple complaints from students, sororities, university staff, and three minor and one major pledge hazing incidents led to a shutdown of the fraternity for twelve months two years ago.

The three-storied house was in decent shape, with a white painted exterior with green trim and a duel-pitched dark shingled roof. There were six chairs of varied make and style situated on the veranda-style front porch. The front door was a combination of a sturdy metal inner door and a black steel reinforced outer door with bars from top to bottom. The black metal mailbox to the right of the front door was overflowing with mail. There were two front windows, two second-floor windows, and a smaller one above those two, presumably an attic window. Typically I wouldn't have thought twice about the front door being extra reinforced being a fraternity house, but each window was reinforced with metal bars also. Hmmm, curious to me.

For fraternity house activity, this one was a dud. Kat a I had been sitting across the street for an hour and forty-one minutes, and we had not seen one frat brother or pledge brother, for that matter. No one came out to drink a beer, smoke a cigarette, throw up over the porch railing, talk on a cell phone or throwing a punch. Boooorrriing. Perhaps they have turned a new leaf. Both sides of the street were littered with discarded fast-food wrappers, crushed beer cans, used condoms, and empty potato chip wrappers. The new SUV is self-equipped with eight cameras with Alpine speakers for audio and can snap one hundred pictures a minute on automatic or at your leisure with remote control access. I was using the remote, all on my command.

"So it would make sense that a fraternity could run a bookie operation.

"How so?" Kat asked.

"Well, for starters, they have a home base with thousands of new customers, they have a solid base of salesmen, the fraternity brothers themselves could network with high school buddies, new college friends, and most of all, a large percentage of students have free and almost unlimited access to federally backed student loans. And there is much money referenced in those journals we liberated," I said.

"Holy Cripes," Kat said.

A newer blue, white, and chrome Harley Davidson Ultra Glide pulled into the driveway and proceeded slowly down the longish driveway. The complete leather-wearing motorcyclist stopped the big bike in front of the garage and dismounted the big bike. The oversized garage was wood and had two floor-to-ceiling garage doors. The rider took a set of keys from his right side and fumbled until he found the correct key, inserted it into the lock on the garage door, and with both hands, slid the door back and into the garage. He then walked the shiny motorcycle into the older garage, took his helmet off, and placed it on the bike's handlebar. Brian Regan then used both hands and arms to close the wooden door before locking it again. I watched him walk the driveway and up the steps to the front porch. He leaned over and grabbed his mail from a large black mailbox affixed to the porch beam. Brian Regan is now officially a clue baked by JD.

Kat and I watched the fraternity house for another forty-five minutes, and then we called it a day and headed home. On the way, we stopped at Mueller's Honey Bee on Manchester Road; Emily Mueller is our dear friend, and her homemade, right-from-the-source honey products are fantastic. Tilly had given us our marching orders with a hand-written list to get some fresh honey, honey jam, elderberry syrup, raw honey, blueberry honey, ginger turmeric honey, and honey sticks for Tilly's nightly tea.

Chapter 38

I knew Enzo Barra was the blackmailer, and I was reasonably sure that Brian Regan and his fraternity were the bookies. I just wanted to prove it. So today, the team was engaged in following Brian Regan on his Tuesday payoffs and pickups. It was a sunny Fall day, and, Bam-Bam and I were in his pickup truck following Brian Regan on Spicer street, then onto Exchange Street. We took a right, heading east, and in three blocks, the big Electra Glide pulled into a large gravel parking lot on the west side of the famous campus bar called Slutty Harry's. We continued past as I caught a glimpse of Sully, Kat, and Tilly turning in behind Brian in our non-descriptive, beige Toyota Camry. Bam-Bam and I parked in a small local check cashing place next door to the bar. Bam-Bam activated the onboard security cameras, and the wi-fi and Kat's button camera would now transmit the video to the nine-inch monitor on the truck's dashboard. We watched as Brian dismounted the big bike, removed his helmet, and extracted a large vanilla envelope from one of the large leather saddle bags on the side of the chromed-out machine. Brian walked across the gravel parking lot towards the bar's entrance, and the ladies followed; in three minutes, the screen on our dashboard flickered, and an HD color video of the inside of the campus pub came to life.

"Hi guys, Scoot my hubby; tell me to stop when you see Brian Regan on the video in case I miss him," Kat said through the earbuds.

"Hey, babe, you just followed him, and we just sat and watched him at the fraternity house. Kat, stop; see the good-looking kid in the booth to your right with the short draft beer, the black motorcycle helmet, and clear goggles resting on the table in front of him?"

"Yes."

"That's our guy," I replied, laughing, and so did Bam-Bam.

"Of all the guys in the world, how is it that I get stuck with you two? Wait, don't answer that."

Kat and Tilly went to the bar, ordered a Corona in the bottle and then used the large mirror behind the bar to record Brian Regan's meeting. Kat wore a baseball cap pulled low, and oversized dark sunglasses obstructed her face. In the next hour and a half, twenty different college kids and some older adults stopped by Brian Regan's apparent mobile office, either receiving or handing out cash payments as secretly as possible. So Tuesdays and Thursdays are pay up days. Also, they are handing out new betting sheets.

Chapter 39

LATER THAT EVENING, after a spectacle of Swenson's Galley Boys, tater tots, fried onion rings, and chocolate milkshakes. I was now sitting in the Denali, actually backed into a spot in a gravel parking lot on the South end of campus. The small parking lot was bordered by mature, tall, and bushy pine trees. I was also waiting on Steve Kapusinski and after ten minutes, he appeared in front of my SUV, and I motioned him to get into the passenger seat. Kap wore a blue baseball cap, warm-up pants, and a white university hoodie. It had begun to rain very large wet drops, and the pine trees were starting to droop slightly from the weight of the raindrops. I turned on the wipers and cleared the windshield.

"What's with the text? and why did we have to meet?"

Kap looked at me confused and said, "I thought you wanted to meet; that's what your text read."

"No, I didn't text you… Oh man, Kap, we have been cloned; get down!" And I looked hard in my left-side view mirror while unholstering my Glock from my right side.

Before I could fully clear my firearm, a dark hooded figure appeared in my driver's side mirror. The window glass next to my face exploded, and simultaneously I heard five distinctive 'pops' next to my left ear; the gunshots were deafening. I heard Steve cry out but could not decipher what he was saying, and I just heard sounds and noises. It sounded and felt like we were underwater. Everything moved very slowly, and my mind wouldn't process that Steve and I were being shot. My mind slowed down again. The first bullet hit me, then the second, then the third. I knew my gun had slipped to the front floorboard, and my right hand didn't function correctly. I looked at Kap; his neck was bleeding, and he was hunched back against his seat. I felt blood running down my side. I tried to reach Kap, but I couldn't get my seatbelt off; I struggled and couldn't do it.

"Car number four, call Bam-Bam," I yelled towards the dashboard.

"Scooter, what's up?" I heard over the SUV's speakers.

"Bam-Bam, we've been shot," And the vehicle's interior started fading to black. I heard Bam-Bam shouting orders to someone while Kap began mumbling, "St. Joe Falcons, Blue Barons…put me in coach…

Chapter 40

I CAME FROM an intense, fierce, and hazy place; my skin felt wet, and I saw blurred overhead lights and heard soft voices; both seemed bright then so far away. My mind couldn't keep a thought for more than a few seconds. Attempting to focus on them and simultaneously trying to move my arms or legs seemed improbable and painful, so I stopped. The darkness arrived and clutched me again. It seemed like a year and I heard the voices again and opened my eyes to total illumination. It wasn't easy to move, so I didn't. The loud and erratic beeps suggested I was in a hospital bed. The overhead lights in the room made me squint, and while I did that, they reminded me of the first time I saw the bright lights of the tremendous dame-Cleveland Municipal Stadium. I moved my head slowly and saw an I.V. in my right hand. I tried moving my extremities slightly, and all four limbs worked on my brain's command; not great, but they worked. My thoughts and feelings were hazy, and I was drowsy. I looked to my left and saw my wife, Kat; her hair was down and falling across her face. And she was focused on something on her phone. She wore a black t-shirt underneath a red and black plaid checkered wool long-sleeved shirt. Her tongue resting partway on her lower lip and her eyes looking on with vibrancy and vigorousness. She was fully engaged, and this was one of her best virtues. Kat could tunnel vision a task better than anyone I knew.

Kat turned and saw my eyes open and jumped off of her chair, and kissed me on the lips. Her lip gloss tasted of honey and lilac.

"Hi, babe." I said; my voice didn't sound like the one that I remembered.

Kat gently held my face with her two hands, "Hi, my hubby; how are you feeling?" She had small tears in her eyes.

"Not sure, can you fill me in?"

Kat lowered the bed's safety rail and sat softly next to me, and began a story, "Well, you were shot three times. You have a collapsed lung; there was some severe internal bleeding that the doctors think they have stopped but are not sure." Kat wiped her face with her right sleeve and began again, "One of the bullets hit the top of your left shoulder. And they say that could be a problem later. And you are having infection challenges."

"Are you sure the food here will not infect me?"

She decided not to engage with my sophomoric behavior. She just affectionately crinkled her mouth and nose as in, no, don't joke. This is terrible stuff, Scooter.

I laid back and tried to think. I couldn't. But then I held a thought and said, "How is Steve?" I asked.

Her eyes got a different thing to them, I couldn't explain what the thing was exactly, but it wasn't good. I knew that.

"Not well, but they are working hard to save him." She replied softly.

I stopped joking and did what I was supposed to do in a hospital bed, shut up and listen or be humble that I was alive. But my heart ached for Steve Kapusinski.

Kat became hushed, and the only sounds in the antiseptic-smelling room were my machines buzzing and chiming. I looked towards the window, and it was gray and drizzly outside. I struggled to think back and couldn't and then the fuzziness came gradually and the hospital room became dark again. In the darkness, I dreamt my toenails on my big toes fell off.

Not sure what day it was or how the clan did it, but they smuggled in bags of food from the eclectic seafood restaurant in the Merriman Valley called The *'Chowder House'*. There were trays of seafood pappardelle, crab cakes, lobster tails, two large loaves of garlic bread, and a whole carrot cake. It was like the scene in the movie Brians's song in Brian Piccolo's hospital room. The football players and coaches brought in pizzas, beer, and cigars. Federal law stopped the cigars today. As we were feasting and cackling, my nurse, Andrea Clark, came in and gasped, "Oh heavens no, how in the heck did you get this in here?'

She had penetrating and large beautiful eyes, and we're now locked onto Summit County Inspector Billy Cunningham and said, "Why didn't you stop this irresponsible nonsense?"

"Hard to tell these folks what to do, you try."

She glared daggers at all of us while crossing her arms. It would have been fearful if her uniform top wasn't pink with hundreds of kittens dancing with dark sunglasses. She stared for a very long time. She had a vein on her forehead performing an epic concert to its angry beat, her jaw was going left to right, and she kept trying to say something and finally did, "You have been shot three times, Mr. Jeanette."

"I know that, do you want a plate? It's delicious."

"I am getting environmental services in here to discard this mess." And she stormed off on an impressive three-point turn that any Nascar driver would have envied.

It was silent in the sterile and quiet hospital room. I could hear a loud metal cart being pushed in the outside hallway with three or four different conversations happening just out my door. The other noises were my myriad of machines buzzing, clanking to justify their existence.

Finally, Billy looked around the room and said, "You guys are going to take care of her for the rest of her life, aren't you?"

In unison, "Yes," we all said.

In three minutes Andrea Clark walked back into the room and walked with intent to my side table and grabbed the large, round carrot cake still in its obnoxious round two-piece plastic container, and said, "This is mine; and no one utter a single word." And she stormed out again.

Again we were quiet until Billy said, "Now, you folks are going to take care of her family for life, right?"

We all laughed and said, "Yes."

Chapter 41

Now, I was sitting in a leather recliner in the marina's den, surrounded by the dogs. My left arm was in a sling, and I felt like I was hit by a train. The dogs were asleep on the plush carpeting at my feet, and they were in full protection mode. They never left my side. There was a diet coke, my tablet, and my cell phone sitting on the side table next to me. I had been out of the hospital for three days now, and my breathing was still labored, and I feared it would never come back. I had trouble walking without a walker. I reached for my diet coke and took a sip. My lips were chapped, and my mouth was dry. Everything felt dry and cracked. My recollection of that night was still hazy. I could vaguely see the outline of the face of the person just before the window exploded. He wanted me to see it; that was the point before Steve and I were to be executed. But this time I recalled a dark hoodie.

The sun was now showcasing her talents by shining through the large front windows of the den. It was two-thirty in the afternoon, and I was freaking bored. But something was bothering me, and every time I was about to catch up to it, it vanished. I knew this, I was misled, and Kap and I were shot as an object lesson. I picked up my cell phone and dialed a number, and proceeded

Chapter 42

IGGY, SABAKA, AND I were sitting on the patio outside of Graceland, in my arm brace, watching the Cleveland Browns play the Cincinnati Bengals on Thursday night football. Guys night, Twiggy was with Kat in our bed in the boathouse. I had the built-in heaters on high; it was snowing with small flakes. I had the volume turned low on the game; the television noise seemed inappropriate and rudely intrusive to the benign evening. The snow gave the illusion that everything was pure and pretty; I was in a business that unfortunately proved pure and pretty inherently wrong sometimes. Cleveland scored a touchdown on their first series. I was drinking a tall bourbon and soda. I twirled the amber-colored glass in slow circles in my right hand. I was also grilling two large ribeye steaks on the outdoor grill. I also had a small aluminum pan with large button mushrooms basting in cooking sherry and real butter. A little snow wasn't going to get between me and a Thursday night football steak. I also had some of Tilly's homemade loaded potato salad and a half loaf of garlic bread. I was wearing my favorite red sweatshirt with a white stitched outline of the State of Ohio with a blue heart that depicted the location of Summit County within her borders. I wore white Nike warm-up pants with red and white slip-on Nike cross-trainers. Kat suggested I was perfect for easy access footwear, but I always laughed as we dressed together, and I slipped into my shoes and boots in seconds while she had to tie hers. Who's smarter now? Well, still here.

I was sipping my Woodford Reserve bourbon and felt the heat of both the bourbon and the two large kerosene patio heaters disguised as metal palm trees. I was nesting and relaxing in a comfortable oversized chair positioned directly under the overhead veranda. It was a room in itself. Tully had placed a seventy-five-inch television on the nearest wall, and this locale was decorated with a dramatic and colorful beach theme. I was habitable this time of year, as everything around me was grasping at the inevitable, just trying to hang on just a little longer. The daylight was trying to exist a little more each night, and around us, the famous and festive Portage Lakes recreation destination was gallantly trying to squeeze out every last moment. Northeastern Ohio had a brief Autumn season and was now ready for another long and demoralizing winter season, according to early reports from the Farmers Almanac. Across Graceland's yard, I could see a small light in our bedroom in the boathouse. Kat most likely fell asleep reading with her tablet on her stomach, Twiggy dreaming of only he knows. I continued to drink my drink. I was almost sixty-five percent back to health. I was also reviewing every journal again. But right this second, I was struggling with mortality, a metaphysical clarity. I was kept here on this giant rotating sphere by a power of pure goodness that needs someone to do this job, to help the people that have exhausted all avenues for justice and can not go anywhere else.

I got up, turned the steaks, placed the foil-wrapped garlic bread onto the hot grill, sat back down, and read some more. I stood again, took the garlic bread from the grill, and set it on the custom-made counter next to the grill. I sliced the bread into four equal pieces, sliced both steaks as well as I could with one arm, and divided one cut-up steak for my furry friends. I plated some potato salad next to the garlic bread and poured the hot mushroom mixture over the perfect-looking ribeye steak I could detect, and I could grill. I walked into Graceland and fixed another drink. I sat back down and swallowed greedily.

After three and a half hours and after another Browns last-minute loss, I saw the pattern in our case; I saw it plain as day.

"Cheese and rice, my furry friends, attorney Milton Haft, and the preppy nerd Brian Regan at the radio station were blackmailing Gunner from the beginning. Gunner, at some point, went to the Chancellor for help, and William Wright, a Chancellor of a major Division I university, wedged his fat corrupt ass into the mix. But it got him dead. After we braced Enzo Barra, he inserted himself into the point-shaving scheme. Enzo crushed Taylor Thompson's last two fingers on her hand to signal everyone that he was back. Not sure how Brian Regan was recruited, but the original letter and radio call-in were both fakes. One or all of these evil people were trying to shake something up. It was point-shaving from the day we were hired.

I would be fully engaged tomorrow, and I was done waiting around. I formulated a quick plan which meant my peeps were engaged. Enzo, Milt, and Brian, I advise going to earth and going very deep. It's your only chance. Man, I had a headache, and I petted my sweet pups.

I took another sip from my drink and watched some of the post-game football highlights. It was peripheral, just like the outside lake noises were at my outer edges; frogs were croaking, fish were restless, and the occasional owl was hooting in the night, all peripheral. As if they were showing me that now was the time to act.

I texted my simple but somewhat complex plan to Bam-Bam and Sully's cell phones so they could use their contacts and connections for '*Code Hunting in the Desert*' it was going to take a series of favors from our associates and contacts.

Chapter 43

AT 6:10 IN the evening, two days later, I parked my SUV next to Coach Darling's university-provided Jeep Wagoneer in a parking spot reserved for the 'Athletic Department.' I wasn't alone; I had Snake and Stella with me. Snake and I walked through the athletic Field House with purpose and intent toward Coach Darling's office, and with each step, my rage increased and my focus more determined. Stella was tucked into her comfortable backpack, but I imagined she was also focused and determined or would be very soon; she enjoyed road trips because sometimes she got to frighten a lousy guy or girl.

A few student-athletes were lifting weights, jogging on the running track, and high jumping, and two were practicing the shot put. I swiftly opened the coach's office door, turned around, locked it, turned back around, and rubber-necked the obtuse coach. My shoulders were as tight as a wound rubber band, and my scalp was hot. I had thoughts of using a few of Bam-Bam's breathing control techniques but decided instantly that I wanted to continue to be mad, real mad.

His secretary was gone for the day, so we had breezed directly into coach Dennis Darling's sanctuary unscathed.

Coach Darling was wearing a blue warm-up suit and sat behind his desk, writing on a yellow notepad.

He looked up and said, "I thought I told you to stay off my damn campus."

Snake took three significant steps and rounded the right side of his desk and grabbed Coach Darling by his hair with his right hand, and yanked him to a standing position, and with his body and his fist full of hair, Snake slammed him against the cement wall behind him.

"You shut the flipping up now, you piece of garbage," I said through clenched teeth.

"Hey, pal…"

Smoke pulled his .9mm from its holster and handed it to me. I pressed the barrel tight to the fleshy underpart of his chin with my good arm and hand and said, "You knew the entire time this crap was going on, and Gunner was a pawn in this whole point-shaving scheme; you turned a blind eye as long as you were winning."

I pressed the gun harder under his chin, and he was now standing on raised toes to try to alleviate the pressure and pain.

"I will destroy you, and no one will ever, ever find the body, you crap bag; you got one of your players laying in a bed in intensive care fighting for his life; I got shot, you self-serving bastard. Let me ask you, Coach Darling, how do you feel about snakes?"

"Why, what the hell are you talking about?" the coach asked; it was difficult for the coach to enunciate words right now.

I smiled and said, "Because it's going to be highly relevant this weekend, old buddy, old pal. Oh, by the way, you are calling off work this weekend, and Snake and Stella will assist you in writing your resignation letter. And if Gunner's name ever leaves your lips again, you die by a flame thrower."

"The hell I am. Are you nuts?"

"Right now, yes."

"Oh Stella, come out and play," I said.

"Who is Stella?"

Stella had already pushed the top of the backpack open, and she was restless. Her majestic diamond-shaped head popped up and out of her mobile home.

"Jesus Christ, Ok, I am sorry," Coach Dennis Darling said.

"Nope, too late; penance you earn and peace and closure we sometimes find through kicking ass," I replied

I swiftly pulled the gun from underneath his chin, simultaneously clicking the trigger safety on, turning the gun butt-forward in my hand; I motioned to Snake, and he swiftly grabbed the coach's right hand, forced it flat on his desk, and I slammed the heavy gun butt down on his knuckles. If I wasn't so tough, the sickening sound of knuckles splintering might have affected me.

"You best pray that Taylor Thompson regains some range and motion with no pain in her two fingers after her surgeries. Again, think flame thrower. Snake will get you some medical help, as the kids say, on the down low.

I turned to leave, and five tremendous football players were standing outside the door; I could see them from the vertical windows on each door. I wondered why they had not tried to enter. The locked door would not have deterred these prominent burly young men for very long. I opened the door, and I saw the reason why these men were not moving. Kat, Rhino, Sully, and Bam-Bam were standing off to the side, firearms on their sides.

I looked at Snake, pointed with my right index finger, and said, "Watch his every move; you are joined at the hip; take him to a safe house, and if he tries anything stupid, feed him to Stella, no mercy on this one Snake."

Chapter 44

THE SMALL EXECUTIVE jet was a Cessna Citation XLS, and it would fit Kat, Bam-Bam, Sully, Tilly, and myself comfortably. I knew this because we have used this exact aircraft several times. Sully and Tilly own a piece of the Executive Rentals private jet service. We only trusted one pilot; he was one of Bam-Bam's men from a previous life and many combat missions in the desert.

We were flying out of Akron Canton airport straight through to Las Vegas, It's about a four-and-a-half-hour flight, and you lose three hours to the time change. It was nine-fifty p.m. because the team likes to fly at night, especially into McCarran International Airport. It's pure magic, the desert is dark and brown below, and then a tiny penlight of illumination can be seen in the distance. As the lights get brighter with color, they seem to pull the airplane into sin, straight into a very sunny and steamy playground.

Tilly and Sully were dressed in almost matching tourist outfits. Astonish King had bright red and purple flowers on black shirts with white linen slacks, and both had sunglasses hanging from their necks. Bam-Bam was in a dummy-downed SWAT outfit. Black cargo pants, a black combat tee shirt, and black cross-trainers. Kat and I were in Las Vegas casual, matching white Akron RubberDuck tee shirts, blue jeans, and running shoes. My left arm was still in a sling, and my lung was getting stronger, but my body was still in partial shut-down, survival behavior. My breathing and stamina were sub-par. I could still shoot, though. The tee shirts were our lucky ones, and they never hurt while flying, gambling, or tracking a murderer. An hour into the flight, Sully handed us carry and conceal identifications and the correct accreditation for private detective services for our time in Las Vegas. Each had our respective snapshots and today's date.

We would stay at The Mirage Casino, a time-tested classic on the Las Vegas strip. As we exited the limousine and entered the impressive lobby of The Mirage, deep, rich colors of reds, blues, yellows, and greens slammed our senses, and it seemed like the dominant color was all of them. The gigantic fish tank behind the reservation desk was remarkable. You can see it in the movies on your television and on the big screen, but seeing it live was heart-thumping. Every rainbow color was represented satisfactorily, with the various fish swimming hypnotically behind the polished glass. A tall young man dressed in a porter ensemble walked towards us, accompanied by a striking female with short blond hair in a navy blue knee-length skirt with a lacy white blouse and navy blue high heels. She wore small earrings and a large gold chain necklace, and her fingers bore no wedding ring. Her makeup was subtle, and her face was healthy, with a small nose and large green eyes. She appeared to be in fantastic physical shape. She gave Bam-Bam an elaborate handshake with a lot of moving parts and then a big hug. She then handed him a large manilla envelope; Bam Bam handed the envelope to me and said, "Team, meet Tennille, don't let the pretty name fool you. We served a tour in Iraq, and being an official badass, she is also the head of security for The Mirage."

We all took turns introducing ourselves and shaking hands with Tennille. After the introductions were complete, Tennille said, "Your room keys for three side-by-side villas are in the envelope, along with two photos taken at various points inside and outside of Las Vegas International airport of your suspects. Mr. Jeanette, you hit a home run on these guys. Both matched your descriptions when they arrived, two males that arrived separately yesterday on two different flights from CAK."

"That's the call sign for the Akron Canton Airport," Bam-Bam said with a smile.

"Thank you, I have booked flights online before," I said.

Bam-Bam looked at me and nodded, and then he looked back and addressed Tennille, "Scooter is an intense pain in my ass, but he is the absolute best at what he does, and there is no one I trust more to protect my twin sister or my aunt and uncle.

"And what exactly is he the best at?" Tennille asked.

"He finds the horrible people that have hurt good, defenseless people, roots them from their dark holes, gives them a hard shake, and sometimes he kills them," Bam-Bam replied.

"Like our old unit?" Tennille said firmly. She asked this question not to be argumentative but because she seemed curious.

Bam-Bam rocked back then forward on his feet and said, "No, not like us. We worked in a system dictated by rules, procedures, policies, red tape, and bureaucracy. That system was difficult to navigate, and that same system sometimes was broken. The guilty knew we were handcuffed. But Scooter works on his terms and his terms only. During cases, we sometimes are confused about his exact terms. But when he grabs hold of something, that thing is his life. No matter how much time, money, the person, the rules, and occasionally the laws mean nothing to him. Especially if a child or woman is the victim, he doesn't play, his word is his soul, and his determination and skill are his calling card. And he's the best shot with any firearm, short or long barrel, any. The best I have ever seen. Period."

"A modern-day Sergeant York," Tennille said.

"Better," Sully chimed in.

Tennille looked over in my direction, appraising me, and I thought her thinking, "This freaking guy, he doesn't look it?'

"Wow, Mr. Jeanette, that's some amazing praise from this guy."

After another few seconds, she nodded again, smiling as if confirming her thoughts, and continued speaking to our small group, "Also, there is a gym bag in Mr. and Mrs. Jeanette's room as promised Bam-Bam. If the varied types of armament are not up to individual requirements or personal preference, please call me. Also, there are two business cards in the envelope; one is mine with my name, but the other is a plain card, and this phone number is the only cell number of its kind. Please use it if trouble finds you in Las Vegas, and you have exhausted all resources. Commit to memory and destroy."

The sounds of slot machines, player exuberance, raucous noises from the table games, and a smooth, soft jazz singer wafted throughout the lobby. I looked around, and four middle-aged tourists, two women and two men with bright, wild Hawaiian shirts, straw hats, and very pasty white legs, were checking in at the reservation desk. They appeared a little drunk, and they were probably a couple of insurance salesmen with their wives from Columbus or Chicago, or Indianapolis. That reservation specialist better speed things up, or she may be the proud owner of a new fifty thousand dollar term life insurance policy with a nineteen dollar a month payment auto-debited from her checking account. Many tourists and gamblers walked past us with eagerness and sanguinity.

"We would like one bill for all rooms and expenditures from the hotel if we could, please," and Sully pulled out an American Express black card from his wallet."

"That is impossible; all charges will be directed to a house account. I owe everything to Bam-Bam. One night in Kandahar, it got hairy real quick, and I was pinned down and taking more fire than I thought imaginable; I was losing ground fast and, well, Bam-Bam, and two of his men showed up and opened up a can of American whoop-ass. I wouldn't have the wonderful life I have today without Bam-Bam."

"We can't let you do that." Sully persisted.

Tennille cupped her left ear with her left hand and said, "Shhh, listen, hear that? If you listen closely, you can hear the table dealers yelling, 'Changing a thousand, changing a hundred, changing a fifty' and pressing it into the table and down to the counting room where they count in shifts twenty-four hours a day, seven days a week.

"Still..." Sully interjected.

"See that staggering line of limousines?" And Tennille pointed to the semicircle directly in front of the Mirage doors and blocks further down South Las Vegas Blvd. All the limousines were black or white, and most but not all had the Mirage's recognizable logo of five colorful palm trees in blue, yellow, orange, purple, and green embossed on the side of each. They were lined up for five Las Vegas city blocks. They looked like planes awaiting take-off at Chicago O'Hare airport.

"Those are our gamblers we call whales because their line of credit starts at one hundred thousand and ends at sixty million. They show up and throw money around in our restaurants, resort staff gratuities, in our shops, and mostly throw it at our dealers."

Tennille continued, "Take that sharp-dressed Asian gentleman waiting to get into that black stretch limousine; in the last four days, that extremely wealthy gambler continued to push into a heater that went cold, and he kept pushing in, and it never came back. He has paid for your stay five hundred times over, and it won't even register a minuscule blip to his actual net worth." And she smiled radiantly and let out, "Vegas Baby."

The four of us looked over to where Tennille had motioned with her head. We all smiled, and Sully replied, "Vegas, Baby."

The villa that Kat and I would be occupying was massive, and that's like saying Fred Astaire could dance. Twenty-five-foot ceilings with a large rectangular skylight. Our suite proudly consisted of a living room, a dining room, two bathrooms, a fully stocked mini-bar, and one enormous bedroom with a king-size bed with a fantastic view of the private heated pool. The suite was designed with large pieces of furniture in royal blues and bright whites. I assumed the other two villas were prepared similarly. Barnum and Bailey could bring two elephants in here while performing a trapeze act, and they wouldn't be in our way. Looking through the sliding glass doors, the in-ground swimming pool was bordered by beautiful blue and white ceramic tiles. Colorful lounge chairs edged the pool.

On the dining room table sat three medium-sized leather gym bags next to a giant purple orchid arrangement in a large Waterford crystal vase. Our luggage was already in our rooms, hanging neatly, and undergarments, socks, and t-shirts were tucked into drawers in the large dressers. I unzipped one of the leather bags, and there were two white towels; I unfolded them and arranged them side by side. I moved the fresh vase of orchids to the wet bar countertop. I began removing the contents of the leather bag while placing them carefully on the white towels. When I was finished laying items and resting peacefully were two dark Springfield Armory .9mm handguns with a twelve plus one bullet capacity and red dot laser sights, two Taser Pulse taser guns in the black camp finish, two black nylon holsters, two army knives, four extra clips, two for each handgun and three boxes of Gold Dot ammo, two canisters of pepper spray, two sets of black handcuffs, and five large and five small mag lights. I arranged them by category. The other two bags contained the same.

Kat leaned over my shoulder and said, "Babe."

I walked over to the minibar and grabbed the first cold can of beer I saw; it was from a local brewery called 'Bad Beat Brewery,' and the name of this beer was 'Ace in the hole,' an excellent reputation for Las Vegas. I studied the aluminum can for a bit, and it told me this was a herb and spice beer. I usually avoided these beers because the barley and alcohol content was lower due to the flowers, spices, and some vegetables in the brewing process. And since it was the first beer, I grabbed it, and in Vegas, do as Vegas does. I had a little trouble pulling the aluminum tab towards me and very much hoped Kat hadn't noticed, but I took a big drink, lowered the can and pointed at Kat, and said, "Ten cases of this are going home with us."

Kat rolled her eyes at me, then walked over to the wet bar's granite countertop, smelled the orchid, and pulled a bottle of white wine from the ice bucket; then she grabbed two wine glasses and a wine opener that was embossed with the casino's name and logo and headed for the doors of the villa.

"I am going to Sully and Tilly's room; I'll send Sully and Bam-Bam over."

I was going to tell her that Sully and Tilly's villa would have wine glasses and a bottle opener but thought better of it, and I chose to remain quiet. After I let Bam-Bam and Sully into my room, I grabbed each an 'Ace in the hole' from the mini-fridge.

After taking a long pull from the aluminum can, Bam-Bam said, "Damn Scooter, that's good; I don't usually drink from a can, but that is good stuff." And then he began to study the label on the cold can. After a moment, Bam-Bam took a pack of Marlboro green cigarettes from his right pocket and started walking around the room with the electronic Marlboro pack extended from his left arm. He started at the doorway of the suite moving from room to room. Slow and methodical, his searches for wireless or wired electronic audio and video RF devices were always neat, logical, orderly, and organized.

Sully took a small sip from his can and let it sit in his mouth for a minute, and said, "I concur, lads."

Sully wasted no time inspecting the weapons I had laid out on the white towels on the dining room table. He sat in a chair and grabbed a small black bag similar to a shoe shine kit and grabbed his small pen light from the bag, and began inspecting each gun. Tennille would have done this before she
packed them, but Sully never left anything to chance with firearms. While they were doing that, I thought it prudent to finish my beer and grab another one. Being a man of reasonable intelligence and above-average deduction skills, I had deduced the beginning of the second one was as good as the first.

My cell phone dinged, and it was a text from Kat informing me that she had ordered a tray of sandwiches for us and that she thought it a good idea not to shoot any room service employees. Man, I love that woman.

I grabbed the file folder Tennille had put together and went outside, found a double light switch, and flipped both up, and the patio was illuminated in soft yellow lighting. I ventured out and sat in a bright orange patio chair with a matching footstool. The small pool was rectangular and crystal clear; underwater pool lights and a small purple-colored fountain were in the middle of the pool. Around the entire patio was an eight-foot beige concrete wall with assorted desert flowers in various pots and holders strategically attached to the wall. I opened the folder, and there were twelve, eight by ten clear pictures of Milton Haft and Brian Regan as they each arrived separately on two different days and other flights. There were various pictures taken of each of them in the airport, exiting the plane, walking throughout the airport, two at the baggage claim, and one each of leaving the airport and getting into a black Alani Nu Casino limousine. The second batch of pictures paper clipped together showed ten pictures dated and time stamped. They were of Milton Haft making bets inside the Alani Nu sports book and all with a sports book employee named Jimmy Morrison. The third set of pictures was about the same, but they were of Brian Regan placing bets with only Jimmy Morrison. The fourth set was of the Chancellor doing the same thing. Tennille included a full background check, including financial information on Jimmy Morrison. He was in so much debt his cash wasn't any good. But there were deposits of nine thousand dollars every Monday during the season. Anything under ten thousand and the bank doesn't have to report to the IRS. Jimmy Morrison had a couple of O.V.I. and a couple of evictions but no felony criminal record, all misdemeanors, no felonies. A casino uses two criteria data points for hiring employees, no financial crimes and no violent convictions. That's why he was able to be hired. Also in the file were Milton Hafts and Brian Regan's room numbers at the Alani Nu and all credit card information at our disposal.

I grabbed my cell phone, found and texted Gigabyte a synopsis of this information, and told him to try to back door into Milton and Brian's bank accounts. We were going to find the money to pay for the best orthopedic surgeons at the Mayo Clinic in Scottsdale, Arizona, for Taylor Thompson's fingers. We could pay for it, but it needed to come from them; accountability is enormous on this one, and we would deal with Enzo Barra later. His men may or may not have swung the hammer without his orders, but he and Milton Haft and Brian Regan were aware and fully engaged in the blackmailing at the time. I went back inside, and I was getting hungry. It was one-thirty-five a.m. out here in the expansive desert.

There was a significant knock on the door, and Sully and Bam-Bam each grabbed a Smithfield Armory .9mm that Sully had finished inspecting, each slapping a loaded clip of ammo into the butt of each handgun and jacked a round into the chamber almost at the same time, the clicking sounds were right on top of each other. Bam-Bam walked to the suite's front door standing to the right side while Sully took a post on the other. Neither peeked through the door's peephole; Billy Cunningham had taught me years ago that looking through a door's peephole was a great way to get shot in the eyeball.

"Leave the tray outside the door, please," Sully asked.

Bam-Bam and Sully, we're in full murder case mode. Trust but verify. The sandwich platter was resting on a silver two-shelf room service cart on wheels. After Bam-Bam wheeled the cart in, he pulled his RF-detecting device disguised as a pack of Marlboro's and ran it around the room service cart. After he was satisfied we weren't being bugged, he placed the device back into his pocket.

The tray had thick slices of rare roast beef, hard salami, prosciutto, turkey, thick-cut sliced maple ham, sliced cheddar cheese, sliced swiss cheese, sliced provolone cheese, a big wedge of horseradish cheese, and assorted loaves of bread and buns. It also was tastefully decorated with black olives, banana pepper rings, sliced red onions, fresh tomato slices, three different types of pickles, and a pile of leaf lettuce. On a smaller tray were red and green grapes, pears, apples, and bananas. Assorted bags of potato chips and pretzels sat on the cart next to the platters. There were five small glass bowls with mustard, ketchup, mayonnaise, fresh horseradish, and spicy mustard. White Versace china dinner plates and matching silverware were sitting on the right-hand corner of the cart.

I texted the ladies to join us. We all dug into making sandwiches; I chose roast beef and the cheddar cheese, pickles, lettuce, tomato, and mayonnaise on a large sliced pretzel roll. I grabbed a bag of chips and plopped down on the couch. Sully, Tilly, Kat, and Bam-Bam arranged their gastric feasts and took chairs at the dining room table. We each ate in silence for a few minutes.

"So, what's the plan, Scoot?" Sully asked between mouthfuls.

"Thinking of surveillance on Jimmy Morrison, Milton's guy in the Alani Nu sports book room," I said, rising from the couch and retrieving one more canned beer.

"And?" Kat asked.

"Nothing else, just that, oh wait, maybe run into Wayne Newton."

Sully was eyeing me over his reading glasses, and after a short minute, he said, "That's not all; you are looking for the thread to snatch and pull so they all fall out. and you will never rest until you find out who made the call on smashing Ms. Thompson's fingers. Gunner is a gifted and bright young man, and if the point-shaving comes out and the dream of playing on Sunday afternoons is gone, well, you will try to prevent that. Chancellor Wright's death is tragic, and that needs to be solved, but no, Ms. Thompson is the driving force. Taking her two fingers away from her and ending her piano-playing days was cruel and intolerable to you."

I thought about that for a moment and pointed my right index finger at Sully and said, "True Dat."

"Scooter, let's look at those files," Bam-Bam said.

We shared the contents of the file folder that Tennille gave me. After a half-hour, Bam-Bam, Tilly, and Sully procured their share of weapons, placed them into the two empty leather gym bags, and retreated to their villas. Bam-Bam would call Rhino back at the marina, checking on Twiggy, Iggy, Sabaka, and our mean cat Colonel Tom Parker. Rhino was in charge of the family pets, and guaranteeing our furry family member's safety was more pressure than his six tours of duty in Afghanistan ever produced. Nobody wanted to relay bad news to Bam-Bam ever.

I slipped my brand new white with red stripes Tommy Bahama swim trunks on, grabbed my can of beer, and headed out the patio doors. I stepped gingerly down the three pool steps. I found a rock and roll station using the Google device that sat on a small table by the pool. Bob Seger's, 'Hollywood

Nights' flowed from the blue tooth outdoor speakers. It was comfortable with dry heat right now. I was in waist-deep water drinking my beer and concentrated on not getting my left arm and sling wet. It dawned on me that the older I got when I multi-tasked, it usually involved beer drinking. Something was bothering me again, but I couldn't grab it; almost when I had the thought again, it slithered underneath a locked door in my brain after a few seconds. I was sure I knew the shooter; I couldn't grab the face right now. The bearded boy from Detroit was now singing '*Night Moves*' quite soulfully when Kat walked through the sliding glass doors with a can of beer and a large yellow towel; she was also wearing a black bikini that could have fit Barbie. Her arms and legs looked toned and firm. Her stomach was flat, and her calf muscles were athletic. The subdued, yellowish patio lights were a sexy backdrop to my wife and her incredibly sexy bikini.

"My sexy husband in a swimsuit, I am staying in a villa in Las Vegas with a heated private pool, a cold beer in my hand, Bob Seger crooning me, and we are going dirtbag hunting. I do believe I just hit the lottery." And she put the back of her left hand on her forehead.

"Come on in the waters, fine baby girl," I said.

Kat tossed her towel on a blue and white striped linen armchair and eased into the water. She waded over to me and kissed me on the lips, and said, "Oh wow, this water is great; I could get used to this very much."

"We will come back soon, I promise."

"The best part of Vegas is no sense of time," Kat said.

"Until this afternoon, Tennille's intel has Jimmy Morrison starting his shift at four-thirty p.m," I said.

We finished our beers, and Kat swam to the opposite side of the pool and raised her right hand, and showed me her bikini bottoms. I swam over to her, and we tried some very intimate adult synchronized full-touch swimming. It was difficult with my left arm in a sling and above my head. But we managed pretty well.

Chapter 45

I WOKE EXTRAORDINARILY startled and mindful at the same time. I moved the king-size bed's blankets off my body slowly; I didn't want to wake Kat. The room was bright with sunlight, and my cell phone read eleven-forty-four a.m. I grabbed a furry white robe with The Mirage logo from the bathroom and padded out to the dining room. I located the card with Tennille's number and texted her my request. In the nightmare the night Steve Kapusinski and I were shot as my driver's side window exploded, I caught just enough of the shooter's silhouette. The dream was an exact reenactment of that dreadful evening. Some sleep experts suggest dreams can reveal traumatic events that were recessed in your subconscious. And I leaned back in the dining room chair and exhaled, and said softly, "Holly crap on a cracker, so that's who shot Steve and me."

I entered the kitchen and found a fully stocked coffee bar with a single-serve brew dispenser. I chose a whole roast, inserted it into the machine, filled the water to the proper level, and pressed the button. I cinched the belt on my robe tighter while I pondered how I was going to inform Kat that Miss Bethany had put five slugs into Steve Kapusinski and me.

After three cups of coffee, Bam-Bam, Kat, Tilly, Sully, and I were gathered and in distinct states of readiness in our Mirage Villa dining room. Kat was pacing and murmuring to herself. Tilly, Sully, and Bam-Bam, we're rechecking our weapons. Our villa had turned into a mobile command center in a short time after I received confirmation of my hunch. The pictures I requested were sent over by courier from Tennille. The new information told us that Miss Bethany arrived at Harry Reid International airport at two-twenty yesterday afternoon from Akron Canton Airport. Milton Haft greeted her at the baggage claim with a string of R-rated public displays of affection. Kat and Bam-Bam were in full combat mode and gear. They were decked out in black shirts, black cargo pants, and black tactical boots. Each had strapped themselves with Tennille's borrowed armament.

"I fed that little bitch my homemade whoopie pies," Tilly said through clenched teeth.

"I don't know how I missed this, son of a bitch; she was gathering information for Milton Haft," I said.

I was looking at an eight-by-ten-color snapshot of Milton Haft and Miss Bethany in an affectionate embrace at the baggage claim.

"If it helps, she was a Drama and Arts major in college," Sully said while typing on his iPad.

"Thanks, but no it does not," I replied.

"This makes it much more difficult to execute top-notch surveillance on Jimmy Morrison efficiently," I said out loud.

"Not true; they have never laid eyes on Sully or Bam-Bam." Tilly declared.

"I failed Gunner, his mother, Darris, Steve and Todd."

Tilly came over and kneeled in front of me and took my face in her two hands, and said, "Scooter, you are upset because you think she got us, and you have to be mainly on the sidelines for now. If I were these people I would be damn grateful that you are on their side. And I promise you it's only temporary that you think they have won, but, that bitch will know pain like she never imagined, I promise." And she kissed my forehead and stood and walked over to Sully.

Tennille had a white Ford Taurus and a silver Ford Minivan waiting for us in front of the resort. Kat and I took the Taurus, and the other three took the minivan with Bam-Bam driving and Tilly riding shotgun.

Kat and I were the lead car, with Kat as we headed to the Alani Nu casino and boutique hotel. The Alani Nu was at the furthest end of the strip, away from the Mirage. Traveling on South Las Vegas Boulevard was slow due to construction as the new Sphere entertainment ball was being constructed.

"What is that?" Kat asked.

As we sat in traffic I pulled out my cell and looked it up.

"The Sphere is being built by Madison Square Garden Entertainment and The Venetian for one and a half million dollars and a couple of Google executives are overseeing the construction. It's a giant entertainment complex shaped into a ball and overhanging the strip. It will seat eighteen thousand when completed." I replied.

After thirty-five minutes we had both vehicles in parking spots in front of the Alani Nu. The plan was to have Sully and Bam-Bam observe Jimmy Morrison. It was now four-ten, and the two of them exited the vehicle and entered the main entrance to the casino. Tilly switched cars and took a seat in the back behind Kat. Bam-Bam's choice of clothing is black. Sully wore gray dress slacks, a short-sleeved white polo golf shirt, and tan Vans casual shoes. They looked harmless, but that was the point. We all were wearing our earbuds, and Sully also had a button camera attached to the middle button on his polo shirt, so at least I could hear and see what was going on being stuck in the car. The video was being transmitted on my cell phone.

We were on full alert, so Tilly and Kat were on the lookout while I watched the video transmission. They stopped at a row of slot machines, and Sully took a seat in front of the Rich Crazy Asians slots. After fifteen minutes, he won forty-six bucks. I couldn't see how Bam-Bam did, but by the earbuds, he didn't win big. They continued through the casino; the Alani Nu's decorating scheme and prevalent style are the Hawaiian Islands. Fake banana trees mixed in with palm tree's, large banzai trees, fake coconut trees, and many man-made volcanoes. The place was shameful, and an adult's-only swimming pool added to the sleaze factor. The good guy's arrived at the entrance to the casino's sports book room. There was an enormous overhead sign announcing the Big Island Sports Book in large white lettering on a piece of dark and light brown driftwood. They entered, and Sully stopped and looked in all directions, moving his body so I could view the entire room. The large room was tacky with red carpeting and dark walls throughout, the sports-book was sunken down with three steps. Large televisions decorated the three walls. There were live horse races from tracks worldwide, an open-wheel F1 Series race from Europe on two televisions, an LPGA golf tournament, and a Korean ping pong tournament, Vegas Baby. There were two massive electronic video boards loaded with the current odds of every college, professional football game, every European soccer game, and every professional tennis match. It was a rotating board so it also listed the odds on winning the MLB Pennant and World Series Commissioners trophy, it was the same for the NFL and the Lombardi trophy. I counted twelve males and two females sitting in leather recliners betting on the ponies and many others standing around studying daily racing forms. Sully and Bam-Bam walked down the three red-carpeted steps and approached the sports book window. There were five open windows at the sports book counter, similar to a bank teller counter except, the Alani Nu sports-book counter was all black. I grabbed the file folder and reviewed Jimmy Morrison's photo, and not one of the attendants that I viewed through Sully's button camera was him. At the second counter, third in line, stood Milton Haft. My heart started racing faster than the start of the Olympic one-hundred yard dash. He sported obnoxious orange slacks with white golf balls spread all over them. His polo shirt was a bright and sharp yellow. His belt was orange. Flipping tool.

"Sully, please place a large wager on the Bills to win the Super Bowl and make sure Milton Haft hears your bet loud and clear."

Sully maneuvered directly behind Milton and tapped Milton Haft on the shoulder. As he turned around, Sully said, "I am thinking of placing twenty-five thousand on Buffalo to hoist the Lombardi Trophy; what do you think?"

The university attorney turned and looked at the electronic odds board and said, "Plus 650, great bet, but twenty-five G's is heavy."

In Sully's earbud, I began scripting Sully's conversation, "Hell, that's nothing; I will drop that today on eighteen holes today."

This perked Milton Haft up, and he said, "Where are you playing?"

"Shadow Creek."

"Jesus, I have been trying to get on that course all year."

"It's expensive," Sully replied.

Milton Laughed, "Money I got; I have been on a hot streak betting on college football; it's the referral to play there that I don't have."

"Any favorite team?" Sully replied.

"Nope, but if you get me on Shadow Creek in the next three days, I will share some inside information with you."

"Fair enough, do you have a business card?" Sully asked.

Milton reached into his wallet, retrieved a business card, and handed it to Sully, and he held it up so I could see the card. It was a plain card that read 'Milton Haft Attorney at Law' with his cell phone number at the bottom.

"It could be an hour's notice. Are you staying close to fill out our foursome?" Sully asked.

"Yes, right here."

It was Milton's turn at the betting window. He placed a bet by sliding a piece of paper on the shelf. Milton was paranoid, that was good for us. I told Sully to wait for a second after Milton was done and to speak softly and place a smaller bet.

When Milton was finished he casually and by design stepped two small steps to his right but, still in earshot of Sully's wager.

Sully said, "Oh, what the hell? You can't take it with you, fifty thousand on the Buffalo Bills to win the Super Bowl."

The Alani Nu was currently the second casino in Las Vegas to accept credit card payments. Sully inserted his black American Express card into the credit card reader. In ten seconds the bet was approved, and the female attendant handed Sully his bet slip and a receipt. Milton heard the bet and sauntered away.

"Sully, please go to another window and place a small bet on anything on the board. And casually inquire about Jimmy Morrison's absence today."

Sully walked up to a vacant window and an old-timer attendant with a name tag that read, 'Tom Jansen-Baltimore MD,' "Hi, can I get five hundred on Houston to win the men's basketball National Championship?"

As the attendant was scrolling his computer, Sully casually asked, "I usually deal with Jimmy Morrison, I don't see him, he on break?"

"Jimmy has been a no-show, and we could use him; no one wants to work anymore."

"It's the times we live in," Sully replied sympathetically.

I turned to Kat and Tilly and said, "We need to get over to Jimmy Morrison's apartment right now."

We got Jimmy's address from Tennille and her contact information software, and I plugged the apartment in Summerlin in my GPS, and it told me Summerlin was fourteen minutes away. Bam-Bam and Sully were back in the van, and they followed us. We followed North Casino Boulevard and merged onto Route 95, to Route 93. We quickly merged back onto Route 95 for five miles and took Exit 81A to Town Center Drive to Summerlin and into The Summerlin Motor Lodge Apartments. We took two parking spots in front of the apartments. It was a motel in a previous life, a two-story faded blue painted exterior, a black asphalt shingled roof missing many shingles. Outside doors opened directly into the rooms. There was a courtyard in the middle of the apartments with a filthy, half filled swimming pool. Jimmy's apartment was on the second floor 13B.

"Bam-Bam can you get in that apartment?" I asked.

"Single cylinder lock, piece of cake," Bam Bam said while looking at Jimmy Morrison's apartment door.

"We are on it, I can provide some cover," Sully said.

Kat, Tilly, and I watched Sully and Bam-Bam ascend the gray steel grated steps on the right side of the L-shaped apartment complex. They arrived at 13B, and Bam-Bam acted like he was tying his shoe and Sully stood with his back to Bam-Bam, totally focused. Bam-Bam took a lock pick out of his wallet, and after thirty seconds, he opened the door a tiny bit.

"Whoa, Son of a….," Bam-Bam said.

"Only one smell like this; once you smell it, it stamps the day, location, and time into your brain," Sully said.

Sully and Bam-Bam entered the small one-room apartment that had an outdated chest of drawers, and a small flatscreen television perched on top. A single sink and mirror were affixed to the far wall. A queen bed with Jimmy Morrison lying on his stomach in a pool of stale blood.

Chapter 46

WE RETREATED TO our villas to regroup and take showers; it was now eighty-one degrees in Las Vegas. When Kat and I walked in, and as I shut the villa's front door, Big Waddles and Frank Nagurski were on either side of the door, and they placed handguns with suppressors screwed into them against our skulls. They ditched their signature .44 Magnums for silence and probably for mobility.

"Shush, one word, and we spatter your brains all over this elegant room," Big Waddles said. And he reached into our ears and retrieved our earbuds. Then he frisked us and took all of our weapons. He then took his left hand and ran it through Kat's hair, and a small handcuff key dropped to the floor. Kat usually carried one on dangerous or out-of-town cases. Conceivably these two weren't bumbling idiots after all. They marched us out to the patio, and there was a small step ladder sitting against the eight-foot wall. Big Waddles climbed the ladder and, with much difficulty, made it to the other side.

"You first, no funny stuff or pretty boy dies real fast," Nagurski said to Kat.

Kat did not hesitate and climbed the wall, and disappeared.

"Now you."

I struggled a little with my left arm in a sling, and I wasn't even close to one hundred percent. But I made it. Nagurski came over the wall next using the identical small step ladder on the other side. Big Waddles forcefully removed my arm from the sling and told me to place my hands behind my back. I did, but I nearly passed out from the pain. Kat did the same, and our hands were zip-tied, tight. There was a black limousine idling at the curb. We were shoved into the back seat onto the rear bench seat, and Big Waddles followed us in and took a seat opposite us. Nagurski took the driving duties.

We rode in silence down the strip. Through the tinted windows, I watched the hotels and casinos pass by. We were heading south as we drove by the Venetian, then Harrahs, and after Paris, we turned east onto Tropicana Avenue, and then we turned west onto a street I didn't catch, and the only view was a large building to our left. We then drove down a dark ramp into an isolated parking deck.

We exited the limo, and the parking deck was dimly lit with few cars. There were two large silver luggage trunks on wheels. And two males dressed as Caesar's Palace porters, complete with black porter caps stood next to the trunks. If you paid attention to beneath the gold and black outfits, they were no porters. These two were on Enzo Barra's payroll.

The porters each opened the chests from the top.

"Pick one and get in; now hurry the fuck up," Big Waddles yelled.

I was in extreme pain but picked one and curled in a position that felt the most comfortable. It seemed like my stitches were coming undone. We began moving, and I tried counting the time that we were in the trunks. After thirty-five seconds, we went up an elevator with no stops. But it felt like we were going to the very top. After forty-nine seconds, the elevator stopped with a gentle rocking motion, and then I heard the elevator doors open with a swoosh sound. We started rolling again for one hundred and twenty-one seconds until we stopped, and I heard a knock on a door. And then we moved again for five seconds.

Suddenly the lid of the trunk was lifted, and the light was bright. I had to squint. We were told to get out of the trunk, and it was challenging to accomplish still being in zip ties. Big Waddles pushed my trunk over, and I spilled onto very thick blue carpeting. Kat was already out of hers, and she rushed over to me and bent over.

"Baby, are you okay?"

Big Waddles shoved Kat in the back with his right foot, and she turned over onto her right side, then he hoisted her back onto a gold dining room chair. The twenty-foot ceilings and walls were well-lit, with enormous gold chandeliers evenly spaced and running the entire ceiling length. Everything was expensive and elegant. The walls were gold with tasteful artwork, neoclassical and a period famous for its exquisite art that recaptured Greco-Roman grace and grandeur. There were also large statues with Greek influences. I could see entrances to three other rooms. There was a second story with a pool table and a fully stocked bar.

Enzo Barra was sitting on the end of an oversized, white couch. Sitting next to him was Brian Regan, Milton Haft, and Miss Bethany sat together on a matching loveseat a few feet away. Enzo was in all black from head to toe. His beady eyes looked angry. His lower jaw was so offset and prominent that he looked like a shark. He was drinking amber liquor in a thick glass. Milton Haft looked like a pre-pubescent clown in mismatched colors. Miss Bethany wore tight white shorts and a pink halter top with brown woven sandals on her feet. Her hair was styled differently than when we saw her at the marina. Her make was applied heavier, she wore open flat white sandals, and her toenails were painted pink. This wasn't the same Miss Bethany I had previous contact with on two occasions. Brian looked like a young, privileged, and preppy jerk.

Kat had a cheeky grin as she said, "Babe, why don't we ever stay here? This place looks nice."

"Shut up," Enzo Barra said.

Kat looked at Miss Bethany and said, "I am going to kill you with my bare hands before sundown tonight."

Miss Bethany stood, walked over, grabbed Kats's face with her right hand, bent over, and kissed her on the mouth hard. Kat fought her off. Miss Bethany then calmly returned to her seat on the couch.

In the middle of the wall above the couch that Enzo was sitting on was a re-creation of 'The Final Judgement,' was massive, at least four feet wide and six feet high. The original was painted above the altar inside the Sistine Chapel in Rome, Italy, by a young Michael Angelo, and it had taken him four years to complete between 1508 and 1512. It is a remarkable depiction of every human being awaiting the thumbs up or thumbs down from God. I wasn't sure if this was a good or bad omen for Kat and me. But after all, we are in Las Vegas and inside, probably the most recognizable casino ever; I was betting this was a bad omen for Kat and me.

"So you assholes think you can fuck with Enzo Barra?" Enzo said.

"I love when you speak in the third person, it showcases your mental instability, Enzo. Did your neighbors enjoy their Chicken sandwiches?" I replied.

Nagurski took giant steps and hit me on the right side of my face with an overhand right. His fist was the size of a cantaloupe, and he had a punch like a mule's kick. I saw stars but stayed in my chair and concentrated on not passing out. I've been punched before.

"After we kill both of you, we will systematically erase your entire team, one at a time, so the others can watch until all of you punks are dead; more funerals mean more grief," Enzo Barra said.

"Hey, you psycho bitch, best you focus on us because the rest of my family will eat you alive," Kat said.

Nagurski stepped towards Kat, raising his big fist, and as he got closer Kat jumped up and kicked him in the nuts. Nagurski went down hard and heavy. He was in the fetal position holding his crotch while simultaneously dry heaving. In hindsight, they should have secured our legs.

As Big Waddles raised his firearm with the silencer, the door to the suite opened, and five men walked into the room like they owned the place. Enzo Barra immediately recognized at least one of them, and he jumped off the couch like his ass was on fire.

"Mr. Rossi, what are you doing here?" Enzo said with complete panic in his voice.

The four other men were obvious bodyguards and Mr. Rossi had struck fear into Enzo Barra. The man who touched a nervous chord with a sociopath was wearing a gray custom-tailored ten thousand dollar Italian three-piece suit. He had a slight belly, and the vest didn't bunch at all, the sign of excellent tailoring. He was tall and had salt and pepper hair and he walked like a man that had a give damn button but it was currently broken.

I knew him as Luca Rossi, the most feared and respected mobster on the planet. The bodyguards were also dressed in expensive custom-tailored suits, two in black and two in gray. Two of Luca's men, closest to Big Waddles and Nagurski, took their firearms quickly and efficiently. Luca Rossi walked to the extensive wet bar and studied the selections for a moment. And while he was doing this, the room was utterly still and quiet. Kat and I were silent because we were confused. The rest of the house party was silent due to unadulterated fear. Luca made his choice and poured it neatly about three fingers into a sturdy rock glass. He reached down and opened the small refrigerator and grabbed a bottle of Perrier water, opened the small bottle and poured some into his rocks glass, and tightened the cap back on the bottle. He then went over to an oversized gold armchair and sat. He took a sip of his libation and set it on an end table to his left. Then he twisted the cap off the water bottle and took a couple of small sips. He replaced the lid and then sat it next to his rocks glass.

"Mr. Rossi, what the fuck is going on?" Enzo said.

One of Luca Rossi's men quickly grabbed Enzo Barra by his shirt and pulled him to an instant standing position. Enzo was frisked head to toe and retrieved a dangerous silver .9mm handgun from his waistband. And when Luca's man was comfortable that there were no other weapons on Enzo's body, Luca's man pushed Enzo roughly back onto the couch. He did the same with Milton Haft, Brian Regan, and Miss Bethany.

The extremely well-dressed gangster looked at Enzo's henchman writhing on the floor and said, "What the heck is his problem?"

"I kicked him in the balls, Mr. Rossi," Kat said proudly.

As Mr. Rossi smiled, he said, "Ah, you must be Katrina.

"I am," Kat replied confidently like she was recognized by a violent and impeccably dressed gangster daily."

"Seriously, what the fuck is going on?" Enzo blurted out.

The front door to the suite opened again, and Tennille entered the room with Bam-Bam. There was also a beautiful female in a splendid sparkly and gold long-sleeved shoulder-to-floor extremely revealing dress. She wore elbow-to-fingertip gold and silver sequined gloves. She appeared to be in her late fifties or early sixties and close to six feet tall. Her hair was blondish gold. Directly behind her were two Asian women wearing matching gold pantsuits; they looked like twins. They both wore identical large gold medallions around their necks. They weren't six feet tall. One of the women had a large black leather satchel strapped around her neck and resting on her right side. They held matching Glock .19 pistols like they knew how to use them. Luca nodded to one of his men, and he walked over and secured a sizable gold-in-color dining room chair. He then brought the chair into the living room for this extraordinary lady. Their were different colored jewels and emeralds running up and down each leg of the chair. The pain in my shoulder was becoming severe, the stitches had been ripped open, and I was losing blood.

Tennille stood next to the large dining room table while holding her Walther PPK. The table was serviced for dinner for eight. In front of each seat were a large dinner plate and a smaller plate with a smaller salad plate resting on top. There were gold-rolled cloth napkins with white circular sleeves holding all gold utensils, a wine glass, and a water glass. There was a stunning bouquet of fresh flowers acting as the centerpiece of the table. Tennille's handgun made the dining room table appear trivial and inconsequential.

Bam-Bam walked over to Kat and pulled out a folding knife, and in a flash cut through her zip tie. Kat stood and rubbed her wrists and shook her arms. Bam-Bam then removed my plastic zip tie, and I performed the same stretching techniques as Kat. I needed to be in an emergency room rather quickly. I looked over at Enzo Barra, and he was confused.

"Mr. Rossi, these two and a few others have been fucking with me and disrupting my operations. I want to kill them."

The suite door opened again, and Sully and Tilly strolled into the suite; the place quickly turned into Grand Central Station; Sully was holding a .38 Special, Tilly was holding a room key card.

Mr. Rossi stood and shook Sully's hand and said, "Sully, how the hell have you been?"

"Hello Luca, it's been a while; I have been better; these scumbags have been making chaos in many lives; Also, they shot a young man and my niece's husband, Scooter, over there. I may kill him in a bit."

And Sully pointed to Enzo Barra and his two thugs. At present Nagurski was seated with his head between his legs, practicing slow breathing movements.

"You wait a minute, you silly old man. Nobody talks to me like that; I kill you, you old prick," Enzo said.

Sully spread his arms and cocked his head, and laughed, "See what we have been dealing with here, Luca?"

Tilly walked over to the lady in gold, stood in front of her, and then they both grinned ear to ear, and Tilly said, "Lady Scorpion, my love, I've missed you."

"Tilly, my darling." And the two ladies embraced.

Hearing the name Lady Scorpion, Enzo snapped his head in her direction and said, "Lady Scorpion, no way, I thought you were a myth, some made-up bullshit."

A small Derringer pistol appeared in Lady Scorpion's right hand faster than the eye could see; she shot Enzo Barra in the right shoulder just below his collarbone. Enzo began whimpering. The shock would come soon, and the pain was about three minutes away.

"Are you nuts, lady? Nobody shoots Enzo Barra," Enzo screamed.

"I can guarantee I am not a myth, and that bullet in your shoulder should be the proof." Lady Scorpion said. She then nodded to the lady wearing the satchel. The lady lifted the satchel from over her neck, walked over to Enzo, knelt, extracted a wide roll of silver-tape, and with speed and efficiency, secured Enzo's hands together in front of him. She then pulled a pair of black-handled heavy-duty medical scissors from the satchel, and cut his clothing around the small bullet wound. She grabbed a syringe from her pouch, held it up to the light, and tested it to ensure the needle was working correctly. Swiftly she stuck it into Enzo's right shoulder and properly pushed the medicine into his body.

"What did you just drug me with lady?"

"It's morphine for the pain that will be arriving soon."

The skilled female then retrieved a pair of tweezers, gauze pads, and sterile tape from her bag. She then took a rag, rubbing alcohol, and swiftly ripped a piece of duct tape from the roll, and shoved the rag into Enzo's mouth. She then roughly placed the duct tape over his mouth. Her movements were swift and precise. Enzo's hands flew to his mouth. But the way his hands were taped together there was nothing he could do.

"You touch that tape around your mouth, and the next shot is a direct hit to your crotch, I promise," Scorpion Lady said.

The bravado and cockiness immediately left Enzo, Milton Haft, Brian Regan, and Miss Bethany. The makeshift nurse took the rubbing alcohol and, disinfected the tweezers with it, poured some directly on the gunshot wound. Enzo Barra was bucking on the couch screaming, red-faced, and hopping mad. Taking the tweezers and rooting around for a few seconds, she removed the small slug from Enzo Barra's upper body. She secured the gauze pad with the medical tape and placed the tools and rubbing alcohol back into the bag. Ensuring that the suitcase was closed tightly, she re-took her original position.

"Miss Scorpion Lady, if there are any pain relievers left, I could use a smidgen," I said.

Lady Scorpion looked at me for the first time and saw my pained face and the blood soaking my shirt and said, "Hell to the yes."

She nodded again to the quite capable satchel women who, in turn, gave me a big shot of morphine and dressed my bandages once again.

Kat stood, took two significant steps, and, in a blur, kicked Milton Haft in the throat with her right foot positioned diagonally. His head snapped back, and he began grabbing at his throat, and a sickening gurgling noise was percolating from his mouth.

"I'll be damned, Milt Baby; I was sure she was going to punch you in the throat; huh, a kick in the throat, wow."

"Kat, if you could refrain from kicking or punching anyone else for just a moment, I have a plan moving forward; I have a one hundred thousand dollar buy-in for a Hold Em poker tournament downstairs," Luca Rossi asked politely.

"Sure, Mr. Rossi." And Kat took her seat next to me.

"Thank you, and it's Luca to you."

"Sully, I believe I have the entire story. The goal has always been to free Gunner Thompson to finish and enjoy his collegiate football career and perhaps eventually pursue his career in professional football. But, could you hit the highlights for me?" Luca Rossi asked.

"Scooter?" Sully asked.

"Sure." And for the next fifteen minutes, I started telling what happened and what I knew about the blackmail scheme. Nobody spoke, and the room was quiet except for the gurgling sounds coming from Milton Haft's throat. He was breathing. Although it was a chore, his trachea wasn't crushed, but it worked overtime.

When I was finished, Luca Rossi nodded his head in acknowledgment. He stood and grabbed a bottle of Blanton's Special Reserve bourbon from the bar; he tipped the bottle to Sully, and Sully shook his head yes, then held up five fingers, indicating the entire team could use a drink. The highly respected gangster grabbed five other rocks glasses and poured the bourbon into each. Sully retrieved our drinks and delivered each to us. I took a big sip, and it hit me how tired I was, but mostly, I hated these people. I was mainly nauseous of these horrible people, all of them.

"We have a question for Milton Haft, Mr. Rossi, if I could?"

Mr. Rossi shook his head while looking at Milton Haft with confident amusement.

264 • Artie Reed

I looked at the frightened felon and asked, "Which partner or partners were you trying to scare away with the fake death threats? Enzo or Chancellor Wright?" I asked.

After a few seconds of silence, Milton whispered, "Enzo." Enzo's head snapped up, and he was speechless.

I took a sip of my drink and smiled to myself; we got these people; we finally got them.

Luca began, "Ok, it's time to get honest and come to a reckoning. Miss Bethany did you kill the Chancellor? And did you shoot with the intent to murder Mr. Jeanette and this young man Steve Kapusinski who is currently residing in a hospital unit? And did you also enter their home, their private residence, and their safe place? for deceptive purposes?" Luca asked.

Miss Bethany was shaking on the couch, and she was trying to get truly small like a rabbit in an open field. Our team was impressed with Mr. Rossi, I had only used Kap's full name once.

"Well?"

"Yes." She replied with her head down.

Luca looked at the Scorpion Lady and said, "That's one."

The Scorpion Lady nodded to one of her ladies, and that lady pulled a zip tie from her suit coat pocket and roughly pulled Miss Bethany from her seat and, with blazing speed zip tied her hands behind her back.

"Go stand against that wall." Luca said as he pointed to the wall next to the front foyer.

"Now, were you two, with Enzo Barra's direction, prepared to shoot their family pet on a nature trail? And how many family pets have you killed?" Luca asked in a calm and controlled voice. But it was his eyes, his eyes were incensed.

The small Derringer .22 suddenly appeared in Lady Scorpions' right hand and she fired a shot three inches from Big Waddle's into the leg of the chair.

"Six or seven," The visibly shaken thug mumbled.

Luca shook his head back and forth slowly in disgust and repeated, "Six or seven; Holy Hell, I have three dogs who are family to us. First and this is a two part question, which one of you kicked Ms. Thompson's defenseless dog's ribs in and which one cruelly destroyed Ms. Thompson's hand?"

"I did the dog," Big Waddles Replied.

"That"s number two." Luca said.

Again same routine and in twelve seconds Big Waddles was zip-tied and standing against the wall with Miss Bethany.

Luca Rossi took a big pull from his bourbon and looked at Frank Nagurski, and said, "So you smashed two fingers of an innocent woman's hand for no reason? Just so she couldn't play the piano anymore?"

Nagurski remained quiet.

"I have two daughters who have operations to one day be concert pianists, and this makes me fucking furious." Luca was at a snapping point. He nodded at Lady Scorpion twice, and she shot Nagurski in the forehead; a small hole appeared, and then blood ran down his nose and face."

Miss Bethany yelped, and Brian Regan began to cry; Nagurski slumped over to his side and bled on the luxurious carpet.

Luca's attention was now fully engaged on Brian, "Young man, if I understand correctly, you didn't kill anybody but did participate and profit handsomely in the blackmail and forced point-shaving scheme. So you will transfer every penny you have to your name to Sully right now, bank account to bank account, and I am assuming there is probably a safe with additional funds at your fraternity house, am I correct?"

Brian Regan was trying to wipe his tears and reach in his front pants pocket at the same time for his cell phone, "Yes, there is."

"How much currently resides in that safe?" Luca Rossi asked Brian in a calm and soothing voice.

Brian was shaking and having trouble thinking clearly.

"Come on, hurry up," Luca said.

"About thirty thousand, I think," Brian answered.

"Let's hope there is at least thirty thousand when Sully opens that safe with you, your life depends on it. And you will drop out of the university and move away from Ohio within fourteen days; I will watch your movements in the future."

Brian nodded his head up and down vigorously while wiping his nose with the back of his right hand. Sully walked over and grabbed Brian by the arm to a standing position, and guided him into another room.

Luca raised his empty glass towards one of his men, who walked over, took the glass, and walked to the mini bar.

"So, Attorney at law, did you kill the Alani Nu sports-book employee?"

Milton was having trouble speaking, so he nodded his head up and down, confirming 'yes.' This was not the same man we witnessed that evening inside The Diamond Grille restaurant.

"Ok, hand Mr. Jeanette, your wallet, wristwatch, and cell phone and assist him in locating your banking information and do it swiftly. See, if you go to trial, you will throw the Thompsons and the other young men under the bus to the prosecutors to save your pathetic ass. Trust me; I have experience with this subject, Luca asserted.

The room now was a series of whimpers and moans. Twenty minutes later, Luca looked at Milton Haft after being led back into the living room; he was zip-tied and guided to the wall next to Miss Bethany.

Chapter 47

LUCA TURNED HIS head and focused totally on Enzo Barra for a full minute and then said somebody please remove the tape from Enzo's mouth. Be careful. He can't be germ-free."

"Sure," Sully honored Luca's request.

"Screw you, Luca; I demand to be allowed to leave right fucking now; I don't give a crap who you think you are. A war has begun." Enzo shouted.

Luca smiled and said, "Enzo, you should think before you speak; I am The Fixer. Nonetheless, you will leave soon and return to your life, but with significant conditions."

Kat, Tilly, and I panicked, but Sully motioned with his hand to be calm.

"Enzo Barra, you will pay Ms. Thompson three million dollars within fifteen days, and my men will monitor that transaction.

"The hell I will; that will wipe my cash out," Enzo replied defiantly, with his trademark spittle forming in the corners of his mouth.

He would not be a good poker player. He had one of the worst tells ever. But the morphine was giving him false brashness.

"Sell your assets quickly, and you will sign your cigar bar over to Scooter."

"Not a chance." Enzo snarled.

Luca nodded to Tennille and she picked up the remote that controlled the giant television. She searched and found an auxiliary channel, and the screen filled with Enzo Barra's home.

"What the…" Enzo said

"Tennille, please fast forward to the high points, the critical aspects, pay attention Enzo, my associates have been extremely busy the last four hours with this project that we are about to reveal to you. After my friend Tennille spotted you on video surveillance per Mr. Jeanette's request, she then contacted me. Tilly then got hold of the remarkable and dangerous Lady Scorpion and walla," Luca said, spreading his arms.

Tennille followed Luca's instructions and fast-forwarded the picture to one of Enzo Barra's garages, specifically the underside of his Silver Lexus sedan. There was a small black box with a flashing red light attached to the luxury car's frame. Tennille did this three more times, showing a red Cadillac SUV that was bomb free, so was a black Porsche 911, and so was Enzo's metallic green Battista sports car.

"Please pause it here, Tennille, Enzo, you will sell this rather expensive mid-life crisis to fulfill the obligations I am outlining. Okay, Tennille, please forward to the star of the show."

The next frame showed a black box similar to the others but much, much larger, and it was encased in a heavy plastic outer box with a large padlock in the corner of the basement.

"Enzo, you will also transfer the title for your Porsche 911 into Scooter and Katrina's name, and these two will see that it is donated promptly. After these requirements are met, my men will disable the incendiary devices. Enzo, if you tamper with these explosives, they will explode. And if you do not follow my instructions in the letter, I will strap a bomb to your chest permanently. And most importantly, again, if Gunner Thompson's name ever gets associated with the public concerning point-shaving, Kaboom." And Luca screamed the Kaboom part, we all jumped a little after that one.

"What are you going to do with us?" Miss Bethany asked.

"I will defer to the lovely Lady Scorpion," Luca replied.

"We are going to drive you to a remote spot in the desert and bury you in the sand up to your necks and watch the sun fry the skin off of your faces. After that, the desert predators will feast on your rotting flesh; you can't be trusted with the future of the Thompson's lives anymore," Lady Scorpion said as a matter of fact.

Miss Bethany fainted, and Luca retrieved his cell phone, dialed a number, and said, "I have three packages for delivery, two male and one female. Extra large packaging needed for one."

Chapter 48

IT WAS A cold, crisp day, and in the turnaround of the marina beside Graceland, I was watching on our big screen television a breaking news story covering Coach Dennis Darling's abrupt resignation from head coaching duties for the university. A familiar long gray Rolls Royce turned halfway and stopped. Buster and Joseph Votto Senior exited the elegant motor car in that order. Buster was again head-to-toe brown, but if I had to pick today's shade of brown, I would say gingerbread brown. Joseph Votto Senior was an exact match to his million-dollar automobile; gray. His gray three-piece suit, dark gray dress shirt, light gray tie, and highly polished gray, expensive Italian loafers. By the time Buster had turned towards the house, Bam-Bam, Rhino, Snake, and Mongoose had them in a loose circle, firearms at the ready. I looked down and had my Sig Sauer in my hand while I sat at the window inside Graceland by the desk. I didn't remember picking it up.

As I watched from my vantage point, Sully quickly appeared, Glock .9mm in his right hand. Kat and Tilly appeared in the doorway of Graceland, both carrying a shotgun in both hands.

After a minute, Bam-Bam's men took a post outside not too far away from the windows. Everybody else entered Graceland.

Sully took up his prioritized spot behind the bar. Bam-Bam leaned at one of the two stand-up tables. I stood from the desk chair with one hundred percent maximum effort and loads of pain. I walked to the bar and took a seat. Joseph took a chair and a couple of stools from me. Buster took a position in the left rear of the room. My family was still wound tight. Joseph Votto took a seat at the bar.

"May I have a cocktail?"

Sully gazed at Joseph Votto Senior for a full forty seconds and then nodded his head and turned and lifted a bottle of Stone Castle, a moderately expensive twenty-five-year-old scotch. Sully pulled a thick crystal rocks glass from the back shelf and filled it to about three fingers, and placed it in front of Joseph Votto Senior.

I was looking at the aging mobster as he sipped his scotch. He appeared twenty years younger than when we saw him in the parking deck. Amazing, just amazing.

"Scooter, I am pleased that you and that young man Steven Kapusinski did not die."

Everyone remained quiet. Joseph Votto Senior had more to say and we wanted to hear it. After three long and silent minutes, Joseph Votto cleared his throat and said, "I am a man that when I was younger, could detach and disconnect my feelings and emotions. But the recent events have me very clear about my current feelings. I am outraged, saddened, furious and now overwhelmed with gratitude."

Sully nodded as if all was well and safe and started grabbing tall pilsner glasses and poured each of us beers. He set them on the bar, and I grabbed two and walked over to Buster, and handed him one of the draft beers. Sully also placed a draft beer in front of Joseph Votto Senior. After taking a sip of his beer, the gangster nodded his head in total approval. Then he began again, "I received an unexpected call from Luca Rossi yesterday afternoon and he relayed the events that transpired in that suit in Las Vegas, although I believe he held some information back as he deemed it confidential."

Joseph Votto Senior took a big pull from his draft beer and continued, "He also explained the determination, guts, and bravery to pursue this to the end. He said you are the most admirable people he has met in a very long time; I agreed."

Joseph took another gulp of his draft beer and a sip of his scotch and said, "I am rejuvenated, and so is my entire organization. This includes my many employees, and we are always at your disposal, no questions asked. Tell us who, what, when, where, and we ride."

Chapter 49

THE SNOW WAS falling with much enthusiasm from the sky and had blanketed the entire lake, our patio, and all of Northeastern Ohio. It was January 5th, and Kat, myself, Tilly, Sully, Bam-Bam, Taylor Thompson, and Gunner Thompson were sitting in Taylor Thompson's ample living room. Everybody had one of Taylor's homemade hot chocolate drinks with mini marshmallows and a heavy dollop of peppermint schnapps, and hot buttered rum. They were served in large glasses.

"Kap, please open your envelope," I asked.

He was enjoying his winter drink so much that he forgot that he was holding an envelope. He sat his glass down on the coaster sitting on the table. He pulled out the letter and the check that was inside the envelope.

"Holy freakin moly."

Steve leaned his head all the back on the couch and handed the letter and the check to Darris, and after Darris read the letter and then gazed at the bank draft, and said, "You people are the dream team."

Todd looked at the letter, then the check, and said, "One hundred and ninety-five thousand dollars, and you folks paid off the mortgage to his mom and dad's home."

"Yes and no, Milton Haft and Brian Regan did, also I hear Belize is perfect this time of year," I replied.

While this was going on we heard soft crying. Taylor Thompson held a bank statement depicting her new money market account containing three million dollars. Her hand was still bandaged but on a lower scale than previous times. Only the last two fingers were bandaged together.

"I don't know what to say," Taylor Thompson exclaimed.

"No need to say anything," Tilly replied and put her left arm around Taylor's shoulder.

I nodded to Sully, and he reached behind his body and obtained a large yellow envelope. He placed it and a long silver letter opener in front of Taylor Thompson.

"Go ahead open it," Kat said.

Hesitantly, Taylor Thompson used the letter opener and opened the envelope, she then began to read the one-page letter that was nestled inside and after a few seconds her left hand flew to her open mouth and she began to cry softly. Her delicate shoulders trembled.

"You are scheduled for next Friday at the Mayo Clinic in Scottsdale, Arizona for orthopedic surgery on your two fingers. There are two roundtrip airline tickets but due to current NCAA regulations it is wise for Gunner to not accompany you so I am going to go with you," Kat said.

Taylor's shiny and wet eyes went directly towards her piano.

Chapter 50

KAT AND I were waiting just outside of the hospital parking surface lot in the staff parking lot. We were leaning against the black Porsche 911, waiting for nurse Andrea Clark to finish her shift. After ten minutes, she emerged from the hospital's electronic doors. She walked briskly while checking messages on her cell phone. As she got close to us she recognized us and said "Mr. Jeanette hello, you look healthy."

"I had a great nurse," I replied and pulled the title for the sports car from my back pocket and said, "If you can sign this, you can take your new car home with you."

Andrea looked at the shiny Porsche and the big red bow on its hood and said, "Wait, are you serious?"

"Yep." I said

"I don't understand."

"It was a donation, and we chose you, and there is a certified check on the dashboard for car insurance, car maintenance, and gasoline for three years or so," I replied.

Chapter 51

THE FOLLOWING DAY Kat, Tilly, Sully, Bam-Bam, Darris Blackford, Todd Carothers, Kap, and I were standing on the sidewalk in front of what used to be Enzo's cigar bar. Kap stood proud and straight in his walker. His doctors have diagnosed him with a full recovery in due time, and the walker is only temporary.

"So guys welcome to your new cigar bar," I said.

The three turned and looked at each other, then back at us, and Darris said, "Are you joking?"

In unison, our team said, "No."

I handed Darris a large yellow envelope and said, "All details are inside, including the keys and security codes. We have installed a new state-of-the-art security system. There is also a set of instructions complete with phone numbers for our attorney to guide you on incorporation and taxes. We have contacted most of the cigar and alcohol reps to come in and train you on the various products. Those phone numbers are included; also, there is a check in the envelope that will cover all expenses for two years."

"Wow, just wow," Kap said.

Crud jumped up and down and said, "Can we get a snake as the store's pet?"

"No." His two teammates said together.

Also, I pointed to the two Harley Davidson Electra Glide motorcycles, one red and one blue, sitting inside the large trailer behind Bam-Bam's pickup truck.

"The blue one was liberated from Brian Regan, and we purchased the other pre-owned. These are for Darris and Todd, and you two can fight over the colors. Kap, we have one on order for you in midnight crimson, and it should be delivered about the same time your doctors deem you fully recovered. The cigar bar has a garage to store these bad-boy bikes."

And Kat and I retreated to our SUV and headed home. As we drove, Kat said, "Damn, Luca Rossi is The Fixer, and we met The Fixer, babe."

The   End

Made in the USA
Middletown, DE
19 April 2023

28888659R00156